Praise for *The Good*

"Fresh, sexy, and fun... McCoy always adds depth to stories that makes them impossible to put down."
— Catherine Adel West, author of *The Two Lives of Sara*

"A hilariously fresh take on dating in the modern world: the good, the bad, and the love that's been there all along."
— Charish Reid, author of *Mickey Chambers Shakes It Up*

"The hallmarks of a Taj McCoy romance are all here: delicious food, ride-or-die friends, spicy sex, and swoon-worthy love."
— Danielle Jackson, author of *Accidentally in Love*

"Taj McCoy's writing positively crackles with energy, wit and humor. *The Good Ones Are Taken* is just the right amount of sweet and salty. Delicious like kettle corn. Yum."
— Jayci Lee, author of *Booked on a Feeling*

"A heartfelt, delicious, joy-filled, friends-to-lovers journey I'll never forget!"
— Courtney Kae, author of *In the Event of Love*

"I laughed, I yelled 'oh hell no!' and most importantly, I couldn't stop smiling anytime the two main characters were with each other. That's the sign of an incredible love story."
— Darby Baham, author of *Her New York Minute*

"What a joy of a book! It's a novel where our heroine Maggie neither shies away from nuanced conversations nor the heart-thrilling heat of romance. A true HEA!"
— Tif Marcelo, *USA TODAY* bestselling author of the Heart Resort series

"This book was enchanting and delightful from start to finish."
— Elle Cruz, author of *How to Survive a Modern-Day Fairy Tale*

"Taj McCoy speaks TRUTH about the travails of modern dating with sass and heart... A steamy (*fans self*) reminder that the best man for you is sometimes right there all along."
— Susan Lee, author of *Seoulmates* and *The Name Drop*

"A sizzling friends-to-lovers romance that's as grown and sexy as it is tender and sweet."
— Myah Ariel, author of *When I Think of You*

"Sexy, swoon-worthy, and hilarious. *The Good Ones Are Taken* has a charming heroine with an unforgettable voice and a love triangle that had me turning pages well into the night."
— Riss M. Neilson, author of *A Love Like the Sun*

Also by Taj McCoy

Savvy Sheldon Feels Good as Hell
Zora Books Her Happy Ever After

Edited by Taj McCoy

Even If the Sky is Falling

THE GOOD ONES ARE TAKEN

Taj McCoy

mira

ISBN-13: 978-0-7783-0542-2

The Good Ones Are Taken

Mira
22 Adelaide St. West, 41st Floor
Toronto, Ontario M5H 4E3, Canada
BookClubbish.com

Printed in U.S.A.

To anyone searching for love—you are deserving, you are enough.

1

HER EYES LOCKED WITH ANOTHER PAIR ON THE OTHER side of the bar —deep brown eyes framed with black, curly lashes and bookended with laugh lines. Maggie's heart flopped in her chest as she inhaled a breath, almost willing the scent of his cologne to travel the fifteen feet to where she sat. *He looks like he smells good.*

The man looked back at her, eyeing her intently. His long locs were pulled back into a messy bun, random tendrils reaching toward his bearded jawline—a lone streak of silver to one side of his manicured chin. His full lips spread into a wide smile bright enough for a toothpaste ad, and he raised two fingers in the air before beckoning her over. He jutted his thumb toward a booth behind him where the table was set with a bottle of champagne on ice and two empty flutes.

Maggie's eyebrows shot up, and she pointed at herself. "Me?" she mouthed.

His smile widened and he bit his lip as he nodded slowly. The carnal look in his eyes spread warmth to her belly.

She swiveled her bar stool to the side, a moment from stepping down and crossing the room before she caught a glimpse of the woman standing directly behind her. Late twenties, svelte and a dress that hugged every curve of a Coke-bottle figure. She had deep dimples, and her honey-blond goddess locs were pulled up and away from her face, showing off her sparkling green eyes and fluttering lashes. The woman strode to the other side of the bar confidently in stiletto sandals tied just below muscular calves. The sexy, loc'd-up couple embraced tightly, kissing twice before they slid into the booth and poured themselves some bubbles. They snuggled close as he raised his glass to toast the occasion, his beautiful date beaming as they clinked their glasses together and tenderly locked lips.

Damn. Strike one.

Maggie turned back to face the bar, sipping the final dregs of her cocktail before running her fingers over her glass of water. The ice had melted and the glass was slick with condensation. With the pad of her finger, she drew a figure eight before dabbing it on a cocktail napkin. She opened her mouth to ask the bartender, Matt, for her check when someone spoke behind her.

"Anyone sitting here?" The rich baritone voice sent a delicious shiver down the back of her neck.

Maggie peeked coyly over her shoulder, her right brow arching slightly as her eyes swept over the tall specimen behind her. The man wore a tailored black suit with a loosened silk tie and a white dress shirt unbuttoned at the collar. His easy smile widened as she regarded him. "Seat's all yours," she responded slowly, her voice a sultry whisper as she swept a loose coil behind her ear. She turned back toward the counter, sending an amused wink in the direction of the bartender.

"Thanks." He slid onto the bar stool and unfastened his tie, tucking it into his jacket pocket.

Matt nodded a greeting. "Hey, man, looks like you could use a drink. What can I get you?"

"Yeah, let me get a Maker's Mark old-fashioned, and another drink for the lady." The handsome stranger tilted his head in Maggie's direction, turning to observe her. His salt-and-pepper fade contoured down to a closely cut beard; a few grays speckled the sections framing his mouth.

Matt nodded and set to making the drinks.

Maggie eyed the man next to her, notes of spiced oud and sandalwood invading her senses from his cologne. "Thank you."

"What you drinkin'?" He crossed his arms, setting his elbows on the bar. He leaned toward her slightly, pointing to her empty cocktail glass.

"A filthy gin martini, extra olives." She accepted a fresh glass from Matt and took a slow sip, savoring the briny liquid. Her heel crooked over the stool's footrest, she flexed her foot and then pointed her toe, her feet still sore from enduring a long day of meetings. She'd braved the day in her favorite Cole Haan pumps, mistakenly deciding that she didn't need to carry her customary pair of flats in her laptop tote. *Never again.*

"Long day?" She eyed him curiously, the stem of her martini glass between her index and middle fingers, her palm flat against its cool foot. Slowly, she swirled the contents of her drink, her shoulders finally beginning to relax, courtesy of Tanqueray.

He nodded. "You could say that. Divorce mediations. You?"

"Tax attorney, and it's nearing April." Maggie sipped slowly, willing the gin not to take hold of her too quickly. "I'm sorry about your marriage."

His brow lifted. "How did you know the settlement was mine? I could be the attorney."

She pursed her lips, considering that statement before shrugging a shoulder. "You could, but your thumb keeps rubbing against the space between your middle and ring finger, like you're missing something."

The bartender slid over a glass tumbler filled with an oversize ice cube, amber liquid and an orange peel. The man took a big gulp before jutting his chin upward in thanks. "I guess as an attorney, you know all the tells."

Her face softened slightly. "Not all of them, but I've seen enough to know it's not going well." She regarded him out of the corner of her eye for a moment. "Sorry."

His shoulders slumped a little. "Not your fault. All mine, really." He took another gulp, almost finishing off his drink, gazing at her in her cream pantsuit and camel pumps. He leaned a little closer, his voice barely above a whisper. "This may be forward of me, but you are a very beautiful woman. Would you maybe want to get out of here?" He raised his eyebrows as he pressed his lips together.

Maggie's eyes widened as she sputtered, almost choking on her cocktail. "Damn, you just go straight for ass, huh?"

Shocked, he laughed awkwardly. "Wow. I'm so sorry. I didn't think about what I was saying until after it came out of my mouth. Please don't be offended. I just— My eyes were immediately drawn to you when I walked in and, honestly, I've been out of the game for a long time." He put a hand to his chest as he apologized, frustration furrowing his brows.

Maggie tilted her head as she employed the poker face she used with her clients, her gaze moving back and forth between her drink and the bartender, who had frozen at the proposition. "Well, I appreciate the compliment and the drink, but I'm going to have to pass. I'm not really the type to bust it open when I don't know your name, we're not dating and you're still married. That's a lot to ask of a stranger." She shook her head, chronicling this proposition among the many things she intended to share with her girlfriends over dinner. *Who does that?*

The man pressed his lips together and nodded, chuckling. "You're right, and I'm sorry. My wife and I, we've been living separate lives for a long time, though I can understand why it still sounds fresh. I didn't mean any harm."

Maggie smiled down at her drink and flipped her wrist at him. "All good, and thanks for the drink. Honestly, I'm still getting over my own breakup, so I wouldn't make great company tonight."

The man turned his entire body to face her, his knee bumping the outside of her thigh. "Do you want to talk about it? I'm obviously not a relationship expert, but I can listen."

Sweet Jesus, that was not an invitation. She shook her head slowly, her lips pressed together in a tight smile that didn't reach her eyes. "Not tonight, but thank you."

It had been a few months since Rob left, and the sting of his betrayal still burned right below the surface of Maggie's skin. She thought they were getting close to moving in together, but he had already set his sights on someone else. Now she wanted nothing more than to junk punch him in front of his new girl. Too embarrassed by the fact that he chose someone else, she preferred to brood over a cocktail rather than air out her hurt, even though her eyes had opened to the potential for someone new. *Just not this guy.* Being in the midst of divorce proceedings didn't exactly signal emotional availability. Now, if only he would take a hint.

The door opened, and a couple of women breezed toward a high-top table in dark corporate suits, their identical bobs parting bone-straight hair with recent highlights. Maggie's neighbor perked up, and she prayed silently for his departure.

"Will you excuse me? I think I recognize someone," he murmured, his eyes never leaving the newcomers.

"Of course. Thanks again." Maggie raised her glass and watched with amusement as he moved quickly across the room and greeted the pair, neither of whom seemed to recognize him. That didn't stop him from planting himself at their table, oblivious to the panicked look on their faces. Maggie winked at Matt, who rested his hands on the bar, an easy smile spreading across his face. "That was...a lot!" She rested her chin in her hand, shaking her head as she laughed.

He whistled in agreement. "One more for the road, Mags? On me. You deserve it after—" he gestured around chaotically "—whatever that was."

She grinned. "You know what, Matt? I think that I'm going to save myself from strike three and head on home. Can you cash me out?" She handed money to him to cover her drink and tip.

"You got it." He moved over to a digital register—a tablet connected to a cash till and a printer. "Thanks, Mags. See you next week?"

"Uh-huh." Maggie's eyes were drawn across the bar to the-booth-that-could-have-been: the loc'd couple entwined and oblivious to the world around them. Their lips and hands were in constant movement, connecting fervently, and when they broke apart to breathe, the intensity of their gazes told everyone in the room what time it was. These two were going to ravish each other, probably before they even made it home. Their kisses made Maggie ache low in her stomach.

I want that.

Maggie stepped into her Santa Monica condo and immediately kicked off her shoes as she shut the front door. "Penny!"

The communal living space was open concept—Maggie

loved a great room. A giant U-shaped couch faced a mounted flat-screen TV. Behind the sofa, bar stools framed the kitchen island. A floor-to-ceiling wall of windows on one side held bifold doors that led to a long balcony. On the other side of the couch was an eating nook and a hallway leading to Maggie's bedroom and her home office.

The wood floors felt cool against her aching feet as she removed her blazer and hung it on the back of one of her bar stools. "I know you're hungry! Where are you?" She crossed into the kitchen, the travertine tiles even colder against her skin. Maggie reached into the pantry for a package of Fancy Feast. "Hmm…what's on the menu tonight?" she murmured, turning over the small tray of food in her hand. "I've got grilled salmon for you! Your favorite…"

"Meow." A fuzzy shadow of Penny slinking into the living room appeared. No doubt she'd spent most of her day sprawled on Maggie's king-size bed. A Himalayan with a deep gray face and paws and big blue eyes, Penny's snub-nosed glare could rival the resting bitch face of any local celebrity avoiding the paparazzi. She'd been a surly kitten when Maggie adopted her—the only one at the shelter who stood away from the others with her incessant "fuck around and find out" expression. A girl after Maggie's own heart. It was love at first scowl.

"Hello, my lovely. Did you have a good day?" Maggie crooned.

Penny leaped up onto a bar stool and then hoisted herself to the island counter, nuzzling the palm of Maggie's open hand as she stepped toward her saucer. She tapped a paw on the plate and looked up at Mags as if to say, "What are you waiting for?"

"Okay, okay." Maggie grabbed a spoon from a drawer and ladled half of the portion in the tray onto Penny's dish. Once she'd tapped the spoon on the plate to drop the last morsel,

Penny licked her lips and went to work. Maggie ran her fingernails along Penny's back and tail, accumulating a small ball of fur, which she tossed in the trash can under the sink. "We need to have a good brushing session this weekend, ma'am."

Penny eyed her for a brief moment before returning to her meal. Maggie held up her hands and walked away slowly, heading down the hall to the bedroom. As she walked, she untucked her camisole from her slacks, easing it over her head and throwing it into a hamper in her open walk-in closet. After unzipping her pants, she stepped out of them and dropped them onto a pile of clothes to take to the dry cleaner before walking into her bathroom on the other side of the closet.

She unfastened her bra, relieving her full breasts from their wiry detention, and exhaled happily. Once she brushed and pinned up her hair, wrapping it into a silk scarf, Maggie dropped salts and tulip-scented bubble bath into her tub, running hot water and humming to herself. "Hey, Alexa, play the wind-down playlist."

"Now playing 'Wind Down.'"

Goapele's "Closer" began to play softly through the speakers that Maggie recently had mounted into her walls. She tugged her lacy thong down and off, examined herself in the mirror before washing her face carefully, trying not to disturb her lash extensions. She patted her face dry with a fresh hand towel before easing into her steaming cloud of bubbles, the fragrance and heat easing her muscles as she sat and relaxed. Maggie rested her neck against a soft pillow at the lip of her tub, allowing the hot water and bath salts to melt away her aches and the stress of tax season. Exhaling deeply, she let go of the day, but the couple in the booth clung to the edges of her thoughts, and she wondered what they had gotten into as she lathered her body with a rich cleanser and exfoliating gloves.

After her bath, she sat on a teak bench and slathered body butter over her brown skin, still unable to shake the couple from her mind. Flashes of them kissing and pawing at each other ran through her head, and she closed her eyes, imagining that those lips and hands were on her own body—the two were equally sexy, so she let her mind wander as she considered what it would be like to experience the two of them together. Maggie had never been with a woman, but that didn't mean she hadn't thought about it. She pulled a silk robe over her shoulders and padded toward her bed, stooping to pull her favorite purple toy from the bottom drawer of her nightstand.

Maggie climbed on top of the fluffy white comforter and leaned back against her pillows, propped up against her upholstered headboard. Her robe fell open, and she squeezed her eyes shut, imagining the man with his megawatt smile running his lips down her neck to her chest as the tendrils of his hair tickled her bare skin. She grazed the flattened tip of her G-spot stimulator against each spot where she imagined his partner's lips connecting with her flesh, biting her lip the lower her toy traveled. She eased her legs apart, rubbing the toy against the seam of her folds, allowing it to slicken with the moisture building at her core.

Maggie's mouth fell open as she gasped, pressing the small round control panel on the front of the device—the toy began to hum at a low frequency. Turning its tip back against her skin, she eased small circles around her clit as she increased the settings with her thumb from a light hum to a heavier pulse. Maggie swore as her hips reacted, winding slowly as her inner thighs began to shake. Delicious pressure and heat began to build at her apex as she undulated against the device. As Maggie's back began to arch and her head pressed deeper into the pillows, the toy sputtered and stopped abruptly. "What? No!" Maggie shrieked, pressing her face into one of her satin-covered pillows.

Strike three.

Maggie whined, dramatically tossing a pillow across the room before pushing herself off the bed and wrapping her robe around her waist. She trudged back out toward the kitchen, thighs slick with arousal, unable to remember where she'd stashed her charging cable. She grabbed a bag of popcorn from the pantry and threw it into the microwave until the series of pops began to fade. Grumbling, she sat on the couch next to Penny, who had sprawled out on Maggie's favorite throw blanket.

Penny eyed Maggie before closing her eyes as if to say, "Don't start none, won't be none."

Ignoring the glare, Maggie turned on the television to her favorite comfort show, *Living Single*. She loved that she could stream it whenever she wanted, and her favorite singles could surely relate to all of the foolery she'd faced that day. She tucked a few kernels of buttery popcorn into her mouth as she watched the scene unfold, but she had forgotten that the last episode she'd started was the series finale. Her mouth dropped open as Kyle and Max happily went home together after accepting that their baby would tie them together forever. And Regine was engaged to her rich guy. And Synclaire and Overton were happy. And now Khadijah finally had Scooter?

"Ugh, all of these bitches end up happy… Where's mine?"

Penny sat up, her stare shooting daggers in Maggie's direction for the disturbance. She leaped off the couch and sauntered toward her bed in Maggie's office, where she could relax in peace.

Maggie watched her leave as her TV auto-streamed *The Golden Girls* as final credits rolled. *Even my TV is judging me.* "I'm going to die alone," she muttered, shoving more popcorn into her mouth.

2

"HERE WE GO AGAIN, BACK ON THE DATING MERRY-GO-round." Maggie sighed into her bourbon old-fashioned. "I can't believe I'm back on this bullshit."

Savvy squeezed her shoulder. "It's going to be okay, sis. Don't even sweat this. Honestly, I'm surprised you're still harping about this dude. It's a minor setback."

"How is this minor?" She flailed her arms around. "I thought we were gonna move in together, and instead he dumps me. On our anniversary." Her hands moved to her hair, which she pulled back into a ponytail puff secured by a thick hair band she kept around her wrist. "He was going to be the one."

"Mmmkay." Joanie Kotter pulled Maggie's cocktail across the table and out of reach. "You can't *make* someone the one if they don't actually want that for themselves. Better you know now than after years of marriage and kids. You deserve someone who's sure."

Maggie reached across the table for her drink, her long limbs working to her benefit. She squeezed her belly against the edge of the table, her heavy breasts resting on its surface. "I know that, logically, you're right." She pouted, her face scrunching up as she began to whine. "Rob wasn't the one. I can see that now. I just want to wallow for a while anyway."

"But, ma'am, what's a while? It's already been months, Mags," Savvy emphasized. Her heart-shaped face was framed by a freshly cut bob with textured waves. "It's time to get over it."

"And how do you propose that I do that?" *Everyone acts like that part is so easy, but it isn't.*

"Get under someone else, Counselor. It wasn't that long ago that you were pressing me to get over a certain someone, you know." Savvy's thick lashes framed her widened eyes. A sarcastic smile spread across her face. "If my memory serves me correctly, I barely had a week before you were trying to get me to create an online profile."

"Ugh, don't even think about it. I'm not going to do that." Maggie gagged at the thought. "I believe in meeting people organically. I am not equipped to handle the nonsense that frolics online."

Savvy raised an index finger. "And I was? Remember the lizard tongue guy? Spencer *still* won't let me live that down." She curled her fingers around the collar of her blouse and shuddered. "You were the one that talked me into going out with someone from the app so that I could feel like I'd 'explored my options.'" She used her fingers to quote that last bit, and dammit if she wasn't right.

"See, but you're the one percent who had a positive experience. You're with Spencer now. And stop right there—you didn't actually *meet* online, but the fact that you *matched* online after meeting in real life was like confirmation that it was meant to be." Maggie shrugged, willing anyone in earshot to pivot the conversation from her love life.

"I thought you said you weren't going to be about the bullshit?" Savvy's arched brow indicated her refusal to drop the conversation.

Joanie chuckled, looking between her two best friends, her fiancée, Beth, sitting quietly at her side, enjoying the show. When Savvy and her ex had their falling-out, she'd hired Beth as her personal trainer for some get back, and as their friendship grew and Joanie and Maggie showed support, romance ignited quickly between Beth and Joanie. Joanie only needed a few months to feel certain that Beth was her forever.

Playfully, Joanie raised a fist to the side of her face, pointing her thumb toward her ear and her pinkie to her mouth in a makeshift hand phone. "Hello, Karma? Is that you?" She nodded, as if someone on the other line responded. "Okay, I'll tell her." Holding the phone toward Maggie, she grinned. "It's Karma. She wanted to let you know she's come back around."

Maggie slapped her friend's hand, fighting the urge to smile. "Ha-fucking-ha. Shut up, heffa. This wasn't supposed to happen! I don't need to explore my options. I just need 'the one' to show up on my front door ready to start our new life. Is that so much to ask?" Realizing her friends were mouthing every word that she said, Beth included, she shifted in her seat. "What, now y'all are psychic?"

"No, bitch, you've literally made this speech the last six Fridays in a row." Joanie took a sip of her peaty scotch. "Frankly, you need a little more flourish, because that soliloquy is getting a bit stale."

Savvy hid a smile. "And either way, you're going to start dating."

Maggie shook her head. If pouting had been an Olympic sport, she'd have a medal. She pouted her way out of tickets, working on the weekends and giving head. Surely Maggie could pout her way out of online dating. "Nope, I refuse." Her lips pursed, and she hoped her friends could read the words *hell no* written across her forehead.

"I thought you might say that," her friend said with a grin. "That's why I took the liberty of creating a profile for you. Consider this payback for when Jason and I broke up."

"No." Maggie faked a tantrum, whining nasally and imitating Kevin Hart's stand-up. "Please! No. I'm not readyyy."

"Sorry, babe, we took it to a vote." Beth rubbed Maggie's shoulder.

"You voted without me?" She couldn't decide which offense was worse—that they'd voted on what to do about her love life or that they'd done so without her present.

"Of course we did. You weren't going to see reason, so we had to do this on your behalf. You'll thank us later." Savvy raised her gin and tonic.

"I'll thank you from hell," she muttered.

"Phone." Savvy held out her hand.

"No." Maggie shielded it from her, but Joanie was too fast. Snapping up the phone, Joanie tossed it to Savvy. "Seriously, you didn't give Savvy a choice. What makes you think that you're any different?"

Maggie's eyes explored the ceiling. "When are y'all going to accept that I simply know what's best? For *all* of us?"

Her friends burst out laughing. Joanie patted the corners of her eyes with her napkin as she tried to catch her breath. "Good one."

"Chile, please. You better get it together, too, because you've got two weddings to attend this year, and we expect you to bring a date for both of them," Savvy added.

Ugh, can they stop reminding me? She rolled her eyes and pretended to gag. "Yes, yes. By all means, please paint the picture for me again of your fairy-tale love lives. You give me so much hope that I'll find love again," she droned, staccato embellishing each syllable.

Joanie leaned close, the perfect spirals of her golden-brown twist-out framing her freckled brown skin. "You betta quit. You were more than happy to volunteer yourself to be the maid of honor in both of our weddings." She gestured between herself and Savvy, who'd only recently gotten engaged to Spencer. Her diamond ring sparkled every time the light hit it. *The ultimate reminder.*

Happy as Maggie was for her friends, seeing where they were in their relationships just made her stomach churn. In her mind, the three of them would have been planning their weddings together; she wouldn't be the odd one out. Too bad Rob had other plans—he'd already moved on to some professional tennis player who decided to give him the time of day. *Ugh. Men.*

Beth, who'd introduced Maggie to Rob in the first place—they were both tennis coaches—all but disowned him after discovering that he'd ended things to jump into this new fling. She didn't believe that he'd cheated physically, but there was obviously a connection between the pair before Rob made his move to depart. To Maggie, that still fell into the unfaithful category. He had permission to look, but being emotionally connected to someone else was crossing the line.

Maggie could appreciate that her friends wanted to help her get past a guy who wasn't worth another thought, and she welcomed help, but she didn't appreciate the rush. "This is just too fast. I feel like things are still too fresh for me to try to move on."

Savvy sucked her teeth and glared. "You were with Rob for a year. I was with Jason for over six years, and you wouldn't let me go two weeks before you set up a Tinder account for me. It's now been months for you. Kotter, let me borrow your hand phone." She held her thumb and pinkie toward the profile of her face while staring at Mags, her unamused, deadpan expression giving not one inch. "Hello, Pot? Yes, this is Kettle. You're black."

Joanie snorted, covering her face with her hands. Beth put her drink down and bit her lip.

"You're getting a little too much pleasure out of my pain here, Joanie," Maggie warned. The daughter of a retired police officer, Joan Kotter had always preferred to be called by her last name. She was constantly using random police jargon that made no sense to anyone but her, but she had a heart of gold and was the epitome of a ride-or-die chick, so she got a pass. Maggie refused to call her friend Kotter; she preferred Joanie because of her obsession with Joni Mitchell after *Love, Actually* came out.

"Listen, Savvy's right. You've had more than enough time to move forward. And quit playing. You're over Rob. You *want* somebody new. But your little plan to just sit around and wait for Prince Charming to show up with a glass slipper that fits one of them big-ass boats you call feet just ain't gon' happen."

"Ugh. Shut up. Maybe I want someone new, but I'm not ready to give up on Prince Charming finding his way to me. It could happen, you know." Maggie sulked, holding up a hand when Joanie opened her mouth. "Just accept that I am embracing my inner hermit for a while, sis. Soft life. Maybe Prince Charming will randomly be visiting a relative in my building when I am picking up my mail or something."

"Oh, no, I don't need Wednesday Addams helping me plan my wedding. I need sassy, energetic, colorful, happy Mags to come back to us. The sprite version who gets her back blown out on the regular." Savvy pointed. "When you're in your li'l hermit era, you're bound to make choices that fit your mood, and I refuse to have an all-dressed-in-black bridal shower."

She and Spencer had decided to do an intimate backyard wedding followed by an extended honeymoon. Her chef friend, Sarah, was catering, and the entire wedding party and guest count was planned not to exceed forty people. Joanie and Beth were planning something even smaller, a destination wedding that would be just close family and friends willing to fly wherever they ended up. Maggie had scheduled the dress fittings, and she was responsible for helping with invitations, the bridal shower and the bachelorette party. She had enough work to do. Did she really need to find a plus-one?

"Seriously," Joanie muttered. "When Beth and I asked you for destination wedding suggestions, you actually recommended the tar pits."

Beth's lips curved as her eyes swung in Maggie's direction. "That was…a thought."

"It was a joke." Maggie threw up her hands.

Joanie cocked her head to the side. "I believe your exact words were 'the La Brea Tar Pits are a good place for love to go and die.'"

"Okay, I wasn't that dramatic, but whatever," she lied. She *had* been that dramatic, but she'd die before owning it. Seeing others happy when she wasn't sucked. It was exponentially worse to be surrounded by lovebirds when vultures and crows would better suit her mood. "Obviously, you should just go somewhere sunny and warm." She shuddered at the thought of an island getaway.

"Will you come out of your coffin to join us in the light, Dracula?" Savvy poked Maggie's shoulder, her rich brown skin with a hint of shimmer exposed over the ruffle of her top.

"Ow!"

Ignoring her, Savvy turned to Joanie, her eyes brightening

with an idea. "Hey. What if you and Beth do your wedding destination where we're honeymooning? It would be so fun to have y'all with us!" She and Spencer planned to honeymoon in Thailand—Savvy would connect with a couple of her aunties in Bangkok, but their primary stay would be on the gorgeous island of Phuket.

Joanie sputtered. "That wouldn't be an imposition for you guys?"

"Of course not! What better way to celebrate love than with more love?"

"Blech," Maggie muttered, before she felt a sharp kick to her shin. "Ouch! You know, eventually I'm going to have permanent bruising from how often y'all kick me."

Savvy leaned forward, her eyes sparkling though she spoke menacingly through gritted teeth. "Then don't give us a reason to kick you, ho."

Maggie scowled, her glare fixing on her friend. "You know I could take you, right?"

Beth's and Joanie's jaws dropped, and their eyes darted around the table as if furniture was about to start moving. Maggie might as well have slapped Savvy with a white glove and proposed a duel.

Savvy's head tilted slightly, and her eyes narrowed—her lips thinning to a straight line. "You wanna take this outside?"

Damn, she called my bluff. Maggie sat back in her chair. Savvy was sweet as pie, but she was strong as hell. They were roughly the same size—proudly plus—and though Maggie was faster, Savvy was definitely stronger. Maggie would never admit it, but if their trio ever got caught in a scenario where they had to fight, Savvy was the one who would whomp on anyone who threatened their squad until the threat was eliminated. She had the advantage of older brothers who'd been her sparring partners from a young age. Suddenly parched, Maggie sipped her old-fashioned. "Nah, I'm good."

The other three burst out laughing, Savvy and Joanie slapping each other five. "What were you thinking going up against Savvy?" Joanie asked incredulously.

"Lapse in judgment. I forgot who I was dealing with," Maggie laughed lightly, waving it off.

Savvy shook her head, her lips curved into a smile. "Well, my dear, I'm glad you got that out of your system. And here you go. Your profile's been set up and is one click away from going live, so get to swiping." She tossed Maggie her phone. "You'll have to be quick to find someone in time for the weddings."

"Ugh, nine months to find someone I'd be willing to travel internationally with... Do I have to?"

"Yes," her girls responded in unison.

Maggie clutched imaginary pearls, leaning back from the table. "Really, though, the surround-sound answers?"

"It's time, sis." Joanie nodded. "Time to move on, because Rob sure has. Consider this a high priority on your list of maid-of-honor duties."

"You want to come play some tennis with us? Maybe you could aim a few balls at that shallow prick for opting to be the Stedman of tennis?" Savvy still trained with Beth. When she'd first started sessions, Joanie had joined in, and it wasn't long until Maggie got roped in for talking too much shit. *Even if it was the truth.* That's how she met Rob in the first place. *And now it's Rob and Clara.*

The possibility of the two of them being on a neighboring court was too much. "I'll pass, but if you see him, can you kindly tell him to fuck off?"

"Bet."

They clinked their glasses together in agreement.

★ ★ ★

After arriving home, Maggie kicked off her shoes and plopped down on her sofa. The balcony doors were still folded ajar, and the rustling sound of the evening waves immediately melted her shoulders. Staring at her phone, Maggie read through the profile that Savvy and Joanie had written on her behalf, and she shook her head softly at the content. They made her sound like a legal advocate dynamo—and they weren't wrong—but the truth was that she was a tax attorney with towering student loans, a mortgage and an addiction to steamy romance novels that made her long for the kind of happily-ever-after that most people assumed was the stuff of fairy tales.

But that was the problem—she knew that fairy-tale love was possible. She'd watched her parents her whole life—high school sweethearts who, as they'd approached their fortieth wedding anniversary, were even more in love than she remembered them being when she was a kid. Sure, they'd gone through a rough patch when she and her siblings left home, and they had to adjust to being empty nesters, but they'd rallied, finding new interests in common and new ways to enjoy each other's company. They never questioned their willingness to put in the work, and watching their love continue to bloom and grow just made Maggie that much more determined that she'd find her own happily-ever-after someday.

In the end, her mother hadn't made it to their fortieth anniversary. She'd passed away eight years ago, but even in her final months, she'd been surrounded by love and had time to prepare, having outlived her terminal diagnosis by two years. The way Maggie's dad had doted on her mom, the way they let go of any petty quibble before it could drain any energy from their day, showed her that even in really hard times, if you remembered who you chose and why you chose them, the tone of the relationship was set for the long haul.

Where is my Prince Charming?

She blinked away tears when her cell phone pinged with an incoming text message.

Garrett: Hey gorgeous, WYD?

Maggie's lip curled slightly. The first time he'd ever called her *gorgeous*, they'd had a movie night, and she'd swooned at Dermot Mulroney referring to Julia Roberts in that way, though they were best friends. Garrett started calling Maggie *gorgeous* to tease her for how mushy she'd been over Dermot, but she dared him to find anyone who didn't find that man attractive.

It wasn't lost on Maggie that Garrett's voice was even deeper and more gravelly than Dermot's. Her eyes fluttered closed briefly recalling his playful growl that mirrored Dermot's seemingly smug amusement. *G should have gone into voice acting instead of sports journalism.* She shook her head before she could fall into a daydream of him reading her favorite erotica and returned to her phone.

Maggie: It's official. The girls are forcing me to start online dating. UGH.

Garrett: Yikes, LOL. You really called it. We still on for tomorrow?

Maggie and her college best friend, Garrett, had a standing date on Saturday nights to order takeout and watch a movie. They'd started enjoying movies together years ago, with it becoming more frequent after he finished grad school and moved back to Los Angeles, though making it weekly was a newer development. It was Maggie's turn to pick a movie, and she relished opportunities to make Garrett watch romantic comedies with her. He teased her about it endlessly, because no one would guess from her demeanor how sappy she got over happily-ever-afters. A huge fan of action series like *Die Hard*, *Fast and Furious*, or just about anything involving Jason Statham or Gerard Butler, he only ever wanted to watch movies with some epic chase or fight scene. *Boring.*

Maggie: Of course! You know it's my turn, right?

Garrett: What are you going to make me suffer through this time? Please don't make me sit through *Pride and Prejudice* for the 600th time... Can we at least watch something with some representation?

Maggie: Hmmm... How about *Just Wright*? Common does the sports.

Garrett: See... You know it's called basketball. SMH. What do you want me to pick up?

Maggie: I've got food covered this week—Savvy cooked up too much food and told me to pick some up.

Garrett: Please tell me she made oxtails...

Maggie: IKR, I wish! Nah, she was trying out a bunch of recipes for her next cookbook, so she said she'd surprise us.

Garrett: Gotcha. I'll bring some wine.

Maggie: Bet.

She set down her phone, leaning back against plush throw pillows. Her eyes closed briefly before fluttering open again at the sound of her phone.

Garrett: Don't get too swipe happy over there. ☺

Maggie: I'm dreading it, tbh.

Garrett: We can look at some together tomorrow.

Maggie: Thanks, love. See you soon.

Maggie looked out toward the ocean. *Why can't I find a good guy like Garrett?*

Back at Georgetown, they'd met freshman year commiserating over an Intro to Journalism class with a professor who had an affinity for redlining. Garrett was a lanky nerd in metal retainers and oversize basketball shorts, and she'd had her eyes set on the star football player who was two years older. Too bad her crush wanted nothing more than late-night benefits and lost interest in her within a couple of weeks. She'd been decimated, and Garrett had been the friend whose shoulder she had cried on, since Savvy and Joan were both on the West Coast at UCLA. Of course, her girls had threatened to fly out to DC and castrate the fool who'd rejected their beloved Mags, but she soon moved on, rebounding and dating Garrett's roommate, Kyle, for most of college. Kyle was on track and field, same as Maggie, and he appealed to her competitive side.

Garrett dated women on and off, but never for long, and whenever Mags was visiting Kyle, she'd often stay over and then study with Garrett, the aspiring sports journalist, offering to proofread his articles and essays in exchange for a home-cooked meal. Cooking was never Maggie's ministry, and Garrett's Southern upbringing had included learning how to cook some of his mom's best recipes. After a while they settled into a routine, and Kyle settled down with someone else. She never missed him once they'd called it quits—she'd spent more of her quality time and energy with Garrett anyway, so they simply relocated their hangout spot to her place to avoid upsetting Kyle's new boo.

They'd never dated, but that was by design—after the roommate debacle, Maggie and Garrett agreed one night that the friendship they'd built was far more important to the both of them than some fling. Neither of them wanted to risk losing the other. Sure, Garrett was attractive, supersmart, generous and genuinely an all-around good guy, but after watching him date for two decades, Maggie was certain they'd never have worked—he had the attention span of a gnat.

At present, Garrett was dating some cute yoga instructor that he'd met through his childhood friend Kenny. He always fell into the same cycle—meeting someone that he immediately wanted to bed but could never take home to his mom. As a sports journalist with dreams of eventually becoming a broadcaster and a connection to ESPN that was getting stronger by the day, he attracted a lot of women who were along the periphery of the industry looking for a come up.

That was one thing about people in LA—everyone was trying to get ahead and genuine connections could be hard to come by. If Maggie remembered correctly, Garrett and his current significant other were nearing their three-month mark, which meant that she was probably showing her true colors and he was getting close to letting her go. Besides, he and a colleague were starting their sports podcast, and his articles on the upcoming NBA players' strike were starting to pick up steam. He didn't have time to try to help her find celebrity athletes to plug her yoga retreat.

Maggie shook her head, not out of disapproval, but because she wanted her best friend to find some happiness and stability—things that she craved for herself. She figured if she couldn't have those things, then the people around her should so that she could live vicariously. *Though jealously.*

Picking up her phone, she opened the dating app and scrolled through her profile, making changes and adding preferences so that she could tell her friends she was making an effort. As soon as she published her profile, she started getting notifications to tell her that she was being "liked" by potential Prince Charmings. Tentatively, she began swiping, mostly left. The first few "princes" didn't seem promising. *Where do I even start?*

Finally, she eyed a profile for a handsome man who did copywriting for an educational company. His eyes crinkled at the corners, and his low fade had a faint sprinkling of gray visible in the waves of his hair. She scanned through his profile, where he described himself as "ambitious but chill" and "the rare good guy looking to settle down." Heaving a deep sigh, she decided to take a chance and swipe right.

"It's time."

3

AFTER RUNNING A COUPLE OF MILES ON SATURDAY
morning and doing her normal strength routine of squats,
lunges, planks and push-ups, Maggie stopped by Savvy's house
to love on her best friend and praise her incredible cooking
skills. Savvy's response was to load Maggie's car with three
bags of food—enough to feed an army—complete with heating instructions and recommendations for wine pairings. An
accomplished home cook, Savvy was working on her second
cookbook with a popular local chef, and they'd spent all day
Friday testing recipes. Maggie loved recipe test days, because
she could barely boil water. She'd survived law school on coffee and free pizza from lunchtime student org meetings.

At home, Maggie put away all of the food, hopped in the
shower and exfoliated her deep brown skin. Her coils were
safely wrapped and tied under a shower cap, and she washed
her face and took her time, allowing the steam to open her

pores before she lathered her body in an almond-scented bath oil and stepped into the path of her high-pressure showerhead. As the almost-scalding water kneaded and melted away any stress from her shoulders, the scents from the bunches of lavender and eucalyptus hanging from the showerhead permeated her senses.

After, she moisturized her skin from head to toe and dug through her closet for some of her comfiest loungewear. She loved that she never had to dress up for Saturdates—who needs to dress up when you're relaxing on the couch? If they had to get some work done, they did it from the comfort of Maggie's living room—she always put out extra pillows and blankets in case Garrett decided to crash after a marathon viewing. She pulled on a cropped sweatshirt and jogger pant set in a purply mauve, wrapped her pineappled curls into a colorful headscarf and donned a thin gold necklace that held a pendant made of her mother's wedding ring, fused to a golden orchid—Maggie's mom's favorite flower. Mags never left the house without her necklace on.

"Hello?" called a deep voice from the front door. "You here?"

"Hey!" she called in response. "Wow, you're early." She walked barefoot toward the sound of rustling bags. "What did you bring? I told you Savvy gave me enough food for the entire week!"

As she rounded the corner, Garrett stooped to put down his bags and then stood to his full height. At six foot three, his dark brown skin shone in the light—his face was framed by a taper fade cut and a full, manicured beard interspersed with a few gray hairs. Over the years, his hairline had receded a bit, but his skin was immaculate. He wore his typical uniform of blue jeans and a zip-up hoodie over a black T-shirt with the words *Black, Proud, & Educated*. His shirt, a relic from a decade ago, used to hang over his toned swimmer's physique.

Now, with Garrett strapped to a desk to meet all of his article deadlines, he filled the shirt out more, proudly owning his self-proclaimed dad bod.

His full lips curved into a smile at Maggie's approach. "Hey, gorgeous." He kissed her cheek and wrapped his arms around her for a tight squeeze. "I brought some wine, those olives you like and your favorite ice cream." His voice was deep and smooth, like a velvety dark chocolate accompanied by a full-bodied red wine. She used to joke with him that she could listen to his soothing voice anytime—he could read the phone book, and she'd find comfort in hearing the location and contact information for every person and business from cover to cover.

He gives the best hugs. Squeezing him tightly, she rubbed her hand across his muscular back. "Hey, handsome. You're too good to me, you know?"

"Is that possible?" He stepped back, admiring her lounge-wear. "I like this color on you."

She spun around and hit him with the old-school rap cover squat pose, angling herself to the side and resting her hands on her thighs until Garrett burst out laughing.

"Okay, Maggie-Fresh," he quipped.

"Funny. Hungry?"

He side-eyed her, lips twitching in a half smile. "When am I not? And what did Savvy bless us with today?"

"We have choices! We have her grandmother's green curry chicken, a spicy lamb with red chilies and Thai basil, crab-stuffed prawns with bucatini pasta and blistered Marzano tomatoes, whatever 'blistered' means. She also did a porcini-mushroom-and-Gruyère-stuffed pork tenderloin with a spinach-and-Parmesan risotto, a curried ginger-and-carrot soup with seared scallops, and those green beans with crispy lardons that you love."

Garrett squeezed his eyes shut, his mouth smacking. "Tell me why she isn't marrying *me* again?"

Maggie laughed, shaking her head as she led the way to the living room. "Because Spencer proposed before you did."

He tilted his head as he followed her. "If I remember correctly, I wasn't *allowed* to date your friends." Years ago, before Maggie would agree to allow Garrett to meet Savvy and Joanie, she made him promise that he wouldn't try to date them. At the time, he'd run through half of the women's volleyball team, and she didn't trust that he'd be more serious with her nearest and dearest. Not that Joan would have given him the slightest chance, but Savvy had always found him attractive.

"Well, you still aren't. That's how Spencer got to her first," she deadpanned.

"Mags, you've known me our entire adult lives. Surely you know by now that I wouldn't treat your friends poorly."

"Uh-huh. How's the yoga instructor?" She turned to face him.

Garrett dipped his head as he cleared his throat. "Um, Sasha and I broke up."

"Three-month rule?"

"I'm capable of dating someone longer than three months, Maggie." He exhaled an exasperated breath, but his easy smile and mischievous glare read full-on amusement.

"I don't question your ability to be in a lasting relationship, love. I question your *desire* to do so." She made a face at him, and he narrowed his eyes at her playfully. Stepping behind the kitchen island, Maggie began to remove labeled containers from the refrigerator. "So what are you in the mood for? Because everything looks amazing."

He eyed the neatly packaged food—huge portions that would ensure that Maggie had more than enough of everything even after he left. "I vote for pasta and prawns, pork and risotto and green beans."

"Okay, good, because I wasn't going to share the green curry with you anyway."

"Ain't nothin' new."

"Hush." Grinning, she set about plating and heating the food, while Garrett cued up the movie on the smart TV.

Penny appeared, wrapping her tail around Garrett's leg before retreating back to the bedroom.

"Thank you for not picking a period movie, by the way. I know you love P&P, but you get all soft." He clasped his hands together and blinked profusely with a sappy smile on his face.

"The lies you tell." Maggie glared at him as she shoved a plate under a splatter guard and into the microwave. "I do *not* get all soft." Her firm tone was louder than normal, mostly due to his refusal to love *Pride and Prejudice* as much as she did. She was securely on the bandwagon, and every chance she got, she attempted to drag him along.

He poked his lips out and side-eyed her. "You do, and it's weird. It's so unlike you. You *gush.*"

"I've never gushed a day in my life," she scoffed. "You must have me confused with someone else."

"Anytime that dude starts talking, you look just like this." He mimicked her mannerisms, his eyes widening like saucers as he clutched at invisible pearls. His voice deepened. "'You have bewitched me, body and soul…'" His body fell back against the plush couch as he rolled his eyes, pulling his hoodie from his broad shoulders to fling it over the armrest of the sofa.

She didn't want to admit that he was right, but of course he *had* to quote one of her favorite lines. In her mind, there could never be a better Mr. Darcy than in the 2005 adaptation. *Matthew Macfadyen played the hell out of that role.* She carried the hot dishes with oven mitts over to her coffee table.

Garrett jumped up to help her carry the steaming containers, dipping his nose toward the food to take in the aroma. "Savvy put her foot in this, I can already tell."

Maggie nodded in agreement. "All the way to the kneecap, I'm sure. She's such a beast in the kitchen."

He raised an eyebrow. "How come you've never asked her to teach you how to cook?"

She blew out an exasperated breath, sucking her teeth. "Are you going to ask me that *every* time she cooks for us?"

Shrugging, he grabbed serving spoons and dished out food for the both of them, his portions heaping. "I'm going to keep asking until you respond with an acceptable answer."

"'I am not a good cook' is not an acceptable answer?"

"No, it's not. It's a definitive statement, when you *could* be a good cook if you actually tried—if you bothered to learn."

She chewed on the inside of her cheek. "Okay, maybe I don't *want* to learn."

"But why?" He blew on a tender chunk of pork tenderloin topped with risotto and gingerly placed it into his mouth, closing his eyes, a throaty growl escaping his lips. "Mmmph, my God."

She watched as Garrett shook his head, slowly chewing and savoring that first bite, a twinge of something stirring in her gut. "Because Savvy's too good," she blurted out.

Garrett stopped chewing, his brows pinching together as he turned to look at her, flabbergasted. "Why does it matter how good Savvy is?" His mouth was still full of food.

Maggie squeezed her eyes shut, not wanting to admit the truth. She paused for a few beats before responding. "You know how competitive I am."

He held up a finger. "Hold on a sec." He chewed quickly

and swallowed his food before turning his body to face her. "You mean to tell me you're jealous of Savvy?"

"That's not the word I would use," she huffed defensively. "She's just really good at what she does."

"And you only want to do it if you can be better? Than your best friend? Am I hearing you right?" He pushed himself up from the couch. "We need wine for this."

"For what?"

"To unpack this foolery, Mags."

"What foolery? Of the two of us, *you're* the cook, so why don't *you* take some lessons from her?" She fumbled with an earring the way she always did when she got called out for something. "You actually like doing it."

"Okay, true. If I had the time or the energy, maybe I'd consider asking." He uncorked a bottle of chenin blanc and grabbed wineglasses from a cabinet above the sink. "Plus, I have this amazing best friend who happens to be best friends with Savvy, so I get all the food without the effort. It's like magic." His eyes sparkled as he gestured with the bottle in his hand.

He carefully served Maggie a glass before rounding the couch to sit next to her.

She took a slow sip. "Remember that time we did the relay race at my family's reunion?"

Garrett's face immediately brightened. "That's random. You mean when you tried to carry me so we could win the three-legged race?"

She clicked her tongue. "Well, when you say it like that… Never mind, let's put on the movie. I'm sure you're tired of my shenanigans. By the way, how's the podcast going?"

He watched her intently as she cackled and snatched up the remote. "I can never get enough," he deadpanned. "And we're just about to tape the first episode. Our producer wants to get this editing software before we get started so that everything feels consistent, but after that, we should be good to go. We even found our first sponsor."

Garrett was building his platform and had always dreamed of being a broadcaster on SportsCenter. The podcast was meant to continue building his base, where they'd talk all things sports, interview athletes and share some hot takes on the latest in athletic current events.

"Wow, look at you!" She elbowed him and dug into her food. "Oh, my God, these prawns!" Garlic and butter dripped from her lips as a roasted grape tomato burst in her mouth. The shrimp were perfectly cooked, and the pasta was still al dente, with hints of white wine and crushed red pepper flakes tickling her tongue. "Mmm..." She dabbed at her mouth with a paper towel.

"Man, this is so good." Garrett's eyes closed when a piece of the stuffed pork hit his tongue. When opening music started, Garrett groaned, turning his attention to the screen. "Come on, Mags. What did you just put on?"

Between bites, Maggie grinned slyly. *"Pride and Prejudice?"*

"Wasn't the stipulation that we were *not* going to watch this?"

She shrugged, twisting pasta around her fork. "Shenanigans!"

Hours later, warm breath tickled Maggie's ear. She squirmed and a weight released her head so that she could look around. On the TV, the credits rolled. "Damn, we missed the end," she mumbled.

Garrett stirred next to her. She'd fallen asleep on his shoulder, and he'd used her head as a cushion. "Too bad," he murmured. "I kind of like seeing you go all mushy."

She chucked a decorative pillow at him. "Shut up. I don't do that."

He sat up and ran his hand over his fade. "You do. Gooey soft. It's cute."

"*Cute* should be reserved for children and pets. I'm a grown-ass woman, G."

Standing, he reached his long limbs toward the ceiling, stretching his chin upward. "Chill out, Beyoncé. Contrary to popular belief, women can be called *cute*."

"Agree to disagree." She playfully swatted his hand away when he attempted to pinch her cheek.

"What's that?" He pointed to a notification on her phone, a glint of recognition shining in his eyes. "Is that what I think it is?"

Before she could reach it, he snatched up her phone and entered her passcode. Maggie cursed under her breath. *I really need to stop using my birthday.*

His eyes widened as her phone unlocked and the dating app opened to her profile page. "Wow, it's officially live, huh? And to think, you said you'd never be caught dead on one of these sites, M." He began scrolling, the corners of his mouth twitching. "'Rising attorney searching for a partner in life and love. I speak my mind and intend to live my best life no matter what. If you're looking for a submissive, I ain't it.' Well, if that ain't the truth…" He continued reading silently, but the smile on his face made Maggie grit her teeth.

This must be what it feels like to be on exhibit at the zoo. "Okay, that's enough." She snatched the phone away.

"I can't believe you let Kotter and Savvy push you into this. You said online dating was for the desperate and socially awkward."

"Yeah, but I made Savvy try it when she and Jason broke up, so she's convinced Joanie that they should exact revenge."

"An unwilling participant?"

She shrugged. "I might as well see what is out there. One of my colleagues at the firm got married to some guy she met online, so I guess it is possible to find good ones."

"Yeah, but didn't you say Savvy's experience was pretty bad?" He took the phone back and began to flip through the profiles of potential dates, barely bothering to read their descriptions before he swiped left to the next. "Nope. Nope. Too short. Nope, needs more education. Has too many baby mamas. Too forward."

She craned to see over his shoulder. "What do you mean by *too forward*?"

He tilted the screen in her direction, his face expressionless. "'If we meet, we smashin'.'"

She pressed her lips together, poking them outward as she considered the statement. *Well, damn.* "Yep, too forward. Well... I mean, what does he look like?"

Garrett rolled his eyes and scrolled to the man's photos—a collection of posed pictures in sunglasses, making odd hand gestures and squatting in front of his friends. "Seem familiar? Does he look like a catch to you, Maggie-Fresh?"

"Umm...no." She bit her lip, holding back some of the thoughts running through her mind.

"You sure? Do you see this? What is he doing, taking his pulse?" In one photo, the man was showing off a blinged-out watch while holding two fingers against his carotid artery.

"Maybe he knows CPR." She threw up her hands.

Garrett stared at her with widened eyes and blinked emphatically until they both burst out laughing. He made quick work out of swiping left and rejecting every profile that appeared until they'd exhausted her potential matches for the day.

As the laughter subsided, Maggie's face sombered, and she

looked at her best friend. "Why can't I find someone like you?"

Having taken a sip of his wine, Garrett cleared his throat to keep from choking. "Like me?" He looked at Mags curiously.

"Yeah, someone who just gets me. Understands my moods and my quirks, someone that I don't have to teach anything to. Someone who gets me and loves me regardless. Someone who will ride with me till the wheels fall off."

His eyes shifted to look at something on the floor as he considered her list of desirables. He cleared his throat, but his voice came out strained, like he needed more air. "You want someone like me? I always thought you were looking for the buttoned-up type who makes half a mil each year and still finds time to volunteer at the local soup kitchen."

"Well, I was," she admitted. "But that hasn't seemed to work for me, and Rob was probably too far in the opposite direction. So maybe it's time to try something else and see if that brings about different results."

He cocked his head to the side, and for the first time in a long time, she couldn't tell what he was thinking. "That's true."

"You'll help me weed through these dudes?" She looked at him expectantly. He'd done such an efficient job so far, and only the girls knew her better than Garrett.

"Of course I will. I'm here for you, gorgeous." He put his arm around her shoulders and pulled her close, dropping his lips to the crown of her head.

Wrapping her arms around his torso, Maggie shut her eyes and squeezed. "You're the best."

4

"SO WHAT DO YOU DO? THAT WASN'T CLEAR FROM your profile." Maggie smiled slightly, the server having just delivered wine flights to the table. Sip was one of the hottest wine bars in West LA, and each month, the establishment introduced a fresh menu of small plates and snacks that paired well with their extensive bottle list.

The wine bar had kitschy elevator-style music playing and the well-lit room was filled with people talking and laughing over wine flights and charcuterie boards. From Maggie's seat, Garrett was visible over the shoulder of Ian, the date sitting in front of her. Garrett glanced in their direction occasionally, as he watched college basketball on one of the TVs mounted behind the bar—something the owners likely installed for sports-minded partners to sit and wait while their significant others overdid it on the mimosa flights at Sunday brunch.

"Oh, a little of this, a little of that. You know how it is." Ian took a loud slurp of the boldest red wine in his flight, ignoring the tasting advice of their server to start with the lightest selection. He smacked loudly. "Damn, that's not sweet *at all*, but I bet you are." His voice deepened at the end.

Ew. There went my appetite. Maggie swished her lips to the side as she nodded. She'd never heard back from the copywriter, so she'd decided to take a chance on Ian. His profile, though brief, stated that he was on the search for his future wife and displayed photos of potential date outings like wine tasting, axe throwing and an escape room. "That's what the server meant by *dry*. You started with the boldest red."

They'd both selected the same flight of red wines, which sat atop a cardstock tasting sheet detailing the vintage, the region, the type of grapes, the flavor notes and the percentage of alcohol below. There were circles where each glass should be placed and lines at the bottom for patrons to take notes or place orders for bottles.

"You get wined and dined a lot, huh?" Ian rested his chin in his hand, looking at her through aviator sunglasses with gradient lenses. His dark eyes roamed her features before reconnecting with hers, his lids flittering a bit as the corner of his mouth lifted.

Maggie's stomach lurched. *What is with the sunglasses indoors? And is he batting his lashes at me?* "I do enjoy a good glass of wine." She took a sip of the deep pink rosé, starting her tastes from the intended side. She rolled the effervescent liquid around on her tongue before swallowing it down. "I'm no expert, but with this one, I taste strawberries, a little bit of citrus and maybe a hint of cherry?"

"Oh, yeah? You like cherries?" He pressed his lips together, sinking his teeth into the lower one.

She set her glass down. "I like that it has a dry finish. I'm not usually a fan of the sweeter wines… I'm curious—are your eyes sensitive to the light?"

"Nah, I just like to keep a low profile. You never know who you might run into—LA is such a small world."

"Yeah, I guess so. Is there someone you're avoiding?"

"No one in particular. I just don't like a lot of folks in my business. You said you're a lawyer, right? What kind?"

Maggie nodded. *So cringe.* "Tax law mostly. I advise individuals and small businesses on ways to optimize tax filings in terms of their finances and help them handle disputes with the IRS or the Franchise Tax Board. But what about you?"

He shrugged. "I mean, I already told you. A little of everything. I do some gig work, and I watch my kids some weekends. You're not afraid of a man with kids, are you?"

"No, of course not," she responded slowly. She'd dated a single father before Rob. "How many do you have?"

"Four, that I know of," he laughed lightly.

"Wow, okay," she processed, her curiosity piqued. "Sounds like you have your hands full! Were you married?"

"Nah." He rested his arms on the table. "I got close once, but one girl was pregnant when I was about to make things official with another."

"Oh, I see. So there are two mothers?"

"No, four. The others weren't serious-serious, though." He sampled the rosé, tasting it carefully and rolling it around in his mouth the way that Maggie had. "Oh, okay. That's what I'm talmbout."

"Right…" She swirled a goblet by its stem, quieting the danger alarms sounding in her mind, so she could put all of her effort into controlling her face the same way she often did for clients. "That must be quite the family dynamic. I also saw on your profile that you're looking for something serious?"

"Yeah, it's time to settle down so that I can expand my family. I'm working toward getting my own place. Right now my mama helps me with the kids when I have them."

Maggie almost choked on the second sample in her flight—a pinot noir from Willamette Valley. *His mom?* "Y-you want more kids?" she stuttered.

"Oh, yeah, I love having babies. You don't have any?" He tilted his head as he stared at her, nudging his sunglasses farther up the bridge of his nose.

Get. Out. People probably get pregnant just looking at this guy. She shook her head. "None so far, but I can imagine it must be hard to manage all of the kids' schedules. Are they close?"

"I usually got them different weekends." He eyed her curiously. "You ask a lot of questions, don't you?"

She lifted the palm of her hand. "I'm sorry—it's the attorney in me. I'm just trying to understand the dynamic." She rolled her shoulders back and fixed a doe-eyed gaze on him attentively. "What would you like to talk about?" *Nothing like some piping hot tea to spill at brunch.* She moved to her third glass to sample an earthy cab franc, a tiny sigh escaping her mouth once she swallowed.

"Oh, you like that one, huh?" He watched her mouth, leaning closer. He chewed on his bottom lip as he appraised her breasts, eventually lifting his awareness to meet her eye.

Maggie sat back in her chair, cursing herself for wearing a low-cut tank with jeans and a blazer. "Yeah, I'm a fan of cab francs and bold reds in general. I'm really excited for this last one that you didn't seem to like."

He scrunched up his face. "To me, it's too sour."

"Sour?" Her eyebrows shot up. "As in vinegary? If so, that could mean they poured something that's spoiled." She lifted the glass to her nose and sniffed the Primitivo. "It doesn't smell vinegary." She took a sip. "Mmm, that's good."

"Well, you can have mine." He moved to pour the dark red

contents of his glass into hers, but she swung her hand over it to block the exchange.

"No, no. That's okay. I've got to drive home," she quipped, keeping her tone light. "I don't need any more than this." She gestured to her flight, most of the contents still remaining in each glass.

"You know, I could take you." He lowered his voice, eyelids hooded as he used the tip of his tongue to wet his lips before pressing them together. "Come on, ma. You gonna give me some play?" He jutted his chin toward her.

Maggie looked around to see if anyone else had heard the question before she busted out laughing. "Does that ever work?" she asked incredulously.

He blinked. "What you mean?"

"I just can't believe you talk to women like this and that they let you." She shook her head.

"Well, I mean, if you're gonna be a bitch, just say that." He shrugged.

Maggie sucked her teeth, measuring her tone to be calm and clear. "A bitch? Listen, playboy, I'm not the one or the two. The way you throw that word around, I bet you talk about the mothers of your children like that. Respectfully, do better, especially if you have any daughters." She rose from her seat, pressing her palm against the white tablecloth.

Garrett turned his attention from the game and craned his neck toward Maggie, raising his eyebrows as he caught her eye. He'd promised to leave her be unless she signaled for him.

Instead, she returned her attention back to Ian, who remained seated, his mouth a tight line. She leaned forward and spoke in a hushed tone. "What you not gon' do is call me out my name and think I'll sit here one more second." Maggie collected her purse, which had been hanging on the back of her chair, and turned toward the bar.

Ian grabbed her wrist as she passed him, his lips curled into a sneer. "You look here—"

Maggie snatched her arm away, wrapping her fingers around the area he'd captured. "Nope, not today."

Garrett crossed the dining room in a couple of strides, stepping between Maggie and Ian. "Hey, man. You shouldn't do that."

Ian leaned over to crane his head upward. "And who are you?"

"I was just sitting at the bar. I don't know you, but she don't look like she wants you touching her."

"Man, this ain't got nothin' to do with you. Mind your business."

"Excuse me—is there a problem here?" Joseph, the restaurant owner, stepped closer, having made his rounds to greet tables around them. Maggie was enough of a regular that he knew her wine tastes and would bring her special pours of new vintages to sample.

"Nah, nothin's wrong. It's just that we're here together, and she needs to pay her half before she leaves." Ian glared at her.

Maggie began to fish into her purse for her card, swearing under her breath. *This nightmare can't end quick enough.* "I can't believe this bullshit," she muttered.

"That's not necessary." Joseph held out a hand toward Maggie before turning back to Ian. "Sir, I'll take care of splitting your bill so that you only have to take care of your portion. I'll be right back. I'm just going to escort these two out, make sure she's okay to drive, and then I'll be back with your bill." He gestured his arm toward the door, and Maggie and Garrett stepped in front of him.

Joseph followed them toward the door. "You okay, Mags?" he asked quietly.

"Oh, yeah, I'm fine. Thanks for checking on us." She pulled her wallet out of her purse.

"You barely drank your wine, so that flight is on me." He shook his head.

"No! Are you sure? I really don't want our server to miss out on a tip."

"Trust me, I'll take care of it. Just get out of here before that guy regrets letting you leave and tries to chase you home," Joseph laughed.

"Thank you. I'll be back soon!" She and Garrett continued out the door and down the street toward his car.

"You okay?" he asked, tilting his head to look her in the eye.

"Yeah, I'm fine." She shrugged. "It was getting weird anyway. We were talking about how his mom helps with the kids during his weekends."

"Wow, what a winner." Garrett stopped. "I especially liked his sunglasses. What was that about?"

Maggie rolled her eyes. "He was worried someone he knew would see him and get in his business."

Garrett's brow furrowed. "Think he's married?"

"That, or he's got someone trying to serve him some court papers."

"Classic." His mouth curved to one side.

"Indeed," she agreed. "But it's also reality."

"You hungry?"

Maggie's eyes sparkled mischievously. "Always."

"Well, you know that Peruvian chicken place is right down the street."

"Ooh." Maggie closed her eyes. "That sounds perfect. I just want some—"

"Extra garlic sauce," they said in unison.

"Come on, Mags. You know I know." He wrapped his arm around her shoulders and they proceeded down the street.

"Hey, Daddy," Maggie sighed into the phone.

"Uh-oh, what's that tone, Magnolia? What's going on?" Maggie's father's face illuminated her phone screen on the stand next to her computer. The only person left in the world who called her by her full first name with love. He was the one who'd suggested they name her after her mother's second-favorite flower—orchids were her first, but she refused to even consider them in naming her first and only child. *Orchid Felize just doesn't have the same ring to it.*

Even when she knew she'd be staying late at the office, Maggie made time to have her weekly chats with her dad, every Monday at noon, shutting her door for some quality time. This day was no different; Maggie had a new client who needed advice on whether to file to make their business an S corporation, and she had some research to do before their meeting later in the afternoon, but she gave her father her full attention now. "Oh, nothing. I've just been so inundated at work lately. I'm just trying to stay on top of everything."

"Well," his gentle voice rumbled, "you always are." Geoffrey Jones looked at his daughter with pride, the creases at the corners of his eyes deepening as his bald head and gray facial hair caught the light.

"I know," she teased, and he chuckled at her reply. "I just want to make sure that I'm delivering, because I think they're beginning to consider me for partner." She lowered her voice even though her door was closed and the firm kept white-noise machines outside the doors of all of their attorneys' offices to create sound barriers anyway, due to the confidential nature of most of their communications.

"That would be incredible, sweetheart. Do you feel up to

the task?" He was making his way from one part of his house to another—the shaking screen and changing background made Maggie turn away to avoid motion sickness.

"Oh, for sure. I know that I'm bringing in good clients and they are happy with my work. I've paid my dues and I meet all of my billable requirements," she started, flipping through her client's file to see how much material she needed to cover before her meeting. "I just worry sometimes that they won't see what I know to be true."

"I understand," he replied, "but you've gotta have confidence and faith in yourself and the work that you're putting in. It's all gonna work out. That firm has held you in high regard thus far, so I can't imagine there being any impediment to your progress."

"But what if they just want me as the workhorse and don't see me as partner material?"

"Well, have they done anything to give you that impression?"

"No…" She toyed with her earring.

"Is it possible that this is a bout of anxiety?" Mr. Jones observed his daughter. He was a big fan of encouraging people to go to therapy and didn't mind administering some himself on occasion. "You falling into the trap of automatic thoughts?" he teased, winking at her.

Maggie grinned. "Maybe."

He laughed heartily, propping his phone onto the top of his dresser, his massive bed neatly made in the background. "So, what else is going on?"

"As you know, Savvy and Joanie are both getting married."

"Right…" He began pulling clothes from a laundry basket.

"We're doing all of the things to prepare, and they just decided the destination wedding for Joanie and Beth will be in Thailand."

"Yes! I'm excited to receive my invitations—I love that it's become a group venture. I haven't visited Thailand in years."

"They'll love to have you there. Are you gonna bring Miss Courtney?" Maggie eyed her father, who pursed his lips before he stared into the camera.

"You can just call the woman Courtney, sweetheart. We've been together for over a year now," he reminded her. Courtney had also lost her previous spouse to cancer, and the two had met at a support group for people grieving cancer-related losses. He took their meeting as a sign from Maggie's mother that it was time for him to move on, and Maggie welcomed Courtney with open arms.

"Come on now, Daddy. You know better than anyone how I was raised. I'm not about to disrespect her just because she wants me to call her by her first name. You were the one who taught me that we don't do that with our elders." She grinned, clicking through emails to rid her inbox of inconsequential items.

"Okay, okay, you're right. But yeah, I'mma bring her—she likes to travel. That's why I wanted to have the call today. I'm packing right now, so I won't be able to call on your birthday." He angled his phone so that more of the room came into view and hoisted a hard-shell suitcase onto the bench at the foot of his bed.

"Oh, where you headed?" She leaned forward, trying to get a glimpse of what he had folded so far to pack into his suitcase.

"I'm taking her to Baja for a few days." Mr. Jones had chosen to retire in San Diego after working for forty years in education. He loved the sunshine and the ocean breeze as much as Maggie did, and he'd earned his retirement. He was the best high school English teacher, in her opinion, and he had multiple Teacher of the Year plaques decorating his wall to show for it.

"Baja, huh? Just because?" Remarrying was a sensitive subject, but Mr. Jones would speak up if and when the time ever came to make things more official with Miss Courtney.

"Yep, nothin' but blue water and good food—"

"Yeah, and some good strong tequila. I could use some of that right about now," she laughed.

"You know I'm not big on hard liquor, but I don't mind me a mezcal margarita once in a while. The spicier, the better." He chef-kissed his fingers.

"I don't understand how you like that more than the classic, but I guess it makes sense since you also like that smoky scotch." Maggie pretended to gag.

"It's called 'peated' scotch," he chuckled, folding more laundry at the foot of the bed. "So what's going on with the weddings? Are you helping with a lot of the planning?"

"Well…" Maggie thought about her checklist of things she needed to accomplish. "I have a lot to do. Honestly, I probably haven't done enough," she laughed. "I'm gonna get on it. I just need to wrap my head around a couple of things."

"Like what?" Mr. Jones sat on the bench and looked at her.

"The girls want me to find someone new and bring them on the wedding trip."

"And…you'd prefer to go alone?" he asked, his brows knit with confusion.

"I don't want to go alone, but you know, Garrett is coming, so I don't really need a date."

"Now, baby, I love Garrett, but he's not a substitute for a romantic relationship. Unless you're telling me you want to start considering him in that way." He eyed her slowly.

"No, I'm not saying that at all," she laughed. "We're not dating or anything like that. We don't do that. We're just friends."

"Yes, yes, just friends. You agreed to that years ago," he droned in response, rolling his eyes.

"Okay, Dad, what is on *your* mind?" Her dad had always been her sounding board, and his opinion was the one that she valued over any other.

"Nothin'." He began to fold a pair of pants. "Someday you'll see what I've always seen."

"Okay." Maggie rolled her eyes. "Anyway, I'm supposed to meet up with the girls for a dress fitting soon and all that stuff."

"Uh-huh, and how is Garrett, by the way?"

"He's fine. He's doing big things at work and he's getting ready to start a podcast. He's been writing his weekly wrap-ups and interviewing different players and stuff." Maggie clicked onto an ESPN affiliate page to read his Wrap-Up article, where he'd recently picked the brains of several local NBA players about the possibility of a players' strike. She bookmarked Garrett's article to read later that evening.

"And we'll see him at the wedding, right? Is he bringing a date?"

"Honestly, I hadn't even thought to ask him that," she replied. "I suppose he could. If Savvy and Joanie think I've got time to find someone, he could, too."

"Wait—he's not still dating that yoga instructor?"

It's a damn shame that none of us even bothered to remember her name. "No, they just broke up recently." She watched her dad bring the camera close to his face, a wry smile curving his lips.

"I can't say that I'm surprised that crashed and burned." He trudged into his en suite bathroom and started filling a toiletry bag with travel-sized bottles.

"Come on, Dad. Cut him some slack," she giggled.

"They're never serious. You never even know the girls that he dates. They're temporary."

"Do you think he's afraid of commitment?"

"I don't know. Maybe." He didn't sound convinced. "It's possible he just hasn't met the right person yet."

"Story of my life. I really want to be supportive of the girls," Maggie said quietly.

"What makes you think you're not? You're the maid of honor for dual weddings. I'd say you've got your hands full." He carried his toiletry bag back to the bedroom and placed it into his suitcase before sitting back on the bench to appraise his daughter.

"I know that, but I think I've been a little reluctant because I'm the odd one out this time."

"Now, Maggie," he chided. "You and I both know that there's no way you would agree to a joint wedding scenario, because you'd want your wedding to be all about you."

"That makes me sound obsessed with myself," she replied hotly. "I don't *have* to be the center of everything."

Mr. Jones eyed her warily. "I'm not saying you're a narcissist, Magnolia. I'm just saying you would want your day to be about you. You're too competitive to share a wedding event with your friends. Somewhere inside, you'd feel pressure to have the best one."

Did my own father just drag me? Maggie sucked her teeth and bobbed her head slowly.

"Imagine it this way," he continued. "The simple fact that they're both getting married before you means that you have the ability to try to plan and top that."

Maggie laughed. "I didn't think of it that way, but that does sound very me."

"Yes, baby. It does." He leaned over to his side to prop himself up on his elbow and rested his head in his hand.

"Hmm. Food for thought. Thanks, Daddy!"

"You're welcome. Now, make sure you watch your packages this week, because I do have something coming to you." He jutted his chin toward her.

"The condo or here at the office?"

"You spend more time at the office than you do at home, girl. I do think that it should arrive later today."

There was a knock at her door, and she side-eyed her father. "Later today as in possibly right now?"

"Oh, well, if that's the case, this would be perfect timing," he chuckled.

Maggie looked toward the door. "Come in," she called.

Terry opened the door carrying a cylindrical vase holding long-stemmed white roses. Maggie gasped at the sight, whispering her thanks as Terry ducked back out.

"I've never understood your love of such monochromatic things, especially since you love to wear such loud, bright colors," Mr. Jones started as Maggie hugged the vase close so that he could screenshot her with the flowers. "I'm always surprised that you deviate from flowers with more energy, but I know my baby."

"These are gorgeous, Daddy! Thank you so much, and you sure do. I just think there's something elegant about white decor." She shrugged, setting the vase on the edge of her desk to avoid knocking it over with the massive files she needed to review.

"Uh-huh. There'll be a little somethin' in your account, too."

"Daddy." Maggie threw up her hands. "I'm about to turn thirty-eight years old. You don't have to keep sending me money."

"Yeah, well, I can't take it with me when I go."

She laughed. "Okay, you're not exactly an oil tycoon, Pop."

"Nah, but I've got a little savings."

"Do you still think you want to buy something in Mexico?"

"Maybe. Wouldn't be a bad idea to have a little condo down in Baja—Courtney and I are gonna take a look at a couple of places. Eventually, it would be yours, along with the San Diego house."

"Let me know if anything catches your eye. Maybe I'll put something in on the down payment."

"Not necessary, baby, but I'll keep you posted. You enjoy your birthday and tell everyone we send our love."

"I will, Daddy. Love you and be safe. Let me know when you get there, hear?"

"Yup. I love you, and happy birthday, my sweet Magnolia. Talk soon."

Mr. Jones's face disappeared from Maggie's screen, and she stared at her flowers again, smiling to herself. "No man even comes close," she sighed.

5

"UGH, THERE'S TOO MUCH LOVE IN THIS ROOM." MAGGIE
shuddered, hunching in her chair as she folded her arms across her
chest. She pursed her lips so hard that she could feel the creases of
her smile lines deepening like fissures on either side of her mouth.

Whose bright idea was this dinner again? Where is the nearest exit?

The restaurant dining room was decorated with red-and-
pink-rose centerpieces and crisp, white table linens. Red, pink
and white balloons formed an arch at the entrance of the building, and white votive candles in clear glass holders were lit on
every available surface. Patrons were dressed in suits and cocktail attire, smiling big with their noses wide open to all this
love-day bullshit. Well, everyone except their table. Maggie's
crew ignored that everyone else was on date night. For them,
this was a family dinner to celebrate a special occasion.

Savvy leaned against Spencer, resting her arm on his thigh,
while he put his arm around the back of her chair and kissed

her hair, gently stroking her bare shoulder. Savvy tilted her head as she observed her best friend's anywhere-but-here body language. "Maggie, I need you to focus. We can't help that your birthday is so close to Valentine's Day."

Right. I blame my parents for not having me in the summer.

The Southern California weather had been especially warm for February, so Maggie and Savvy wore colorful maxi sundresses. Spencer wore a button-down shirt with dark jeans. Beth wore a cropped tank top with ripped jeans, her ebony skin glowing everywhere it peeked through her clothes. Joan had donned a tailored short and blazer set over a gray V-neck tee with the word *MELINATED* across her chest.

"How can I do that when y'all are being all lovey-dovey and I'm sitting here by myself?" Lips puckered into a pout, Maggie was surrounded by couples—not just at their table, but across the entire dining room of the restaurant. The scents of garlic butter, seafood and fresh pasta wafted from the kitchen as an orange sunset danced on waves lapping the Santa Monica Pier.

"Thirty-eight is a big year, love. Just think about all the things that you want to accomplish this year in terms of your firm—we're manifesting that you're gonna make partner, you're starting that pro bono project. We know that you're wanting to get some more stamps on your passport, and we're here to help support that and anything else you want to do," Joanie encouraged.

Across the table, Savs and Spencer were practically fused together at their hips. God only knew what Savvy's hand was stroking under the table. To Maggie's left, Joan and Beth sat with a relaxed closeness that Maggie craved. Joan leaned back in her chair while Beth sat forward with her chin resting in her hand. Her smile grew at the same rate as Maggie's scowl. Maggie turned to the right to look at Garrett's empty chair and the view outside of the glass walls to the busy pier and the neon lights of the Ferris wheel against the cerulean-blue and rust hues blending like paint across the cloudless predusk sky.

"Garrett is on his way, love. You'll have someone to take up for you then, but if you want someone in your corner in the meantime, Joan would share me with you, isn't that right?" Beth cooed, wrapping her arms around Maggie and squeezing her shoulder.

Joanie's head perked up. "Hold on. I mean, I love you, Mags, but…"

Maggie nuzzled Beth's shoulder, eyeing her best friend. "But what? You won't share your boo with me in a time of need?"

"Um…hell no." Joan wrapped her fingers around Beth's wrist and tugged her close, leaving Maggie grasping at air. Beth giggled, appeasing her fiancée with a soft kiss on the cheek. She gently rubbed the pad of her thumb against the same spot to remove the residual lip gloss.

"Damn, that's how y'all do me?" Maggie muttered, hunching over the remnants of her cocktail. "Just leave the spinster to herself while y'all go gallivanting around the world? Y'all are going to go off and live your married lives, leaving me to the scraps of the dating world. The dating pool is shrinking, you know," she sniffed. "The closer I get to forty, the more it starts to feel like the previously limitless dating pool is now the size of an ice bucket, and someone peed in there." She knew that her friends would never completely leave her to her own devices, but since everyone decided to up and get married on her now that she was single *yet again*, surely she was entitled to wallow and throw a tantrum.

"Ma'am." Savvy sat up straight, folding her hands on the table—her corporate training fused into her stature and the directness of her tone. Her changed demeanor made Spencer, Joan and Beth each sit up a little straighter, Savvy being the clear matriarch of their friend group. "Who is going around the world without you? If Joanie and Beth get married in Phuket, you're comin', too, ho. So why don't you report your progress for finding a date for our weddings?"

An impossible task. "Y'all are getting married in less than nine months!" Maggie threw up her hands. "I don't think that's enough time for me to meet someone that I want to travel halfway around the world with. Do you?"

"Yes," Savvy and Joan responded immediately.

Beth and Spencer sipped their drinks, clearly determined to remain out of the conversation as long as possible. When Maggie and her girls got into it, the significant others tried their best not to get involved—these women had long memories and weren't opposed to holding grudges.

Maggie's eyes widened as she stared hard at her friends. She blinked, feeling a wave of emotion that she didn't want to identify. She cleared her throat, averting her eyes down to her lap. "But what if I can't find someone?" she asked quietly.

Savvy reached across the table and grabbed her hand. "You will. And if it takes longer than seems feasible, bring Garrett on the trip as your date—if he's not already bringing someone, of course. He's good company, and you know we all love him."

Beth turned in her seat to face Maggie, her voice delicate. "I'm curious, Mags. Has anyone ever asked you why you don't just date Garrett?"

Savvy and Joan both sucked in collective breaths and shook their heads adamantly—Savvy's eyes rolled closed as her face pendulated back and forth.

"What?" Beth searched everyone's faces for a tell. "Did I just open a can of worms?"

"No," Maggie sighed. *But really, yes. At least Garrett isn't here to hear this conversation.*

"That's a question we've been asking for years, B." Savvy

sipped her cocktail. "They're best friends, both about their business, both attractive. They literally have a Saturday date night every week and still don't think about each other that way."

Which was mostly true. Maggie had thought about it. A long time ago. But the one time that she and Garrett started to get close, she suggested the pact before they could take it too far. She kissed her teeth as she conjured memories that hadn't surfaced for a few years—since the last time one of the girls brought up their chemistry.

And they weren't wrong; Maggie and Garrett *had* all of the necessary components to create heat—the magnetism, the spark, and enough of a mutual respect and adoration to fuel intense flames the same way that dropping lighter fluid onto a bonfire could build into an inferno. Only Maggie decided to throw sand on the blaze before it could burn out of control.

Back in college, they hung out all the time, especially after Maggie and Kyle's relationship had run its course. As confident and competitive as Maggie was, Garrett always called her on her shit, even when acknowledging her strengths. She never had to pretend with him. He saw her bumming in her pj's without a drop of makeup, he'd helped her take down her braids and scratch her scalp—honestly, she had his mother and sister to thank for that. Maggie could be herself without an ounce of performance or code switching, in the same way that she could with Savvy and Joan, though he was slightly less likely to drag her when she was wrong.

One drunken night, they were hanging out and studying. Well, they were *supposed* to be studying, but somehow they fell into a bottle of Jameson and began playing truth or dare. Maggie always chose truths, because she hated when people made up humiliating tasks for her to carry out. Garrett never minded dares, but he always was more "go with the flow" than she was. *So what? This is what happens when you're an Aquarius sun with Capricorn ascending.*

Maggie had playfully asked Garrett if he found her attractive. He answered yes so fast that she didn't have time to process, and when he asked her if she wanted a truth or dare, she leaned into the whiskey and accepted the latter. Garrett locked eyes with her and dared her to kiss him. So she did.

It started slowly, softly. Lips pressed against each other in an innocent convergence. But as one led to two, platonic affection combusted, and they began tearing each other's clothes off. Everything about it felt right; there was passion, genuine love and appreciation, and the sensation of Garrett's touch set off pyrotechnics within every synapse in Maggie's nervous system. *It was too good to be true. Had to be.* She couldn't lose him to inevitability.

Maggie pulled back, interrupting a kiss that was melting her insides so abruptly that Garrett looked like he'd been slapped. Her heart was beating out of her chest, and he retreated from her as if he could hear it. "We can't do this," she'd whispered.

"What?" He sounded confused, but something about his face made her want to take it back. To step back into his embrace, where she'd never been unsure about anything. Until now. "Y-you want us to slow down? We can—"

She bit her lip, shaking her head. *I can't lose him.* "I think… we shouldn't cross this line. You're one of my closest friends. I don't want to mess that up." She exhaled deeply, her eyes begging him to agree with her. "I won't risk what we have over something that wouldn't mean anything in the long run."

Garrett's mouth opened and shut just as quickly. He accepted Maggie's decision without any rebuttal. The very next day, he hooked up with another girl in their class, which served as confirmation to Maggie that dating each other would only lead to heartbreak—that they were better as friends. They hadn't spoken about it since, but Maggie was certain that they were on the same page about preserving their unique bond. She never told the girls about the agreement, but they usually didn't press her about Garrett because every time they saw him he was dating someone new.

Maggie shrugged. "We're best friends, and that's where the story ends. I don't know if it's a wandering eye, or he just gets bored, or what, but it seems like he loses interest in anything that lasts longer than a few months, and I don't have the patience for a perpetual bachelor. Besides, his taste in women is trash. These chicks he dates are nothing like me."

Savvy giggled. "There could never be another like you, chile. God broke the mold makin' your stubborn ass."

"Shut up, heffa." Maggie flipped her off and returned her attention to her cocktail.

As a server brought them more drinks, Garrett rounded the corner in his typical work attire—jeans and a casual blazer over a fitted tee. Savvy's eyebrow rose as her lips curved slightly. She lifted her menu to peruse the starters. "Speak of the devil."

"Ladies, the devil hath arrived." He grinned, having overheard Savvy, and took the empty seat next to Maggie. He wrapped an arm around her shoulders and kissed her temple, his deep voice reverberating in her chest as she swayed into his embrace. "Hey, gorgeous."

"Hey, Garrett," Joan and Savvy chorused, smiling wide like Cheshire cats. Beth finger-waved playfully.

"What's up, man?" Spencer held out a hand, and Garrett stood to dap him up.

"What's good, bruh? You lookin' sharp." Garrett dusted off the shoulder of Spencer's dress shirt, grinning before he clapped him on the back.

"Hey there. How was your day?" Maggie leaned into him slightly, nudging him with her shoulder as she took in the scent of his woodsy cologne, and he sat down, easing out of his jacket.

"Good. I had a couple of interviews today for weekend features. What were y'all talkin' about when I walked up? My ears were burning." He stole a sip from Maggie's refreshed old-fashioned, nodding to the server that he'd like to order the same.

Their audience watched in amusement, Savvy's eyes burning holes into Maggie's forehead as she looked down toward her lap.

"Oh, nothing," she answered quickly, transmitting a warning glance toward the others. "Just plans for the weddings."

Garrett leaned forward with genuine interest, turning to Joan and Beth. "Oh, great! Did y'all pick the destination for your wedding?"

Joanie beamed. "We just did a few days ago. Savvy and Spencer were kind enough to invite us all along on their honeymoon! So—" she laced her fingers with Beth's, whose deep brown eyes sparkled in the twinkling lights "—we're getting married on a beach in Phuket."

His eyes widened. "Oh, my God, that's going to be amazing!"

"Yeah, so the gag is that we're trying to help your girl find an acceptable date to bring to the weddings," Savvy interjected.

His eyes narrowed in recognition as he pursed his lips. "Ah, so *that's* where this whole dating profile comes in." He nodded at the server, who delivered his old-fashioned. He side-eyed Maggie. "That dude the other day was a contender to travel around the world?"

She chewed her lip and stared at him out of the corner of her eye.

"Would you want to bring a plus-one, Garrett? We're trying to get our plans together," Beth asked sweetly as Joan hid a smile with her hair.

Maggie huffed, steam coming out of her ears. *Here we go.*

Garrett frowned, his lips pressing together as he shook his head slowly. "Nah, I don't need a plus-one." He cleared his throat and made a sideways glance at Maggie, as if she might combust at any moment. "Any new profiles of interest so far?"

She shrugged, pouting. "A couple of them don't look like serial killers. Nothing I'm interested in pursuing just yet." She rubbed some tension out of her neck. "Honestly, it's stressing me out."

"Well, it's nothing to stress about. If you don't find someone, we'll just go together," he offered with a casual shrug.

Savvy, Joan and Beth exchanged glances around the table as Spencer coughed and looked away. "I said the same thing!" Savvy smiled brightly at Garrett.

Joan twirled the dark, brandy-soaked cherry in her Manhattan. "How's the dating world been for you, Garrett?"

These two are ruthless.

"Oh, nothing really new on my end. I'm back at the drawing board." He shrugged slowly.

"What happened to the yoga instructor? She was cute! Excellent assets…" Joan winked for effect.

Maggie's eyes narrowed at her friend. "Joanie…"

"What? It's true! We wouldn't have kicked her out of bed." She gestured between herself and Beth. Beth shook her head in confirmation.

Garrett smiled into his drink. "She was cute, but you know, these girls Kenny sets me up with don't usually have much substance. They're just nice to look at." He looked up at the ceiling briefly, as if he was searching for the right words. "Half of the time, she'd be staring at her phone while I was trying to talk to her. Nothing to write home about."

Kenny was Garrett's other best friend—they'd known each other since childhood and couldn't be more different. He met Garrett's organization and research with procrastination and an innate ability to wing it. A broker by day, he moonlighted as an author of several yet-to-be published thriller novels. He was too afraid to brave real-world reactions to his writing, so he posted snippets on his blog, keeping the majority of his writing to himself.

"It's a wonder this one lasted so long, then," Savvy interjected. She tilted her head. "What is your type anyway, Garrett? You've never asked us to set you up."

"And he won't start now," Maggie snapped. "Excuse me, but it's *my* birthday. Can we focus?"

Savvy closed her mouth and sat back in her seat, her eyes locked on Maggie, her stillness unnerving. She stared quietly, and no one else made a sound—their other friends darting their eyes at each other but avoiding Maggie's gaze.

A moment passed and Savvy's look shot daggers that intensified with each blink. Maggie couldn't take it. *What is she waiting for?* "Just say it, Savs. I can tell you have something you want to say."

"I'm good. When you're done with your tantrum, you let me know." She sipped her dirty martini silently, maintaining eye contact the entire time, like a mother waiting for the outburst to end before she instilled correction. Savvy was old-school, so correction meant throwing hands; Maggie was the orator of the group.

Garrett nudged Maggie with his elbow playfully, as if to say, "You good?"

An ache built in Maggie's stomach—that sense of foreboding before she got a full lecture on why she was wrong. And she hated to be wrong. "Go ahead, sis. Just get it off of your chest."

Savvy twirled a skewer full of pimento-stuffed olives around in her glass, tucking the one on its end into her mouth and separating it from the rest with her teeth. Returning the stick to her drink, she chewed and shrugged, still waiting. The poster child of sternly unbothered. She rolled the olive around between her teeth painstakingly slowly, staring at Maggie with an intensity that pulled her closer to the brink of explosion as each second passed.

Joanie leaned over and whispered loudly into Beth's ear. "Savvy is the Jedi Master. Just watch."

Maggie rolled her eyes. "You know we can hear you, Joanie." The pressure in her stomach continued to build, as Savvy chewed at the speed of a melting glacier, boring holes into her, channeling a version of Medusa that had Maggie stuck in her seat. "God, will you just say it?"

Savvy took a slow, deliberate sip of her drink, never breaking eye contact. She barely blinked. "Say what?" She bounced her shoulders once more, turning the olives in her drink before taking another bite. The corner of her mouth curved ever so slightly as she began to chew at a snail's pace, but her gaze remained hard.

The pressure reached a point of implosion, and Maggie threw up her hands. "Say that I'm being too dramatic and that putting myself out there will help me forget about Rob. You'd probably also say that I'm being a big baby, and that I don't want a taste of my own medicine, since I did this to you. You'd also be sure to say something to the effect that, no matter what, I have a date to the weddings, so what am I actually worried about?"

Savvy savored the final swallow of her drink—her eyebrow arching in amusement. "If you already know all of this, really, what more is there that I need to say?" She smiled sweetly at the server as they delivered another dirty martini and removed her empty glass. "Why don't you tell us about your date?"

Maggie rolled her eyes hard, dipping her chin to glare at her best friend. "Ugh, y'all are the *worst*, you know that?"

"Come on, girl. You know we love riling you up. And no one can ruffle your feathers the way Savvy can." Joan wrapped an arm around Beth's shoulders, the couple the epitome of relaxed and content.

Maggie huffed. "Not you, too! What is this, bag-on-Mags day?"

"Magnolia Felize Jones." Savvy's calm transitioned into a booming warning projected from the depths of her chest, and others around the table held their breaths. "No one is coming for you right now. If you'd take a moment to gain some perspective, we're looking to help lift you up and move on."

Did she have to use my full government, though?

Beth patted her hand. "We really do want you to move on, love. The sooner you decide to leave that fool in the dust, the better. You deserve to be happy with someone who genuinely wants to build with you—someone worth your time."

Garrett's hand gripped Maggie's shoulder and squeezed, kneading away some of the tension she held. "You know I'll help, right?"

Maggie huffed and nodded. "Anyway, to answer your question, I went on a date with someone and it was an *epic failure*." She emphasized for effect as she gave death stares to Savvy and Joanie. "Four kids with four exes, he lives with his mama and he wears sunglasses indoors to be incognito. Pickings are slim out in these streets."

Beth's eyes widened. "Shut up. Not the sunglasses!"

Garrett nodded his confirmation. "It sounds wild, but I was there."

Savvy tilted her head in his direction. "In case she needed a speedy getaway?"

"Good thing, too." He leaned forward. "Dude called Maggie out of her name and tried to stop her from leaving."

Savvy's face steeled. "I know you fuckin' lyin'." She might give her sis a hard time, but Savvy stayed ready for war when it came to anyone in their circle.

Maggie waved it off. "Whatever, it's fine. We left and I'll never see him again. Besides, today only the people sitting around this table fit the bill of being worth my time. So I want tonight to focus on this group right here. Anyone added to this table in the future is a bonus, but you all are my people. I don't want to think about anyone else. I just want to enjoy your company."

Joan opened her mouth to protest, but Maggie cut her off.

"Yes, I'll go along with the dating plan, and Garrett's promised to help me weed through some profiles, but for tonight, let's just enjoy dinner," she sighed. "And y'all better have gotten me my favorite cake!"

"You mean the triple berry lemon cake with whipped cream frosting that you love?" Savvy taunted, eyes sparkling. "The one that's sitting in your refrigerator at home because you don't *actually* want to share it with us?"

Maggie's eyes widened to the size of saucers. "Damn, no one knows me like y'all do," she gushed.

Everyone around the table burst into laughter as Savvy raised her glass. "To Maggie—happy birthday, we love you, even when you're a hot-ass mess."

"To Maggie!"

6

"EW, NO. I COULD NEVER." MAGGIE PEERED OVER GAR-rett's shoulder at a profile of a man leering into the camera with a look that made her shudder. "I'm looking for a relation-ship, not a grown man looking for a second mama."

Garrett snickered. "He did have a 'let me rest against your bosom' quality to him, huh?"

"Quality? Dude looks like he would be okay sitting on my lap being rocked to sleep. Wait—what about this one? Okay, he went to Morehouse, he's a professor of sociology...tall... *white women only*? Wow..."

"That's...a bold statement." Garrett shook his head, his eyes wide. "At least he told his truth."

Maggie sucked her teeth. "I can't with the foolery. Swipe on by."

His finger dragged across the screen. "Hmm."

She leaned against his shoulder. "What now?"

He poked out his lips before angling his head slightly to look at her. "What are your thoughts on ethical nonmonogamy?"

"What does that even mean?" Lines formed between Maggie's eyebrows as she tried to wrap her brain around the concept. *When did dating turn into such a shit show?*

"Open relationship and both sides are honest about what they're doing outside of their situation." Garrett popped an olive into his mouth.

"I don't think I'm into that. You know I don't like to share." She didn't like to share men in the same way she didn't want to share food. Savvy and Kotter always rolled their eyes at her when they went to the movies—Maggie would buy three of everything to ensure that no one reached into her lap looking for popcorn or candy.

"Hmm..." he rumbled again thoughtfully.

"What?" Maggie turned to look at Garrett, whose lips curled upward slightly. "You'd be into that?"

"Nah, I think I'd be too jealous. But it's interesting to think about. Respect to the people who can make it work." He pointed his fingers toward the screen. "Just couldn't be me."

"True. And pragmatically, maybe it makes sense. Different partnerships can serve different purposes..." Maggie tilted her head to consider the scenario.

"I just don't have the energy to try and keep up with two people, you know?" He leaned forward, resting an elbow on his knee as he turned to look at her.

"Completely. I barely have the energy to keep up with myself."

"Seriously," Garrett laughed. "The needs of two people feels daunting to me."

"Keeping up with one is hard enough, and it's like now we have to worry about catfishing and all of the BS of situationships and entanglements. These folks out here trying to fill rosters... Online dating is awful." Maggie sipped on a glass of wine. "I almost feel bad for putting Savvy through this last year."

"Almost?" Garrett raised his glass to his lips and then stopped.

"She ended up matching with Spencer through the app, so it actually did work for her." Maggie pointed her index finger at Garrett as she wound more pasta around her fork.

Garrett sipped his wine. "True, but they'd already had that organic first meeting and had the chance to feel each other's chemistry. Not the same."

She huffed. *No one wants to give me credit.* "Okay, fine. Well, what about this one? Tall, good-looking, says he's an accountant..." She spread 'nduja onto a cracker and then sprinkled Gorgonzola crumbles on top, drizzling it with honey. She bit into it and her eyes crossed. "Oh, my God, you have to try this."

Garrett bit his lip, watching her happy shimmy as she steered the other half of the cracker toward him. "Hmm, I don't know. Something just feels off." He accepted the bite, his eyes scrunching closed. "Sweet and spicy wins every time. Mmm."

"Off?" Maggie peered at him curiously as she tugged a few red grapes from their vine. "Because he's the most regular guy we've seen so far?"

He considered that for a moment, blinking slowly. "Maybe that's it."

"Well, let's swipe on him and see what happens." She swiped right and reached for her TV remote. "We need some background noise for this."

The Netflix logo appeared on the TV screen, and Maggie scrolled through to her collection of movies she watched in heavy rotation—comfort movies that made her feel good and helped her fall asleep when she couldn't turn her mind off. She scrolled past her favorite romantic comedies through action-packed thrillers to a fantasy series of vampires and werewolves with New Orleans vibes. After deciding to search for something else, Maggie sat back, relaxing into the couch.

Garrett leaned closer as she continued to scroll, the tone of his voice becoming more grim with each swipe. "Well, he looks like a winner…" The profile showed a man named Cory flexing his arm muscles for the camera with one eyebrow risen to the heavens.

"What in the Rock impersonation is this?" Maggie mumbled, swiping her thumb to the left against the screen. *All he needs is a spandex suit and a bottle of baby oil.* The next profile was a man with an olive complexion and baby blue eyes. He had dark hair stuffed under a backward baseball cap.

"Not your type," Garrett quipped, moving his hand to swipe.

"Huh, how can you tell?" She held his hand away from the phone, scanning the photo for anything compromising.

"Come on, Mags. Neck tattoo, second photo is him lying in bed, third picture is him in a men's room…" G scrolled, pointing to the most incriminating shot. The guy, though good-looking in gym attire, flexed into a mirror while curling half of his mouth into a sexy snarl. Cracked white porcelain gleamed in the background.

"Ew, there's literally a giant urinal in the photo! Why didn't he think to crop that out?" Her eyes widened in disbelief. "Y'all think the men's room is sexy?" She gestured to the picture with an accusatory tone, as if Garrett had taken it himself.

Garrett's face screwed up tight, wrinkles bunching on the bridge of his nose. "Of course not. It's disgusting in there."

She elbowed him. "Yeah, okay…lemme see your profile." She held out her hand.

"What? No."

"Let me—" Maggie reached over him, rooting around for his cell.

He leaned away from her and patted his phone in the hip pocket of his jeans. "Absolutely not!"

"Why not?" She pouted. *Come on, puppy dog eyes.*

He sighed. "Don't do that, Mags. Must we share *everything*?"

Maggie gasped in jest and pretended to clutch imaginary pearls. "You'd really keep secrets from me?"

"Quit it, M," he laughed, batting her away as she began tickling his sides.

"Give it up!"

"Not happening." He swatted at her playfully. "Come on— give me a break. You don't tell me everything. You never told me that you were the one who hit a parked car in my truck and knocked off my side mirror back when we were in college."

She snatched back her arms and froze; a look of horror crossed her face as her mouth dropped open. *Shit.* "Who told you?!" she squealed.

Garrett fell over on his side, laughter rumbling from deep inside. So hard that tears streamed from his eyes. He wiped them away as he tried to catch his breath. "Checkmate. I was never sure until this very moment. I asked my mom once if she thought you did it, but she defended you to the high heavens. Your face is priceless right now."

Maggie clamped her mouth shut, her brown cheeks deepening in color. "I—"

"You owe me a mirror." He poked at her arm with each syllable. "And you can actually afford it now, so I plan to collect."

She blinked a couple of times. "I do owe you for that." She nodded, her eyes sparkling with relief. "How are your parents, by the way? I owe your mom a call."

"Yeah, she keeps telling me she misses you. They're fine. They're jealous about the trip to Thailand."

"Have they ever been? They used to travel all the time."

Over the years, Maggie had grown close with Garrett's family. Originally from Louisiana, they'd relocated to Atlanta after Garrett moved to California. "Yeah, they're starting to slow down a bit. Pop hasn't wanted to travel as much, maybe once or twice a year now. He wants me to come home for Christmas this year." They used to come to California every year—they'd even spent a Christmas together at Savvy's.

"It's sweet that he wants you to visit."

"Wanna come?"

Maggie shrugged. "I haven't seen your parents in a while, and I know your mom would be so happy."

"She would," he agreed.

"Can I tell you a secret?"

"Shoot."

"She always knew that I was the one that broke your mirror." Maggie grimaced. "I told her in a panic, and she told me that it would be our little secret, so we agreed to let you think that one of your neighbors must have clipped it in the parking garage."

Garrett's mouth dropped open as he stared at her. "It really be your own people." He shook his head in astonishment.

"But now I have no secrets, so let me see!" She lunged at him.

He held out a hand. "Hold on. Because I seem to remember that there's a big plush box in your closet that I've never been allowed to open." He stood and started toward Maggie's room, glancing back at her mischievously. "So, if there are no secrets…"

The color that had been deepening a moment before drained from her cheeks as she pictured some of her favorite toys on display. The remote-controlled vibrating panties, the crops and feathers, the satin blindfold or the array of vibrators. Things she'd never even let Rob see. "Nooo! You're right. It's not a bad thing to keep a little something to ourselves once in a while." She grabbed at his hand and pulled him back onto the couch.

"Uh-huh." Garrett grinned at her slyly as he returned and sat next to her. "I'm going to find out one day."

She flipped him off and hit Play on the TV remote. "Yeah, right after I see that profile."

This was a terrible idea. Maggie smiled with her lips pressed tightly together, hoping the saccharine sweetness of her expression fooled her date. "So, how was your day?"

Terrance, the accountant, sat across from her, unabashedly eyeing every curve he could see from his seat without leaning onto the table to get a closer look. His neck swiveled left and right to take all of her in, as a voice deep inside Maggie's brain screamed in panic. "Better now," he laughed, licking his lips in the way only LL could pull off.

She smiled through the urge to cringe, praying the conversation moved forward. "So, you're an accountant?"

He nodded. "And you're a tax attorney, right? I mean, I couldn't have asked for a better match." He gestured to her with an open hand. "We could start our own empire, girl."

"I like your ambition," she quipped stiffly. Maggie wore a red sheath dress and blazer set, since they planned to meet for drinks right after work. Her deep red lipstick matched her dress, and her coils were side-parted and fluffed to perfection. The subtle V-neck of her dress showed just enough cleavage to have Terrance close to drooling, which would have been the desired effect if he wasn't leering in the creepy "I might follow you home" kind of way.

The server brought their drinks, and Maggie tried to think of something to say as her old-fashioned was placed in front of her. The server smiled brightly. "Here you go, sir. I have your Hennessy and pineapple."

Red flag. Maggie groaned internally. *That sounds disgusting.* "Have you ever been here before?" Her voice wavered an octave above its normal tone.

Terrance looked around, his dark eyes intense as he sucked his teeth and sipped his drink. "Nah, but it's nice. I like sitting here with you in the candlelight. Makes my mind conjure up some images."

She propped her elbow onto the table and rested her chin in her hand, hoping her body language wasn't too obvious. "Oh?"

He nodded, his tongue overmoisturizing his lips once again. "Do you like candles?"

Her eyes narrowed, but she continued on with the conversation, thrumming her fingertips against her cheek as if in thought. "Sure, they smell good, and I light them anytime I want to relax. One of my good friends owns a candle shop on Etsy."

Terrance leaned forward, his eyes hungry, his voice barely above a whisper. "I can help you relax, you know. Light some candles, maybe give you a little massage. It's such a stressful time of year in our industry." He reached a hand across the table and traced his finger from her wrist to her elbow. "Would you like that?"

Where the fuck is Garrett? Maggie fluttered her fingers against her temple again and swallowed back a bout of bile as her inner voice screeched with discomfort. "Umm—"

"Maggie, is that you?" Garrett appeared at the edge of their table. "Wow, it's been a long time."

Finally. "Wha... Hi. What are you doing here?" Stunned, she looked at him with furrowed brows.

"I know this is out of the blue, but I was at the bar and I

saw you sit down. I just had to come talk to you." Garrett gripped the edge of the table, staring into Maggie's eyes intently. "I never thought I'd see you again."

She stared up at him, her mouth agape. *Damn, he is playing the hell out of this role.* "Well, you know what happened last time." She spoke in a hushed tone.

"Now, who is this?" Terrance sat back in his chair, trying to make sense of the interaction.

"He's my… We were…" Maggie wagged an index finger between her and Garrett. "I'm so sorry. I had no idea he would be here."

"Give me another chance, Mags," Garrett pleaded. He dropped to one knee, and patrons at another table against the wall of glass windows gasped. "Please say yes."

Terrance's face balled up in confusion. "Hold on, now. She's here with me."

Garrett pulled Maggie's hand from the table into his and kissed her palm. "Please."

The warmth of his mouth against her skin made her flex her fingertips involuntarily, her entire arm tingling. "Yes," she whispered. She stood as Garrett rose to his feet and embraced her tightly.

"Un-fucking-believable." Terrance stood up. "You know what? Drinks are on you. Out here wasting my time."

Maggie broke from her hug and turned to Terrance, who had already turned to leave. "I'm so sorry," she called after him, her hand bidding him farewell. *Good riddance.*

He waved an arm above his head, refusing to look back at her. The valet held the door open for him as he exited, stomping his way to the stand to retrieve his car.

She covered her mouth with her hands and turned to Garrett, still aware of the eyes on them from surrounding tables. *I'm going to hell if they see me cackle.* "Wow, that almost felt real," she whispered. She swiped at him lightly with one hand. "You really should consider acting."

They'd planned the entire exchange, from Maggie resting her head in her hand to signal Garrett to come save her, to the faux-mance that they created to drive the date away. Garrett kneeling down and kissing her hand was improv, but the extra razzle-dazzle halfway had Maggie convinced it was real.

Garrett grinned down at her. "I drew from real experiences."

She crooked an eyebrow as she sat back down. "You've begged a woman to come back?"

"I haven't," he started slowly. "But maybe I should have."

The bartender brought his drink over from the bar and slapped him on the back in congratulations. Garrett raised his glass in thanks.

Maggie's eyes widened as she stared at her friend. "I swear, lately it feels like you've got all these secrets. Do I know the ones that got away? Did you just not tell them how you were feeling?"

Garrett looked down at his vodka soda. "Nah, we were young, and timing wasn't right. And none of these are story-level secrets—no one is producing a biopic anytime soon. You know more about me than anyone else."

"Even Kenny?" she chided.

His head bobbed. "Even Kenny."

Satisfied, Maggie sipped her drink. "So do you want to get out of here? I've still got some of Savvy's birthday cake."

Garrett's eyes brightened. "You're actually going to share it? You know I've never been allowed to taste her famous lemon berry cake with whipped cream frosting because it's been declared yours until the end of time."

This cake was the stuff of dreams. Airy, fluffy white cake kissed with lemon zest and with blackberries, blueberries and raspberries folded in. Savvy sandwiched her lemony whipped cream between the three tiers, coating the outside and garnishing with glazed berries and candied lemon peel. "Well, you got me out of a terrible date, so now I feel like I owe you. I mean, could you *hear* what he was saying? Dude offered to light candles and massage me." She shuddered.

He shook his head. "I couldn't hear what y'all were saying, but when he touched your arm, you looked like you were gonna jump out of your skin. That, or rip his arm off and beat him to death with it." His closed mouth curved up to one side as he signaled for the check.

"I was tempted, but I saw you move from the bar in my periphery, and I decided to hold on," she giggled. "After that Academy Award–worthy performance, you have definitely earned yourself a slice of cake."

He grinned wide. "Well, that sounds delicious. Want me to have some of our favorite Chinese delivered? It should get there right as we do." He looked at his watch. Given the hour and the fact that they were still close to downtown, their trek back to Santa Monica could easily take them forty-five minutes.

"Oh, my God, yes," she moaned. "You read my mind."

"Your usual?" He handed the server his card.

"Please." She had a long-standing love affair with the spicy garlic and tofu string beans and Sichuan boiled fish from Hot Wok, a popular family-owned restaurant in Maggie's neighborhood. "We'll have to find a good movie or something to watch."

"Do you remember that show *Kaleidoscope*? I think there's a new series with a similar concept that just came out." Garrett spoke as he typed their order into his phone.

"Another heist?" Maggie perked up. *Kaleidoscope* wasn't exactly a love story, but there was something sexy and exhilarating about a good heist.

He nodded. "A heist, but the money is missing, and the person who was suspected of double-crossing has been murdered."

"Ooh, perfect." She shimmied a little with excitement. "So the double-crosser was double-crossed?"

"Looks like it, but maybe the alleged double-crosser was actually framed." Garrett signed the check and turned his attention back to Maggie as she stood, his head shaking slowly. "I can't believe you wasted the red suit on that guy."

Maggie's red suit had won court cases, gotten her out of speeding tickets that she deserved, had earned countless drinks and meals and even gotten her an impromptu proposal once from a stranger. "Gotta kiss a lot of frogs to find a prince, so they say." She did her best Mae West voice, resting a hand on her hip.

"There has to be a better way," he protested. "That was torturous."

She poked out her lips and nodded. "I don't disagree. But this is what we get as we get closer to forty. Like I told the girls, it's slim pickin's out here! You don't experience it because you're willing to date people a full generation behind us, while I have zero interest in training anyone how to date a professional, educated, grown-ass woman."

"Well, I think I'm going to lay off of the young ones for a while. It's starting to get embarrassing when they don't understand pop culture references from our childhood. Like, what do you mean you never watched *Martin*?" Garrett scowled.

Maggie winced. "Seriously?"

He held up his hands. "I know, I know. Tragic, right? Anyway, I plan on taking my time. No need to jump into anything, especially when I am trying to get promoted to lead journalist."

They waved at the bartender on their way out and stepped out of the restaurant arm in arm.

"How is the promotion quest going, anyway?" The evening breeze ruffled Maggie's hair and she pulled Garrett closer to stay warm. The February weather fluctuated between perfect, sunny weather and breezy days where the sun had to fight to burn through the marine layer. It wasn't cold enough to wear tights, but Maggie's legs were covered in goose bumps. "I should have brought a full coat with me." She shivered.

"Here, stand on this side of me. I'll block the wind for you." Garrett wore jeans and a pullover sweater that showed off his broad chest and arms.

A strong gust blew and Maggie squealed as the draft nipped at her thighs. Garrett wrapped himself around her, blocking the breeze from crawling up the back of her collar. His jaw pressed against her temple as his arms held her tightly. "You know, if I didn't know any better, Mr. Bailey, I'd think you were just trying to get close to me so you could get a little fresh." Somewhere along her statement, her sultry Mae West dipped into a Southern drawl.

Garrett eyed her before proceeding toward the car. "You know, I can't tell if you're trying to be sexy or sound like my aunt Edna."

Maggie groaned. "Not TiTi Edna!"

"A li'l fresh," he mimicked before bursting into laughter. He caught her elbow before it could connect with his midsection. "Yo, quit."

"Wowww, okay." She grinned, attempting to break free as his arms tightened around her.

"It's okay, TiTi Mags." He nuzzled her hair and she pushed him away.

"Fuck off," she scoffed, unable to hide her smile, and he almost doubled over in laughter. "No cake for you."

"No! Okay, okay, you're right. I'm sorry," he mumbled into her hair. "Pleeease let me try some of your favorite cake?" His eyes rounded into his best Puss in Boots impression.

"Ugh, fine. You did save me from candle guy, after all." Maggie rolled her eyes.

Garrett chuckled. "Check me out." He turned to face her and began licking his lips incessantly. "Gimme some suga, girl."

Maggie yelped and broke out into a full sprint, heels and all, with Garrett racing behind her. "Stranger danger!" She strained to belt the words out at the top of her lungs between breathy giggles.

Passersby craned their necks to see what was happening, and Garrett waved his arms to signal that she was kidding. When they reached her car, she tossed him the keys and jumped into the passenger seat. "Um, Miss Daisy, this is your car." He brandished the keys hanging from the ring on his index finger.

"Yeah, well, now my feet hurt. Come on. I'm ready for our Chinese!"

Garrett shook his head, amusement curving the corners of his mouth. "The things I do for cake," he sighed.

7

"I DON'T KNOW ABOUT THIS ONE, SAVS." MAGGIE STARED into the mirror, the blue taffeta itching her skin. "What in the exfoliation is this? It feels like—"

"It's a beautiful cut!" Savvy stood behind her, having pulled back the curtain so that she could see what Maggie was complaining about.

"Yeah, but it feels like I just wandered through a giant patch of poison oak. It's not okay. Don't do this to me," Maggie pleaded. "Besides, don't you want me to wear a brighter color? This is so *slate blue*." Disdain dripped from her lips.

"Well, damn, tell me this wedding is about you without telling me it's about you." Her friend shook her head. "Okay, so what did you have in mind, since it's your wedding and all?" Savvy crossed her arms.

Maggie kissed her teeth as she stared at her friend in the

mirror until something dawned on her and she turned around. "Oh, my God, Savvy."

The bride stood in a lacy white dress that clung to her waist and hugged her curves. Savvy smiled radiantly, looking down at the skirt of the dress as its lower third swayed with her movements.

"You look so beautiful." The detailing was lace along with the sash, with the slight train cascading behind her. "It's so simple but it's so you, Savvy."

Her best friend's eyes began to water. "I can't believe we're doing this right now."

Maggie teared up. "You are a goddess, my friend."

Her hair was swept back into an easy knot, a few wavy tendrils trimming one side of her face.

"I wanna see! Wow! And what do you think about this?" Joanie asked as she stepped out of her fitting room stall in a silk tux, a black lace camisole beneath her jacket. On her feet, she wore block-heeled leather sandals with a simple strap over her foot and another around the ankle. Her twist-out was parted in the center and had been fluffed for volume into a mane of curls. "Damn, Savs, look at you." She rushed over.

"Jesus, this is gonna be the finest wedding ever, if only I can get out from under this Brillo pad!" Maggie wailed. "Am I breaking out in hives? Do I have the pox?" She fanned her décolletage with her hands frantically.

"Okay, okay, that's enough," Savvy laughed, shaking her head. "I just wanted to see you in that dress, honestly. That one is not *the* dress." She gesticulated toward the blue number.

"Well, where is *the* dress?"

"Here." She pulled a garment bag out of her fitting room and handed it to Maggie, who unzipped it to find a formfitting fuchsia dress with a thin gold belt.

"Ooh…"

"Yeah." Savvy grinned. "We decided on light pink roses and lilies for flowers, so this is going to accent them nicely."

"I can't wait to see it all together," Maggie crooned.

"Well, go on." Savvy smiled. "Go put it on. Let's see it."

"Okay." Maggie shimmied her way out of the scratchy taffeta and pulled the fuchsia garment over her head, careful with the seams as the material slid over her bust and her hips. "Hey, can someone help me with the zipper?" she called.

"Sure, I got ya." Joanie stepped behind her to close the back and fasten the clasp at the top.

"I don't usually do strapless, but goddamn I look good!" The insert material pleated just below the bust to create a slight accordion effect over her midriff, the folds opening wider as the material dropped below her waist, fanning out below her hips. As she moved, the pleats opened and bright pops of orange caught the light. Maggie wrapped the golden belt around her waist. "This is a *look*, honey!"

She stared at herself in the mirror, her eyes wide. "How did you even...? Where did you...? What in the...?"

"I feel like there are good ends to these sentences—" Savvy steepled her fingers together, her eyes sparkling "—so I'm just going to take that as a win."

Joan stood back and whistled as Maggie turned, the flowing skirt swishing behind her. "You have no idea how long it took Savvy to find that—she practically scheduled the wedding around being able to find the right dress for you."

Maggie's eyes widened. "Are you serious?"

Savvy propped a hand on her hip. "Do you know how difficult you can be when you aren't wearing what you want to wear? When you don't feel like you look good?"

"I'm not that difficult." Maggie sulked.

"Tuh! Heffa, you better find someone else to believe that bullshit," Joanie quipped.

"Okay, fine, well, I'm not that difficult *all* the time," she responded sheepishly.

"Well, now you have even more incentive to find a date for the weddings," Savvy encouraged. "How's that going, by the way?"

"So, remember that first one was a dud, probably does dirt, and obviously I can't be attached to anything illegal—I'd risk my license."

"True."

"Then the next one had this weird need to be extra glossy—he wouldn't stop licking his lips, but in a very 'I'm giving LL Cool J's perverted uncle on ten' kind of way."

"Ew… Did Garrett go on this one, too?"

"Wait—are you having Garrett go on *all* of your dates with you?" Joanie crossed her arms over her chest.

"First of all, he offered. Secondly, he sat at the bar—it's not like he was at the table with us—and third, that first guy ended up kind of grabbing me, so I'm glad G was there."

"Wait." Joan held up a hand. "That's new information. He put his hands on you? Who is this dude and where can I find him, because I just wanna talk…"

"Now, now, Joanie, there's no need for that."

"I-on like dat," she inflected, imitating Yung Miami.

"Well, it was *somebody's* bright idea for me to go on these dates…"

"Listen, you and I both know that you're wanting someone." Savvy rested her hands on Maggie's shoulders. "And you deserve someone, so whether this person that you bring to the wedding is *the one* or whether you end up with Garrett as your date, just be open to the process of dating.

"I know it's not great out there, and I know there are some frogs, but I think you're going to find your match. I believe that for you."

"Yeah, okay, if you say so."

"Go on, sis."

Maggie pouted. "I wanna believe that that's true, and God knows I have been kind of craving a little something. I just don't think I'm going to find anything this way, but I'm gonna give this a couple more tries because you asked me to, and then I'm probably just going to have Garrett be my date."

"But how do you know Garrett's not gonna bring a date for himself? He may have said he didn't need a plus-one, but he's got time to find someone new—just like you."

A knot twisted in Maggie's stomach. "I really don't know what to say about it other than that he's not going to bring anybody to Thailand."

"How do you know that, though? How do you know he won't just find someone to travel with? Or that Kenny won't introduce him to another pretty young thang? Like, it really can be that simple where it's—you know—it's not like anybody has to propose marriage to be on a trip with you. Just someone you enjoy spending some time with, maybe get a little broken back from here and there, you know, all the things."

"I don't have anybody like that." Maggie threw up her arms.

"You think he does?"

"This is Garrett. He can find somebody if he wants somebody."

"Just like you," Joanie reminded her.

"Yeah, yeah."

"Well, why haven't you asked him to be sure?" Savvy probed.

"I just assumed we would go together. I knew this plan would be futile," she sighed.

"And it will be if you go into it with that attitude. I'm gonna need you to figure it out, ma'am."

"Yeah, whatever."

She blew out an exasperated breath. "You just like being difficult. That's what it is."

"Nobody likes being difficult…"

"I'm sorry, ma'am, look back in the mirror and tell me who you are, because I don't know you if you're not difficult." Savvy motioned toward Maggie's reflection.

Maggie sighed, gazing at herself. "Yeah, okay… I do look good, though." Her coils were pulled back from her face with a headband.

"I actually really do like that look on you—it's very chic but it's also soft."

"You did a good job." Maggie plopped down on the couch that faced a three-sided mirror. "Well, come on and get on this pedestal, girl. I need to see all the angles of this dress and then I need to know if we need second looks, too, because the way that this wedding is about to be set up, I can't even imagine how good Beth and Spencer are about to look."

"Yeah, is Uncle Joe walking you down the aisle?"

"Of course."

"And, Joan, what about you?"

"Now, you know I've got my daddy, but I'm thinking about having both of my parents walk me down, and then Beth could be walked down by her parents so that everybody feels like they have a part."

Savvy clasped her hands together in front of her chest. "That's really special."

Maggie nodded. "That's special for sure." Her eyes welled with tears. A pang in her chest reminded her that her mom wouldn't be there to see her get married when the time came. A hand landed on her shoulder gently, and she reached to grab it.

"You know that Miss Josephine will be there in spirit." Savvy read her mind.

"I do." Maggie swiped at her eyes, and Savvy held her hand for a moment, patting the back of it calmly.

"Which reminds me," Savvy started, "I've been meaning to tell you that we decided to do both wedding ceremonies in Thailand. Spencer and I are doing ours at the same time as Joanie and Beth, so we may or may not need second looks for the reception, but we can figure that out later."

"Oh?" Maggie's mouth dropped open. It wasn't like they needed to ask her permission, but she hated not being in the know.

"You've been busy trying to accomplish the orders we gave you in terms of a date, and it's tax season, so I figured that we wouldn't bring you into this until we had actionable items for you as maid of honor." Savvy fussed with the waist of her dress. "Bringing our ceremony to Thailand makes more sense, since some of the fam is there, and it saves Mom and my brothers a trip so that we can just all meet out there instead."

Savvy's brothers and her mom all lived in the Bay Area, so initially, everyone had planned to come down to LA for the ceremony and then head to Thailand. "Yeah, that makes sense. What do you need me to do?"

Savvy pulled Joan on the pedestal and stepped down so that she could see the full view of the tux from all angles. "We would love it if you'd take care of the calligraphy for the invitations and get those out in the next couple weeks. Everyone on the list is already planning to come, so this is really just so they all receive the keepsake." She pointed to a couple of cardboard cartons with a packet of felt-tipped calligraphy pens and a printed list of names and addresses.

"Okay...what else?"

Joan stepped down from the mirror. "The hotel venue out there has a location here also, so cake tasting."

Maggie interlaced her fingers and stretched her arms out in front of her. "Now we're talkin'."

"By the way, have you talked to my mom lately?" Savvy asked.

"No, but I'm sure we will. Is she going into full planning mode now?"

"She's got like a whole itinerary for when Spencer and I get to Thailand—she's got family members for us to meet and all these things… It's all good, though. You know we're excited to go."

"Yeah, you get to be there a whole week before we get there."

"Yes, but then we get to have the bachelor/bachelorette party." Savvy ticked another item off on her fingers.

"Right, yeah, I really love that you came up with that idea for us all to be together," Joan said as she sat next to Maggie on the couch.

"It was kind of selfish, actually," Maggie admitted. "All of you heffas are so blissfully, annoyingly happy, and I figured including the guys meant I could bring Garrett and have someone who's there for me."

"This is why you're going to bring a date."

"Right." Maggie blew out a breath, rolling her eyes. "Yeah, yeah."

Savvy tsked. "Come on now, girl. You so fine!"

Joanie catcalled her.

Maggie stood slowly and swiped her thumb at her nose, walking with a little swagger in her step. She rubbed her hands together, imitating her last date, her tongue dragging across her lips in a cringey way. "Hey, girl. Why don't you come see about me?"

"Please stop. Ugh, I'm so sorry that you're still in the trenches."

"Girl, these are full-on fissures. The San Andreas fault line is less complicated."

"Jesus." Joan shook her head.

"Yes, call on the Lord. We can touch and agree that someone is on the way for you." Savvy lifted her hands.

Maggie rolled her eyes. "Fighting with the IRS is less complicated. Being closer to forty than not and trying to date in LA is damn near impossible."

"Now you're just being dramatic." Her hands moved to her hips. "I think that you're scared."

"What would I be scared of? It's like you think that I'm going into war or something. I know that dating isn't anything to be afraid of..."

"And yet you find every reason not to do this. Not to give this an honest try. These two dates that you've been on so far, were these honestly contenders? Are you going to tell me that you really went on a date with a guy with questionable employment and another who sounds like he had major proximity issues and couldn't stop slobbing on his own lips long enough to have a decent conversation, and that there weren't tells before the date?"

Maggie considered her friend's question. "I don't know. I guess it's possible," she admitted stubbornly.

"Okay, give us an example." Savvy crossed her arms over her chest.

"So the first guy, I guess you could say it's true that something seemed off. He didn't fill in the job title or industry lines. Come to think of it, he really didn't say much of anything of substance."

"This was the guy who wore sunglasses the whole date, right?" Joanie queried.

Maggie nodded, biting her lip.

"And why did you think that this was a good choice? Was he wearing sunglasses in all of his photos?"

Maggie cocked her head to one side and blinked slowly,

her face scrunching into a frown as she tried to remember. "Maybe?"

"So you never even saw his full face?" Savvy raised an eyebrow.

"Huh, I guess I didn't." *Funny how I didn't really pay attention to that before.*

"So do you think it's possible that you're picking duds on purpose simply to get out of being vulnerable with someone real?"

Maggie avoided her eyes. "I don't know what you're talking about."

Savvy threw up her hands and turned to Joan. "Why is she the most difficult person on the face of this planet?" She turned back to her friend. "Listen, girl, I don't know if this is you trying to protect your heart because of Rob or because you simply don't believe that you can find someone this way, but you and I both know that you don't want to be alone. This is self-sabotage. It's okay to try and not have the results you want right away, but how can you ever have what you want if you don't try?"

Joan nudged Maggie with her knuckles. "Savvy's right. Don't block your blessings, sis. The last thing that you want is for a person who is for you to be presented to you, and you miss them because you weren't open."

Joanie's words landed. "Okay, if you two heffas are so convinced that I should trust this process, I'll give it the college try. But if I don't find someone travel worthy, I need both of you to be okay with that. Y'all know how particular I am, and it's no small feat to travel thousands of miles over the course of two weeks. With *me*."

Savvy and Joan turned to look at each other and burst into laughter. "You ain't never lied, sis," Savvy wheezed. "Honestly, I thought about getting a tranquilizer for you just for the flight."

Maggie swiped her lips to the side. "Ha ha, very funny. Yes, look at Maggie, the most difficult, unlovable person in the world."

"Ah, come on," Joanie laughed. "Nobody said all that, drama queen. You know you're a handful."

Maggie stood again and turned so she could see the back of the dress in the mirror. "Nah, sis, I'm at least four." She cupped her hands over her ass to demonstrate, miming them to measure her backside.

"I know that's right! Go on and shake a li'l somethin'!"

8

"OH, HE'S SUPERCUTE. WAIT—NUDIST? HMM...HERE'S A different one. Okay, he did the 'two truths and a lie.'" Maggie grinned. "You ready for this?"

Garrett smiled as he dropped salt into boiling water. "Shoot."

"'Kay, he said he loves anime, he's slept with three hundred women and he can cook better than the Iron Chefs." She bit her lip.

"And two of these are supposed to be *true*?" Garrett scrunched his face up in disbelief.

She nodded.

"What is there to think about? Swipe left." He dropped pasta into the boiling water and lifted the lid off his Bolognese. "Almost ready."

"And smelling good!"

He smiled in response as he cut into a fresh baguette.

"Ugh, listen to this one. 'I'm looking for a serious, somewhat nonmonogamous partnership, but open to all connections along the way.'" Maggie looked up from her phone. "What does that even mean?"

Garrett scowled as he diced herbs and garlic for bread. "That means that he wants you to be monogamous while he isn't."

"Oh. Welp." She swiped left. "Why would anyone ever agree to that?"

After a taxing workweek, she sat on her couch with her feet up and her back against one of the armrests while Garrett cooked them dinner. He wasn't as accomplished in the kitchen as Savvy was, but he had his mom's entire recipe book and a couple of dishes that he could churn out without expending too much effort, which happened to be some of Maggie's favorites. He poured a glass of Chianti and handed it to Maggie after sampling it for himself. "There are people out there who will agree to whatever just so that they feel like they have someone."

Maggie sipped thoughtfully. "That makes me really sad. I'd rather be alone than accept a situation where I have to share my partner with someone else. I want someone who *wants* me. You know what I mean?"

He glanced at her quickly as he stirred his Bolognese. "I do."

"I mean, I think I'm kind of a handful already. I can't imagine someone having the time to deal with me and someone else."

Garrett's mouth twitched.

"What?"

"You really are a full-time job, Mags," he teased.

"Hey, you knew what you were getting yourself into when you volunteered to be my best friend. Besides, you're probably the only guy who's ever gotten on my dad's good side."

Geoffrey Jones was a lot of things, but trusting wasn't one

of them. When Maggie called home and told her parents that her new best friend was a guy, her father had demanded to meet Garrett the next time he visited. Garrett was sweating buckets the entire time, and while Maggie's mom assured him that there was nothing to worry about, Maggie's dad was as stern and sharp as he'd been in the Navy. A no-nonsense man, he'd regularly terrorized Maggie's dates in high school, and Garrett had heard all of the stories. After a long weekend of good meals, a battery of questions and even a phone call home to Garrett's family, he'd gained the stamp of approval from Maggie's first love.

"That is true. You're lucky that your pop loves me now," Garrett chuckled to himself. He tossed spaghetti noodles in his sauce. Using tongs, he distributed noodles and sauce into two shallow bowls and topped them with a fresh grating of Parmesan cheese and a sprinkle of fresh parsley.

"Mmm, smells amazing." Maggie put her wineglass on the coffee table to accept her bowl of pasta. "You spoil me rotten, G. What man can compete with this level of treatment?"

"Only one who is worthy," he quipped, half of his mouth curving upward. "If they don't treat you like this, they're not worth considering. Most don't deserve you."

Period. Maggie smiled to herself, blowing on her food as she twirled pasta around on her fork before allowing the tender meat and red wine sauce to melt on her tongue. "Oh, my Go— This is so good, G." She struggled with the words, her cheeks full of pasta.

"Uh, Mags?" He sat next to her on the couch, allowing her legs to stretch over his lap as he balanced his glass and bowl in his hands.

She slurped the end of a noodle into her mouth. "Hmm?"

"You didn't want to say grace?" He stared at her expectantly.

Shit. I knew I was forgetting something. Maggie chewed quickly, holding up her index finger as she set her bowl in her lap. Her eyes were pleading with Garrett not to laugh as she tried to swallow down her mouthful.

"Are you really using a church finger when you already forgot to thank the Lord?" His mouth twitched as he set his wineglass down next to hers. "So sacrilegious. Maybe I should scoot over just in case He decides to smite you for your shenanigans."

She swallowed her remaining food and flipped him off before resting one hand on his shoulder and holding up her fork in the other to pray. "Father, thank You for this food. I ask that You bless the hands that prepared it, that this may be nourishment for our bodies and that You guide our minds and hearts to be more like You. In Your Son's holy name, amen."

"Amen." Garrett's shoulders shook as he rolled his eyes. "You really gave me the finger as you started to pray. You know, Jesus don't like ugly, Mags."

"He don't, but tell me what reason I would have to be concerned?" she countered, smiling sweetly.

Flabbergasted, Garrett turned to look at her as she shoveled another mouthful of pasta, slurping obnoxiously.

"What? I'm fucking adorable," she declared, holding a hand to her mouth so she wouldn't choke on her big bite of food, the urge to snort-laugh growing stronger.

His eyes widened at her before he closed them and howled from deep in his gut. "Adorable, yes. Charming may need a little bit of work." He leaned over and wiped some sauce from Maggie's chin. "Well, maybe a lot."

"Mmph," Maggie grunted, dropping her kettlebells to the padded floor after finishing her final round of dead lifts. She ground the heel of her hand into the side of her glutes, kneading the muscle until it stopped spasming.

Maggie loved the gym. She loved to be in public but in a space where most people didn't speak or even look at each other. The collective energy exuded wellness and self-care; her quiet nods exchanged with other regulars were acknowledgments of accountability. She never let more than a day pass before she was back in community with fellow strength trainers—perhaps because she loved feeling powerful. Savvy liked to joke that she could crack a walnut between her thighs, but Maggie always corrected her—only diamonds could withstand the pressure she created. *They betta recognize!*

Slowly, she folded her body forward, picking up her kettle-bells and holding them to her sides as she began split squats, watching her form and posture in the mirror. Her noise-canceling headphones reduced the clanging weights, the grunting, and the electronica blaring out of the gym speakers to a distant garble and filled her ears with hip-hop and R & B tunes with heavy beats.

As Maggie began her second set, movement in her periphery prompted her to set down her weights and move her headphones from one of her ears. As she turned, her eyes locked onto deep brown, muscular arms coated in sweat and a bright smile framed by stubble. "Hey there. Would you mind spotting me? I promise I'll be quick." He gestured to a bench-press station, one of his over-ear headphones in his hand.

"Me?" Maggie's eyes darted around to a few men a couple of stations away that he could have asked, but they seemed engrossed in some sort of pull-up competition. "Yeah, okay."

She abandoned her weights and stepped behind the bench as he straddled it and sat in front of her. There was something about a muscular back and shoulders that always stirred up the butterflies in Maggie's stomach, and this man's physique was exceptional. His gray Georgetown T-shirt was damp and his fresh cut framed the sweat beading on his forehead. He lay back against the bench and smiled up at her. "You ready?"

Maggie's butterflies began a slow migration south as flashes of her being ready for this man in ways he probably wasn't imagining invaded her psyche. From where she stood, the weights were the only barrier stopping her from sitting directly on his face. Well, the weights and the spandex from her shorts. She loved to show off the strength of her thighs and the roundness of her ass. Maggie bit her lip and nodded. "Mmm-hmm."

She widened her stance, bending slightly at the knee while keeping the palms of her hands under the barbell's shaft. Maggie clocked the weight at one thirty-five, which meant he was focusing on repetition over heavy weights. *Tone more than gains.* After twelve reps, she helped guide the bar back to the rack, and he stood, stretching his arms and chest as he smiled at her. "Thanks. Just two more sets, and I'm good."

"No problem. I'm not in a rush today." Maggie laced her hands behind her back and pulled her shoulders back, relishing the stretch while she waited.

"I'm Blake." He reached out his hand, and rough calluses pressed against the softness of Maggie's palm.

"Maggie." Something about his dark brown eyes made her return the smile that spread across his face.

"Are you always here on Sundays?"

"I try to be, but it depends on my schedule. I'm a tax attorney, and it's tax season, so I can use every bit of stress relief I can get." *Shit.* She considered the connotation of what she'd said, feeling warmth flood her cheeks.

"Ah, I can imagine." If he considered the double entendre, he didn't let on. "I'm a surgeon, and this is my main form of stress relief, so I'm here as often as possible." He sat back on the bench for the second set, lying back slowly and looking up at her.

"Wow, what kind of surgery?" Maggie's hands hovered under the bar as he lifted it off the rack.

"Heart." He blew out the word with his breath as he pushed the bar from his chest. Each repetition contorted his face into frowns and grimaces; each push of the bar resulted in a deep exhalation through clenched teeth. He got to twelve and started to move the bar back toward the rack, but Maggie stopped him. Blake looked up at her with confusion in his eyes.

"Nope, gimme one more." She grinned at him slyly.

"What for?" His lips began to curve, a glint of playfulness in his eyes.

"Baker's dozen," she quipped, as if it was obvious.

He pressed his lips together, shaking his head against the bench as he lowered the bar to his chest once more, maintaining eye contact with her. His eyes grew more intense as he pushed the bar toward her, but he never looked away.

Maggie guided the bar back to the rack and gave him a little applause as he stood up again. "Good job!"

He grinned. "So what, you're my trainer now?"

"Hey, you asked me to spot. So I'm here encouraging you to push harder. I'm not gonna gas you up just because you…" She gestured to his physique. *Are fine as hell.*

"I like that. Someone willing to push me."

"Oh, you don't find that very often in your work, do you?"

"No," he laughed. "Most people try their hardest to keep me happy."

The things I would try… "By placating you?" she challenged. "What, are these nurses or something? They have a big crush on you and so they just like to feed your ego?"

"Nah." He blinked slowly, returning his eyes to her with a curious look. "Do I seem like I have a big ego?"

"I mean, you're a surgeon. Don't you all have big egos, or is *Grey's Anatomy* inaccurate in that sense?" They shared a laugh at that. "Come on, McDreamy. Time for that last set."

"McDreamy, huh? If we rush, then this whole exchange will be over, and I'm not quite sure I'm ready for that yet." He tilted his head and looked at her expectantly. "What about you?"

Maggie stood tall and put her hands on her hips, allowing him to observe her and relishing the way his eyes raked over her body. "No one said anything about the conversation ending. That would just be the end of your set."

He nodded, dimples poking through his stubble as his mouth turned upward. "Bet." He lowered himself to the bench once more, completing thirteen reps before looking up at her, a question in his eyes.

She smiled at him. "You know you want to give me one more."

"I think I want to give you a lot of things," he muttered, lowering that bar to his chest. Once the rep was completed, he stood and stretched again. "Did you need a spot for anything you're doing?"

"Well," she thought out loud. "I was planning to do some squats next. Do you mind?"

His lips curved. "I don't mind at all."

When their workouts were done, Blake asked if they could exchange numbers, and Maggie agreed. He handed her his phone and she entered her information. "Great. I'll text you so that you have my info, too."

"Sounds good," she responded with a smile. "Well, I better get into this locker room. I like to take advantage of the cold plunge and sauna before I get going."

"Good for your muscles." He nodded. "I do the same every

time I'm here. If you've never tried the infrared sauna, there's a place downtown."

"Thanks for the tip! So I guess I'll see you next time?" She turned toward the door.

"I guess so."

His words hung heavy in the air as she turned to walk into the locker room. Freezing water followed by thirty minutes of sweat in the sauna didn't take her mind off Blake. As she stepped from the sauna into one of the showers, she let the water knead her shoulders as she thought about his thick lips pressing against her most sensitive parts. His gravelly voice shook awake her sexual cravings and she pictured his hands in place of hers as she lathered cedar-and-lavender-scented bodywash over her smooth brown skin.

As she wrapped a towel around herself and made her way to her locker, she unwrapped her hair, fluffing her curls and pulling them into a pineapple atop her head. Moisturized and dressed, she threw her gym bag over her shoulder and headed toward the exit, only to be stopped by a familiar voice. "Wow, you sure clean up nice."

Maggie looked down at her faded jeans that exposed her knees through shredded threads of fabric and her olive-colored Believe Black Women T-shirt under her open track jacket. Meeting Blake's eye, she smiled. "Why, thank you." Maggie's eyes swept over Blake, taking in his track pants with white stripes up the sides, his Georgetown Medicine hoodie and his sneakers. "I could say the same about you."

The afternoon air fluttered the leaves on nearby trees as the sunlight bounced across their canopies. He gestured upward. "It's kind of the perfect day. Could I bend your ear a little longer? Buy you a cup of coffee?"

Maggie sucked her teeth. "With the workout we just put

in? Brunch is still going over off of Third Street. I could use a protein power plate."

Blake grinned. "Even better. I'll drive."

"Good, 'cause I walked."

9

"HEY, GIRL, WHAT YOU DOING?" MAGGIE HIT THE SPEAKER-
phone button and set her cell phone down on her home office
desk, picking up a pen and practicing the next name on the list
on a piece of scratch paper.

"Oh, just trying out a couple of new recipes. I slept in this
morning and then went and met Joanie for hot yoga. What
are you doing?"

"Girl, I'm chillin' here with Penny, relaxing for a bit. Sitting here doing the calligraphy for some of your invitations
right now, but that's not why I called."

"Oh? Everything okay?"

"Oh, yeah, everything's fine. I'll probably be done with
these within the next couple of days and then be able to get
them out in the mail. But outside of the invitations…"

"Yeah…?" Savvy's tone held a sense of foreboding.

"So I kind of met someone…"

Maggie heard Savvy's chair creak and pictured her sitting up from a casual slouch. "Okay, you have my attention. Now spill."

"I was at the gym, and this guy just randomly asks me to spot him." She dragged her pen across an envelope slowly, making sure to leave little flourishes with each cross of the *T*. The loops on her *L*s, *B*s and *D*s were all consistent, and she added a little flourish at the end of each last name. Back in high school, Maggie used to like to learn different crafts. She collected old fountain pens and inkwells, but these newer felt-tipped ones were so much cleaner. Her handwriting had been so painstakingly neat that she used to forge notes for her friends so that they could skip class once in a while. That was until she got caught. *How do kids even forge parent letters anymore if they don't learn cursive?*

"Cute guy?"

"*Foine* guy." Maggie pulled her pen away from the page as she bit her lip, picturing Blake completing his last sets, sweat dripping from his temples and his muscles twitching.

"Uh-huh, continue," Savvy encouraged, each tidbit adding more enthusiasm to her reaction.

"He was bench-pressing while I was doing split squats. I went over and spotted him, though he really didn't need it."

"Mmm-hmm. He asked you to spot him? Body?"

"*Bawdy.* Strong, very athletic build. Great smile. Short fade, clean-shaven with a little stubble."

"Wow, totally your type."

"Right?"

"Mmm-hmm. Go on… Job?"

"Get this…" Maggie put the cap back on her pen. *I'll just have to work on these later.* "Heart. Surgeon."

"Stop! Ooh, tell me more," Savvy squealed.

"So after the workout, we exchanged numbers, but after I

did my plunge and sauna, I ended up walking out with him, so he took me for breakfast at this cute little spot near the Promenade."

"Bitch, keep going!" She was practically salivating through the phone.

"We are going to see each other again tonight."

"So tonight is a date-date?"

Maggie shrugged. "We agreed to keep it casual today, so we're just going to meet over in Manhattan Beach to walk the Strand."

"Ooh, I love that! The Strand is so pretty. So y'all are having a cute little sunset meetup."

"Yeah, neither of us really did any cardio today—just a quick warm-up—so he thought this was a good way for us to help our muscles recover and have plenty of time to talk."

"Do you think this could be your date to the weddings?" The excitement in Savvy's voice was palpable. Her voice swelled with emotion.

"Girl, calm down. This is a first date. I may be a lot of things, but I am never thirsty."

"Now, Maggie," Savvy warned.

She huffed. "Fine, not *that* thirsty," she emphasized.

"I know, but something about this already feels right! Have you told Joanie yet? She manifested the fuck out of this."

Maggie cracked up. "Right? She'll never let me live it down if that's the case."

"You've gotta admit, you may have just met your person. I mean, how often does a *heart surgeon* randomly pop into your workout and ask you for a spot and then take you to breakfast as a thank-you? Call me crazy, but that shit never happened to me."

"Shut up, Savvy. It probably would have happened to you if you actually knew people were hitting on you in the first place. *You're* the one who thought your man was homeless when he was just trying to say hi."

Savvy giggled. "Whatever, heffa. He got me, right?"

Sure did. "You's married nah."

"Almost."

"Yeah, almost, but it's happening."

"So what time y'all meetin'?"

Maggie looked at her watch. "We're gonna meet at five."

"Okay, so you've got a little over an hour to get ready. What you wearing? I know you got some of those workout leggings that accentuate that wagon you carryin'."

Maggie cackled. "And do! I was thinking of wearing a pair of those with a cropped workout top and a track jacket." Those good, booty-sculpting leggings accounted for half of Maggie's closet. She avoided the honeycomb leggings all the influencer girlies played out, in favor of seamless compression that snatched her in all the right places.

"Okay, crop top! I love how bold you are."

"Girl, don't nobody care about my belly. I'mma set this FUPA right on this man's forehead if he'll let me."

Savvy squealed. "I know that's right!" She lowered her voice. "Spencer loves mine. He practically has to hold on to it to fall asleep."

"And should!" The mental image made Maggie smile. "I would love for someone to do that."

"It's really sweet. Took me some getting used to, because I used to be so self-conscious about my body thanks to Jason." Her ex was the worst and deserved every lick of karma that was coming his way. Last Maggie heard, Jason had tried to branch out on his own and start a business, but his family wouldn't invest and he couldn't come up with the capital. He ran back to work for his mommy with a quickness, though he'd never been a good Realtor to begin with.

Savvy was Maggie's sweetest friend; she'd give the clothes off her back if it helped anyone she cared about. Savvy constantly fed her family and friends, she made sure that they got together regularly and she would call to check in if she thought Maggie was in one of her moods. The thought of a loser like Jason talking Savvy down to her lowest point torched her insides.

"Ugh, fuck that guy."

"Yeah." Savvy was quiet for a moment. "So has Garrett weighed in on the surgeon yet? You're not going to have him tailing y'all on the beach today, are you?" She thought the whole idea of Garrett coming to interrupt her dates with the men from the apps was ludicrous. "You're a grown woman, Mags. You've never needed a chaperone."

"Nah, Garrett doesn't know about Blake yet. I haven't had a chance to talk to him, and this just happened so quickly. I'm sure I'll fill him in tomorrow. He'll probably be happy if it means we get to take a break from meeting all these weirdos."

"Well, don't put all your eggs in the doctor's medical bag just yet, love."

Maggie stilled for a minute and exhaled deeply. "You right. Ugh, I do not like these online guys, though. It just feels so unnatural."

"Trust me, I remember," Savvy agreed. "Remember that one that followed me home and tried to slob me down while Spencer was inside the house hearing the whole thing?"

Maggie shuddered at the thought. "Oh, my God, yes."

"Sometimes Spencer pretends like he's going to swallow my face and chases me around the kitchen."

That's hysterical. And also cloyingly adorable. "You two make me sick, you know?"

"Shut up—you love it. You're a big softy."

Maggie scrunched up her face. "Ew, no, I'm not. Garrett said that mess the other day."

"He was telling you the truth!"

"I refuse to believe that."

"You're stubborn just for the sake of being stubborn, girl, and it's exhausting. It's okay to embrace your squishy center."

"Ew, pause. But also, I'm *not* soft!"

"Ooey gooey, like marshmallow fluff."

"No. But, ooh, make those Fluffernutter egg rolls again, please," Maggie begged. Savvy had been traveling and experienced them in a restaurant, so when she came home, she attempted to re-create what she'd tasted, and they were outstanding—crispy egg-roll wrappers encompassing warm and sticky marshmallow fluff and peanut butter, with a chocolate dipping sauce and chopped peanuts for added crunch. *Divine.*

"See, this is why you're in the gym all the damn time!"

"And they're worth every squat. Anyway, let me go get ready."

"Mmmkay. Turn on the location thingy on your phone in case I have to come rescue you, and call me when you get home."

"Bet."

"Luh you, bye!" The phone clicked, and Maggie set her phone to share her location with Savvy and Joan before heading into her closet to start getting ready.

Early spring at the Strand meant cool breezes, sunsets at seven and occasional dolphin sightings. A walk down the Strand and back at sunset was a popular pastime for locals, while others chilled on the beach to watch the waves and await the sunset. Maggie hopped out of her car and began stretching her legs on the sidewalk, nodding her head at people who walked past her. Her ensemble was all black except for a hint of hot pink—her sports bra under her crop top kept the girls in place. She was startled at a deep voice that approached from behind her.

"It's good to see you again so soon." Blake smiled at her, still wearing his track pants and hoodie.

"Hey, you, too. What have you been up to?"

"I've been running errands since I saw you. Picked up some groceries for my mom, dropped those off, got my oil changed and my car detailed, did a little shopping…"

"Wow, you accomplished a whole lot," Maggie laughed.

He grinned. "Oh, yeah? What did you do?"

"I took a nap." She shrugged. "Spoke to my bestie. It's Sunday!"

He laughed. "Well, you earned that, I suppose. Ready to walk?"

She nodded, and they began down the sidewalk. Maggie admired the large houses across the street with their bright windows and expansive balconies that faced the ocean. The breeze ruffled her curls. "I used to dream about owning one of these houses."

"Yeah?" He quirked an eyebrow at her.

"I can't think of a more perfect view. Not anywhere near here, at least."

"True. Might be different if we were talking about some island waterfront."

"Don't get me started," she whined. "The Caribbean has been calling my name!"

"Do you prefer the Caribbean to Hawaii?" He kept an eye on her as they walked, glancing in front of them to nod at passersby.

Maggie considered the question before answering. "I love them both. They're very different vibes, but I give the Caribbean an edge. I love to be surrounded by *us*. I love the seasoning and the spice, the music." She looked over at him from the corner of her eye. "I wouldn't turn down time in Hawaii either, though. It's paradise."

He nodded.

"You know that feeling when you get off of the plane and the humidity touches your skin? It's like all of your stress just melts off of your shoulders."

"That sounds amazing," he responded slowly.

What is he thinking? "You got quiet." She nudged Blake with her shoulder. "Do you have a preference between Hawaii and the Caribbean?"

"So, you promise not to laugh at me?" He smiled at her.

"No," she giggled. "I most certainly will not make that promise."

"Oh, here you go," he chuckled. "Already laughing."

"I'm sorry! Well, if I'm being honest, it's funny already! I can tell. So just say it and get it over with—you'll feel better."

"Mmm-hmm. Okay, fine," he said. "So I have a bit of a fear of flying."

Maggie stared ahead, her face screwed up because the math didn't compute. "I'm sorry, but you're afraid of flying? You literally hold beating hearts in your hands. You bring people back to life after they've technically died."

"I have, that's true."

"Is it the heights, or is it the act of flying?" She pressed her lips together, biting them between her teeth to keep from smiling. "The act of being in a pressurized tube?"

He reached out a hand in front of him as if to grasp for the explanation. "Maybe both? I'm not great with heights, but I love views. Flying just makes me super-nervous. And then you add flying over an ocean, and I just think the worst."

"Wow, that is fascinating. So you've never been to the Caribbean *or* Hawaii?"

"Deal breaker?"

She shrugged. "Everybody's got something, right?"

"I guess. You haven't shared anything that seems out there yet."

She smiled, keeping her gaze straight. "Not everyone can be perfect, you know."

His mouth dropped open and she dashed forward to jump in front of him.

"I'm kidding, I swear!" Her giggling erupted into full-on laughter.

He stopped. "Yeah, but you believe it to a certain extent, right? It was your confidence that I noticed in the gym. The way you carry yourself and push yourself. At one point, it looked like you were giving yourself a pep talk."

Maggie's eyes widened. "I didn't think anyone noticed when I did that," she laughed. "Sometimes getting to that last set of reps requires some motivation."

His mouth curled to one side. "Normally, I probably wouldn't have seen you do it, but you happened to be massaging your ass at the same time. It was hard to miss."

She clapped her hand to her forehead and closed her eyes, willing away the mental image. "I had just finished hip thrusts before my split squats, and I got a cramp. I had to knead it out."

"I saw. I would have offered to help, you know."

Maggie tilted her head, her mouth curving. "Uh-huh. What stopped you?"

"I didn't work up the nerve in time. You moved on to your kettlebell RDLs."

"So then you decided to ask for a spot."

He nodded.

"I see." She turned, and they continued walking as the sun began its descent toward the horizon. When they made it to the end and turned back, the lower edge of the sun had barely kissed the water.

They walked in silence for a bit, watching families ride by on bikes, seagulls chasing after each other and couples lingering in the sand to watch the sunset. They arrived back where they started, and only half of the sun was still visible. Blake gestured toward a vacant bench to watch the rest. "Hey, I'm just going to grab something from my car."

Maggie nodded and sat, mesmerized by the orange and gold flecks dancing across the waves. Hot-pink clouds hung like fluffy gobs of cotton candy as the sky went from yellow to orange to blue to purple the farther up she looked. The breeze ruffled her curls and made her shiver, so she zipped up her track jacket.

Blake returned with a grocery tote, from which he pulled a large metal thermos and a couple of stainless steel mugs. "I hope it's still hot."

"What is this?" Maggie asked incredulously. She turned toward him, folding one of her legs on the bench while the other hung comfortably over the side. He sat next to her, facing forward as he opened the container.

"I thought it might get a little chilly, but maybe you might stick around for a few and enjoy some hot chocolate." His voice was soft, and she noticed the smile lines crinkling toward his temples. He poured steaming liquid into the two mugs and the aroma of chocolate wafted upward.

Maggie stared at him as he handed her a mug, the metal warming her hands. She shook her head as her mouth pulled upward and turned her body back toward the view. "You are smooth, Doc."

He chuckled. "Every once in a while, I'd like to think I get it right."

"Do you often do these walks and finish off with a mug of cocoa?" She looked at him pointedly.

He shook his head slowly. "Never done this before. Just seemed like a good idea once I knew what we were doing."

"Hmm."

They were quiet for a while. The sun continued to drop below the water, as if it were testing the ocean's coolness inch by inch before taking the deep plunge. The bright pink clouds turned lavender as the orange light gave way to dusky blue.

Maggie watched as the last bit of sun disappeared and closed her eyes, her face peaceful. When she opened them, she tilted her head to see Blake watching her. "Anytime I catch the sun setting, I like to make a wish."

"Why?"

She shrugged. "Habit, I guess. I don't know where it started."

His eyes twinkled. "Was it about me?"

She threw her head back and laughed. "Now, you know I can't tell you what my wish is if I want it to come true."

"Ah, so it was about me." He grinned.

Maggie rolled her eyes as she sipped her cocoa, the stainless steel doing a good job of keeping the liquid warm. "Mmm, this is great. Too bad you didn't bring marshmallows."

Blake's eyebrows shot up. "Oh, I forgot." He reached back into the tote and pulled out a can of whipped cream.

"Oh, come on." Maggie's jaw dropped as he swirled a cap of whipped cream on top of her cocoa. "You're good."

"I'm trying to impress you, Maggie." He eyed her playfully.

"Why?"

"So that you'll let me take you out on a real date."

She sipped on the chocolate carefully, so as not to make herself a whipped cream mustache. "So, this wasn't a date?"

His shoulders rose slightly. "I guess technically it was, but let's consider it a gradual buildup to something a little more formal. Honestly, I just knew I wanted to see you a little more today without putting any pressure on you to do anything special." He reached toward her temple and wound one of her curls around his finger. "You're really beautiful, just like this."

A warmth built in Maggie's chest. "Oh, yeah?"

"Yeah. Makes me wonder what you look like when you're dressed up to go out."

"I guess you'll see soon enough."

"Can you do Saturday night next weekend?"

She grimaced. "Oh, Saturdays are usually reserved for my best friend. How about Friday?"

Blake nodded. "I can do Friday. What do you and your best friend do on Saturdays?"

She waved her hand. "It's like our weekly debrief. We've been doing it on and off since college, but we became more consistent this year. We get food, watch movies, drink wine."

"No pillow fights?" he teased.

She laughed. "It's not like that, but I'd say it's a big part of my self-care."

"I feel that. Saturday mornings, I usually go hoop with my friends. It can be hard when I'm on call, but that time is both stress relief in terms of the workout and then just being in community with the fellas."

"I hear you. Does your schedule get crazy given your line of work?"

He shook his head. "Most of my work is scheduled well in advance, but of course, being in a hospital, there are always other factors that weigh into any shift. Every once in a while I'll get called in to evaluate something or will be needed for something emergent or life-threatening, and then my scheduled patient might get bumped."

"Did you ask for Saturday because of your schedule? You're not on call for Friday, are you?"

He shook his head. "Nothing that pressing. I usually hit the barber after basketball on Saturdays, but I'll go Friday morning instead. It's nothing major, and honestly, I'll be out of there a lot faster."

"This has been a lot of fun. Thank you for being so thoughtful." She gestured to her mug.

"Of course." He stacked the empty mugs and screwed them atop the closed thermos.

"Thank you again." She reached her arms up and hugged his neck, heat transferring between them as her cheek pressed against his. As she pulled away, his stubble tickled her jaw and his musky cologne filled her senses. *Should I kiss him? Nope, not a date.*

Stepping back, she waved a hand. "See you Friday?"

He dipped his head quickly and smiled. "Yeah. I'll give you a call tomorrow evening."

She unlocked her car door, and he opened it for her. "Text me to let me know you made it home safely?"

"Only if you do the same."

"Will do." He shut the door once she was comfortably in the driver's seat, and she waved as she pulled away from the curb.

Her heart thumped in her chest. "Well, *that* was interesting," she whispered.

10

MONDAY MORNINGS WERE THE WORST.

Maggie savored her nights and weekends, because she was able to unplug from her work emails and frantic business clients. Her desk was buried under client files as she sipped on a mug of coffee and assessed her calendar and upcoming deadlines. *Ugh, it's going to get uglier before it gets better.*

"Hey, Mags?" Terry called from the front desk. The managing partner was out on vacation, so everyone else felt free to holler down the hall in lieu of the intercom system.

"Yeah?"

"You have a visitor. He comes bearing gifts."

Maggie made a note to herself so she wouldn't forget a couple of important tasks before she left for the day. "Mmmkay, it's fine," she called.

Half a second later, Garrett poked his head in her doorway wearing his typical hoodie-under-a-blazer-with-jeans look that he'd worn since college. The stitching was frayed and there were a few snags along the left sleeve.

She glanced at him quickly before typing a few lines into a demand letter on her computer. "We really need to do something about your wardrobe, you know. People are going to start thinking that you've been wearing the same blazer since college."

He pulled at the fabric. "This *is* from college. Does it look bad?" He gripped the lapels and turned slowly, a button missing from the outdated, double-breasted design. *If Steve Harvey had a church collection fifteen years ago, this relic originated there.*

"Garrett…" Maggie rested her face in her hands and tried to hold back the laughter that threatened to bubble to the surface. She swiped at her mouth, attempting to wipe away the smirk. "That's the blazer I bought you?"

"Of course it is. Why do you think I love it so much?" He spread his hands at his sides, a boyish innocence in his eyes as if this answer was obvious.

"Oh, my God, that's so sweet. I think I'm gonna throw up," she joked.

"Shut up, you big softy."

"Ugh, what do you want?" She crossed her arms over her chest and leaned back in her leather chair.

"I know it's your busy time, so I brought you some lunch."

"It's not something healthy, is it?"

He side-eyed her. "Snarky today, ma'am. See, I knew your blood sugar was going to be low. You get so mean when you're hangry."

"I do," she sighed. "It's been a rough day already. And thank you, this is super-thoughtful of you, because I probably wasn't going to order anything nearly as good as whatever you brought."

"Well, I figured you'd be slammed, because I know the business filing date is coming up, and I happened to be in the vicinity of The Hat—" He stepped just outside her door and picked up a massive bag and a cup holder.

"Oh, my God, what did I ever do to deserve your kindness?" she crooned. The Hat was a Los Angeles institution known for its pastrami. "And more importantly, how did none of my colleagues steal this from the hallway?"

Garrett chuckled. "Should still be warm, too. I was at the studios recording some stuff for the podcast about that upcoming players' strike, and I remembered they were nearby." The NBA and the players' union had been at odds since their collective bargaining agreement was due to expire at the end of the season, and many hoped that everyone involved learned from the last time.

He set a soft drink and straw down on her desk. "Okay, so I've got you a large Orange Bang, a pastrami dip with avocado and extra banana peppers…"

"Uh-huh, and??"

Garrett shook his head. "How do you put all of this away, seriously?"

"It's not 'all' if you forgot my special fries." She made air quotes before reaching her arms out with grabby hands.

"I never forget, Mags." He set a carton in front of her. "Chili cheese fries topped with diced onions and double pastrami."

Maggie inhaled the scent. "Ahhh, heaven," she sang. "And you brought something nice for Terry since she let you in?" She projected her voice to get past the white-noise machines.

"He took good care of your girl," Terry called, her mouth full of food.

Maggie and Garrett stifled laughs, and Garrett moved to close the office door. By the time he turned around, she'd already tucked into her fries and was slurping her Orange Bang loudly. "You know, someday you're going to make some man extremely happy." He watched her inhale a few bites before she decided to come up for air.

"Maybe sooner than you think," she said through the peppered pastrami. She closed her eyes, her head propped back against her chair. "God, this is so good."

"Care to elaborate, or should I wait until you've emptied the trough?"

"Shut up!" She balled a napkin and threw it at him. "Where's your food?"

"I have it here, but sometimes it's fun to watch you go." He began to peel back the paper on his own pastrami sandwich, which he loved to load up with extra spicy mustard and pickles.

"At least you think so. Beth still shudders at her first time seeing me eat a danger dog." Maggie grinned, a little chili smudge on the corner of her mouth.

Garrett beckoned her forward and wiped her face. "Watching you take down danger dogs is one of my favorite pastimes. If I didn't worry about esophageal tears and other major aftereffects, I'd bet money that you could win one of those hot dog–eating contests."

Maggie grinned. "If law school hadn't worked out, I could have been great."

He rolled his eyes. "Your mom never would have allowed that."

"True, but it still would have been fun to try."

"You gonna take your sandwich home for dinner?"

"Of course."

"I figured. I have a second Orange Bang for you to take home." He set another cup in her office mini fridge. "That one doesn't have ice, so it won't be diluted."

Maggie imitated a chef's kiss. "You are a king among men, my friend. Seriously, you deserve one of those special baths like in *Coming to America*, and then they'll throw rose petals everywhere you walk."

"Who is *they* in this scenario?"

She shrugged, poking her plastic fork through a fry with a perfect smattering of chili, cheese and pastrami. "I dunno. I'm sure there's a local bathing service around here or something. Ooh, one of those spas in K-Town exfoliated me within an inch of my life, and then I had one of those four-handed massages. I came outta there feeling brand-new!"

"Two women scrubbing me clean and then giving me a rubdown?" He parroted the question as if the answer weren't hanging above them on a neon sign.

"I mean, to be clear, these women were auntie age and a little rougher than I expected. Honestly, I was lucky to leave there with my dermis intact. But maybe they're cougars looking for a cub. Want me to look into it for you?"

"I feel like a positive response to that question lands at least one of us in jail," he deadpanned, and Maggie almost choked on her food. "How do you even say some of that with a straight face?"

"Fair." She coughed, sipping more of her sweet orange drink with hints of fizzy vanilla—it tasted like a liquid Creamsicle. "Occupational perk. This really did make my day, G. Thank you."

"Of course." Garrett bit into his sandwich. "What did you get into yesterday?"

"Actually, I may have met someone!"

"Oh? An online date gone right?"

"God, no. At the gym! I was working on legs and glutes, and he came over and asked me to spot him on the bench press."

"Smooth."

"Well, we got to talking, and after we'd both showered,

he took me to breakfast at that little place on the Promenade that does those power plates? And then we met back up later to walk the Strand, and he surprised me with hot chocolate." She popped more food into her mouth. "Wasn't that sweet?"

He eyed her slowly, chewing a mouthful. "Very," he agreed.

"Well, why do you look so glum? What did you do?"

He shrugged. "Nothing really special. I ran some errands, did laundry and some meal prep."

"A lot of good meal prep does you when you stop at places like The Hat," she teased.

He smiled slowly. "Yeah, but you and I both know that you wouldn't want my air fryer salmon with roasted squash and Greek salad."

She made a face. "That's so healthy." Her mouth turned downward.

"You're like a five-year-old sometimes."

"You love me either way."

"True," he sighed. "So when are you seeing this guy again?"

"Friday. He's planning."

"What does he do?"

"He's a heart surgeon."

Garrett blew out a breath. "Wow, what are the odds?"

"I know, right?" She grinned. "And here I was starting to give up hope. The girls were right. You really do have to kiss a few frogs…"

"You kissed him?"

"No, of course not. It was barely a date." She eyed him. "I was speaking metaphorically, or whatever."

"Ah, gotcha."

"Anyway, what's going on with you? Any big articles coming out that I should expect?"

"Just the usual stuff, but I have a couple of bigger pieces that I have been trying to submit to talk about the latest players' strike. That's why I was over recording a podcast—I'm trying to get some airtime."

"Uh, that's amazing! Could this turn into a regular feature? Or maybe TV?"

He grimaced, rubbing the back of his neck. "I don't know if I can do TV."

"What do you mean? You know sports better than anyone I know, you're easy on the eyes and you've got a great voice. You've dreamed of broadcasting for as long as I've known you."

"Yeah, but I'm not as 'in your face' as you are…"

"You mean extroverted?" she corrected, one eyebrow perched higher than the other.

"You know exactly what I mean," he said, looking deadly serious. "Every time I think of the camera lens focusing on me, I get overwhelmed and freeze up."

Maggie got up from her desk chair and moved to the other side, sitting next to Garrett. "How have I never known that you deal with stage fright?"

"I just freak out a little. It's different on the podcast, because there are no cameras. It's just me shootin' the shit with a couple of other sports heads, so even though a mic is in my face, I don't really think much about it," he explained. "But when I see that red light illuminate on a camera, I just—" His eyes glazed over and he froze in place.

"That's awful. Total deer in headlights?"

He nodded. "Facing a freight train head-on."

"Jesus. Well, but we can practice so that you can get used to having a camera on you. Maybe it'll help?" She rested her hand on his forearm, which flexed under her touch.

"Yeah, maybe."

"Saturday. I'll set up a camera, and you'll talk to me about the strike and all its intricacies."

"You'd listen to all of that? Most of the time it makes your eyes cross, and you look like you wanna die."

She gestured around the room. "Look at what you just did for me. You're keeping me alive! Of course, I'd do anything for you."

"You're the best, Mags."

"Nah, love, you take far better care of me than I usually admit." Her voice took a serious tone. "We're talking about your career here. You've always wanted to be one of those guys on ESPN talking about all the things. You could be over at L.A. Live dropping sports gems on a national broadcast."

"You really see me doing that? Tell the truth." He poked his lips out.

"I believe you're capable of reaching your dreams, G. You got it. Point-blank, period." She gazed into his eyes and spoke with authority. "When have I ever lied to you?"

"Never."

"Exactly. Now I have a client coming in ten minutes, and she's a hot mess in a lot of ways, but I also think that she'd catch one glimpse of you and try to follow you home."

"Say what now?"

"She's a little eccentric, but yeah, she has already had a crush on two of my paralegals. The managing partner now actively avoids coming in on days she has appointments."

"If she's harassing people, why not just fire her as a client?"

"Eh, because she owns forty beauty supply stores between here and San Diego. As long as she works with me directly and the menfolk run for cover, we're good."

"Should I take the stairs?"

She mulled it over, glancing out the window into the heart of Century City thirty floors below. "Nah, you should be okay. She might have gotten stuck in traffic. But if you see a woman with a red-and-blue headband wig with reddish-brown hair in big curls, just walk in the other direction."

"All right, bet. But first, gimme hug."

He pulled Maggie to standing and wrapped his arms around her shoulder blades; she wrapped her arms around his waist. "You're the best," he murmured against the crown of her head.

"I'll share that title with you today." She grinned, stepping back behind her desk.

He playfully poked his head out into the hall, looking either way before heading back to reception. "Call me later!" He waved.

"Will do!"

"So where are y'all going?" Savvy sat on the bench at the foot of Maggie's bed. She ran her fingers over a fuzzy throw blanket that Penny loved to curl up in for naps.

"Girl, I have no idea. He said dinner at a nice place. I don't know what kind of food, if we're by the water or not. I feel like I should be dressy, but I don't know how far I'll have to walk. Questions that need answers!" Maggie called from her bathroom, where she was applying the finishing touches to her makeup. She gave herself another quick spritz of her favorite vanilla coconut perfume.

"Hmm." Savvy tapped her bottom lip with the pad of her index finger. "What if you ask him for some environmental clues so that you can make sure you're dressed appropriately?"

Maggie shrugged. "Worth a shot. Let's see what happens." She typed out a text message, narrating as she typed. "'Hey, B, curious about whether we'll be inside/outside, how much walking we might need to do? Currently out shopping for a cute 'fit for Friday night—you know I gotta come correct.'"

As they waited for a response, she ran her fingers over a crepe blouse.

"You could always go with a dress and then have a light duster coat situation. You have that light gray trench that I'm always trying to steal."

"Uh-huh, you were almost successful last time."

Savvy grinned. "I'm just saying, if there's ever a day you can't find it, know that it's being well cared for." She always threatened to take Maggie's clothes, but Maggie was usually the one grabbing clothes and accessories from Savvy's closet. Today, Savvy's black jeans hugged her curves perfectly, and she wore a lacy bra under a button-up cardigan.

"I could say the same for that cardigan. Ooh, come here, I love the buttons!" Maggie looked at the tiny flowers painted on the wooden buttons coated in a shiny lacquer. "These are pretty," she murmured as her phone pinged.

Blake: Hey, Gorgeous. Minimal walking, unless you feel like taking a stroll after dinner. We'll be inside, but it'll be a good idea to bring a wrap in case the restaurant has the A/C blasting.

"Okay, I don't know what the man said, but I can tell you how your face looked."

"How'd it look?" Maggie's head snapped up from her phone to stare at Savvy as she tried unsuccessfully to quell the butterflies in her stomach and remove the smile from her face.

Savvy peered over Maggie's shoulder to see the message. "Okay, Gorgeous," she purred.

"Ugh, shut up."

"Why? He can call you that, but I can't? It should mean more from me. I know all your dirty little secrets." Savvy wagged her finger in Maggie's direction.

"I mean, true, but also, shut *up*!" Maggie laughed, shoving Savvy lightly. "So what do you think? What should I wear?"

"Do you still have those super-high black boots? And that

leather motorcycle jacket with the stand-up collar?" Savvy's mouth moved to one side, like she was deep in thought as she peered into the open door of Maggie's closet.

"Of course. I love those boots."

"You look amazing in those boots," Savvy responded. "I say you wear your signature color." She stood and pulled a red faux-wrap sweaterdress from one of the closet racks directly in view—the light, ribbed material was perfect for the spring, and a button detail started at the waist down one thigh above a generous slit. The neckline was a standard V with a few buttons trailing to the waist.

"Oh, this is cuuute." Maggie ran her fingers over the fabric.

"Yep, and you can do your red lip."

"Mmm-hmm, hair pulled back?"

"I'm thinking twist-out curls in a low ponytail, light baby hair, little swirl or curl at the sideburns."

Maggie nodded. "Gold hoops?"

"The big thin ones? Yes, and that really pretty herringbone necklace and bracelet set your dad gave you."

"Perfect." She high-fived Savvy, who handed her the dress. "This is just right."

"I think so. Not too much skin, a little edge, a sexy red lip…" Savvy eyed her friend. "You're gonna go get a manicure, right? You know you bite your nails when you're in your busy season."

"Ugh, yes, fine. I'll go get my nails done."

"Don't go superlong, because we know you won't be able to type, but just something cute. Almond shaped, but on the shorter end, or oval."

Maggie held out her hand before gnawing on her cuticle. "Oval looks funny on me. I'll go almond. French?"

"Or a pretty neutral. Either way would work." Savvy sat

back down, Penny sauntering into the room to greet their guest.

Maggie surveyed her nails again as she plopped down on the edge of the bed. "Hmm. How's everything on your end? I swear you've been the calmest bride I've ever known."

"Well, when you're getting married on a beach in another country, what is there to really worry about? We just booked our flights for Thailand—the hotel was booked months ago. What about you? Have you gotten your tickets yet?"

"Girl, yes, I got mine using travel rewards points. Garrett's, too."

"And how goes the road to partner?"

Maggie sighed. "Honestly, I've upped my client intake and my billables as far as I can really go. I don't think I have the bandwidth to take on more."

Savvy searched Maggie's face. "Are you worried they haven't noticed all that you've taken on?"

Her shoulders slumped. "Sort of. Like, maybe they see it, but everyone is so busy that I don't actually know, and I haven't had my performance review—we don't do those until May, once the partners return from vacation." After taxes were officially filed, several of the partners immediately dipped for a few weeks of sunshine and rejuvenation, leaving Maggie and the others remaining to deal with any clients who hadn't made the deadlines and were scrambling to get things done.

"Do you not feel comfortable asking someone? Is there a partner that you could pull aside?"

"Maybe? It can be tough to gauge sometimes, especially because everyone is so swamped right now. But I've got a couple of clients who are potentially facing some major penalties, and right now I think the best thing that I can do is really kill it when it comes to their cases and making sure they don't end up under the jail."

Savvy shivered. "Lord."

"Right? Anyway, thanks for coming over here on such short notice. I was having a wardrobe emergency."

"My pleasure, my love! You know, I think that means dinner is on you."

"Sushi?" Maggie offered hopefully.

"As if there were another option!"

11

"BLAKE, HEY." MAGGIE SMILED AS HE TURNED TO THE sound of her voice. He looked good in a fitted charcoal suit, a thin sweater under his blazer.

He reached for her hand and held her at arm's length to get a look at her. Just as Savvy predicted, the red dress fit her like a glove, accentuating all of her curves. Its hem hit just below the knee, allowing about an inch of moisturized skin to show before the expanse of her leather boots—their stilettos increasing her height by close to five inches. The leather jacket hugged her torso, and she gave a little Vanna White wave to make him laugh. "Maggie, you look spectacular!"

He held his other hand to his chest and Maggie tsked. "Now, if something happens to your heart, who comes to save you?"

He chuckled. "You've got nothing to worry about. It's nice

and strong." Still holding her hand, he pulled her closer and rested her palm against his chest. "See?"

Warmth radiated through his sweater to her hand as his heartbeat kissed the center of her palm. "I do," she breathed.

Blake removed her hand from his chest and looped it into the crook of his arm. "I take it you haven't been here before?"

She shook her head as they stepped through the open doors into a dimly lit dining room. When she'd looked up the restaurant, she'd seen that it was Italian and that the chef was someone famous, but Savvy knew way more about that world than she did. The food photos posted online looked beautiful and indulgent, so she anticipated a delicious meal, though her mind raced to Garrett teasing her about how she ate. *Not everyone thinks inhaling food is endearing...*

"Do you like Italian?"

"I like *food*," she laughed. "You don't have to worry about me—one of my best friends might as well be a chef. She's got a couple of cookbooks and tests out all of her recipes on me. I've never been a picky eater."

"That sounds like a lucky job to have." He smiled.

"I barely buy groceries! I guess I should tell you now that I don't really know how to cook." She grinned. "But why learn when you have best friends who are gourmets? In exchange, I take her to her favorite sushi restaurants whenever she wants. I think it's a fair exchange."

"I love sushi." His eyes lit up. "You'll have to show me your favorite spot."

"I think that can be arranged," she replied, glancing in his direction slyly as they walked.

Blake held her hand against his arm with his other hand, and heads turned in their direction as they were guided to their seats. "Want me to help you with your jacket?"

"Please?"

He pulled the jacket from her shoulders gently, and she adjusted the three-quarter sleeves of her dress and her bracelets as he pulled out her chair with a smile. "Red is truly your color."

She laughed. "When I was a kid, my mom told me that women in red made power moves, and it's been my color ever since. I've always been one to speak my mind. I went to law school to make power moves and I hit the gym the way I do to feel powerful." She lowered her gaze. "My friends would tell you I boss them around to feel powerful, too."

He threw his head back, a rumble coming from deep within. "I bet they find ways to push back. I can't imagine you being friends with a bunch of pushovers."

"Nah, they check me pretty regularly." Maggie fidgeted with her nails.

Blake watched her. "Is the all-powerful feeling some nerves?"

"Hush." She smiled. "This place is beautiful, Blake." The room was massive, yet intimate. Chandeliers composed of uniquely shaped bulbs and exposed filaments hung above each booth. Large, family-style tables spanned the center of the room for larger parties, and a large chandelier with crystals the color of champagne hung above the bar.

"A colleague brought me here for lunch one day, and I thought this might be a cool place for a date. Do you like pasta?"

"Who doesn't like pasta?"

"True," he chuckled. "Well, I took the liberty of making a special request, so the chef has selected some of his favorites for us."

Maggie's eyes lit up. "Really? Daaamn, you have it like that?"

Blake nodded, the edge of his tongue wetting his bottom lip. "I can't stop at hot chocolate, can I?"

"Good evening. I'm Lily, and I'll be your server this evening. Welcome, Dr. Hamilton and...?"

"Maggie."

"Maggie, welcome. Have you dined with us before?"

"I have not."

"Well, you're in for a treat. Chef DiSalvo has prepared a special meal for the two of you, including a couple of wine pairings. Chef is from Sicily, so he brings a lot of flavors from home to his cuisine. To start, we have an orange-and-fennel salad, Catania-style monkfish, pasta con le sarde, and since we're approaching Easter, we have lamb chops with a potato crust served with a spicy sauce, sweet onions and saffron. For dessert, we have a chocolate Savoie cake."

Maggie smiled. "That all sounds amazing! Wow, thank you so much!"

Course after course, Maggie marveled over the food, taking pictures so that she could show Savvy. Blake got a kick out of watching her savor her first bite of something new. He watched her eat, taking small bites of the dishes, leaving the lamb chops completely untouched.

"Are you full?" Maggie asked after sampling the saffron sauce.

"Actually, I'm not much of a red meat eater, but they're supposed to be the best in town, so I didn't want you to miss them." He motioned toward her plate. "How are they?"

Maggie took her first bite and closed her eyes, the tender meat falling apart as it landed on her tongue. "Divine. Oh, my God," she marveled.

Blake's phone buzzed and he pulled it from the inside pocket of his blazer. "I'm sorry. I've got to take this—it's the hospital." He rose, a look of concern on his face as he placed his hand on hers.

Maggie nodded. "Of course."

He walked toward the front of the restaurant and out the front door. She sipped on a smooth red Barolo, picking over the last of her lamb chop. When he returned, the look on his face gave Maggie a sense of foreboding.

"Bad news?" she asked.

"Let me preface this by saying I've had such a good time with you tonight, and I in no way intended to have to cut this short. I'm so sorry, but I've been called in to assist on a surgery. Lily's going to box up dessert for you, and everything else has been taken care of. Do you want to stay and have another glass of wine, or I can order a Lyft or Uber to take you home?"

"No, that's okay, really. And I drove. I'll run to the ladies' room and get the box from Lily, and then I'll head home."

He squeezed her shoulder. "I really had a good time, Maggie, and I promise I'll make it up to you."

She nodded, shrugging. "I mean, you're rushing into emergency surgery—you're not exactly ditching me for a strip club."

"Well, when you put it like that…" He grinned. "I promise, though, next time will be seamless." He checked his watch. "It'll be late by the time I get out of surgery, but would you just text me to let me know you made it home safely?"

"Sure, of course."

He dipped closer and pressed his lips to her cheek, and warmth spread to her neck and chest. "I'll call you tomorrow," he whispered in her ear, his breath tickling her skin.

"Okay," she whispered back, allowing a hint of a smile to shine in her eyes.

He retreated out the front, looking back at her one more time. With a quick wave, he was gone.

"Hello?" Garrett answered on the first ring.

"Hey, you busy?" Maggie maneuvered her car out of the parking lot and toward the freeway.

"Nah, I'm just over here trying not to throw my whole laptop away." She heard the clacking of his fingers against the keys, and the way he pounded on them demonstrated his agitation.

"Writer's block?"

"Times ten. What are you doing? I thought you had a date?"

Her shoulders slumped. "We did, but he had to cut things short. He got called into surgery."

"Not all heroes wear capes," he muttered, breathing heavily into the phone.

Maggie giggled. "Damn, someone is grumpyyy. Want to talk through your article with me? Maybe I can help you shake something loose?" She cared very little about most sports, especially if she wasn't playing them, though she could be competitive in the ones she knew.

"Nah, it's okay. This one isn't on the strike—it's on a charity golf tournament being hosted by a couple of football players. You'd be bored in ten seconds flat," he teased. "When are you seeing Superman again, anyway?"

"I don't know. I'm sure he'll call. Besides, I've got a little lunch ting tomorrow before you come over with another one of the guys from online."

Garrett paused. "You do?"

"Yeah. I can't be putting all my eggs in one basket. Besides, this guy's a chef, and you know the way to my heart." She did a little shimmy, aware that people in the car next to her were staring.

Garrett groaned. "You really need to up your standards. If being fed is all it takes, we have some work to do."

She cackled. "Shut up."

"Anyway, I am glad that you're exploring your options. It's good to see what's out there before you go making any big decisions."

"It's not like I'm trying to be some dude's wife tomorrow. It's not that serious."

"I know it's not, and I'm not trying to say that you're acting any type of way, because you're not."

"Thank you."

"I just want you to take your time and really think about what you want and who might be best equipped to deliver that to you."

"Well, if we're talking equipment—"

"Goodbye, Maggie," Garrett groaned.

"No! I was just going to say I wouldn't know anything about that yet. Remember, I'm adding to my plate with this other guy—I'm actively trying *not* to fall for Blake, because the optics are damn near perfect. Something's gotta be wrong with him somewhere, and I need to know what that is and whether it's a deal breaker."

"Fair, okay, well, I like where your head's at. And I'm sorry I can't be there for your first date with this other guy tomorrow. What's his name?"

"Chad."

"Ugh, already sounds like a mistake."

Maggie snorted. "Something is wrong with you."

He laughed. "If only you knew. Anyway, let me get back to this article. Don't buy food for tomorrow. I've got a surprise for you."

"Ooh, do I get a hint?"

"No, because you'll guess it."

"Ugh, fine. Okay, luh you, bye."

"I love you. Bye, Mags."

12

IT TOOK MAGGIE THREE SHOWERS TO WASH THE IRRI-
tation off her. She was guiding her hair into a topknot when
Garrett called from the front door. "Mags?"

"In here!" She poked out her tongue as she got her hair
exactly as she wanted it, held it in place with one hand as she
grabbed a couple of bobby pins with another.

"Okay." The rustling of bags piqued Penny's interest, so
she leaped from the foot of the bed to go investigate, only to
curl her back and retreat as Garrett got close to the door. He
was her favorite anyway. "You decent in here?"

"Yeah, come on in." Maggie pushed the last of her bobby
pins into place and turned her head to different angles to ad-
mire her work. "I'm all done."

"How was your date?" He kissed her on the cheek before
perching on the storage bench at the foot of her bed.

"We'll have to work up to that, honestly. Want to do some run-throughs for broadcasting first?"

"Oh, boy. Sure, if you'd prefer." He shrugged, his shoulders slumping slightly.

"You're gonna be great, G," she assured him. "Did you bring something to practice on?"

"I did." Garrett leaned to the side to pull a wad of folded paper from his back pocket. As he pulled it apart to flatten it, he handed one copy to Maggie and straightened the copy he kept. "So how do you want to do this?" He eyed her, laughing nervously.

"Come on, G. It's just me!" She moved next to him on the bench and jostled his arm.

"That doesn't make this any easier, Mags."

"Really?" She watched him fidget. *He's serious.*

"Yeah. It's like my logical brain knows it's just the two of us standing here, but I'm also picturing all of the people at home staring at me through the TV screen. Wouldn't that make you nervous?"

"Well, that depends," she replied seriously. "Is the camera focused on my good side?"

Garrett's shoulders dipped. "Ma'am."

Maggie cackled. "Sorry, it was too easy. Okay, how should we lead into this? Do you just want to try to read it to me? Or am I supposed to prompt you in some way, because I can do that." She held an imaginary microphone up to her face and stared off into the distance, a bright smile spreading across her face. "Hello and welcome to another segment of All Sports All-Stars. I'm your host, Maggie Jones." She mimicked her favorite TikTok news reporter, overenunciating her words with added emphasis and enthusiasm. "Today, we've got a special guest live in the studio, Garrett Bailey, with the latest update on the NBA players' strike rumored to start next month. Garrett, what have you got?"

"Come on, Mags. Be serious." He eyed her warily.

"There seems to be a bit of a delay." Maggie maintained her reporter voice and held a finger to her ear as if she were receiving a quick message from the producer. "Garrett, give us the scoop."

Garrett rolled his eyes, holding his paper in front of him. "Thank you, Maggie. Today, a representative of—" He coughed, squirming on the bench. He turned a little, glancing up at her over the paper, so she turned toward him, folding one of her legs onto the bench. "A representative of the NBA players' union confirmed that we are facing another lockout—" cough "—similar to what we experienced in 2011…as the collective bargaining agreement nears expiration."

She nodded encouragingly. "Take your time."

He continued. "As we near the playoffs—" he squirmed in his seat, his knee bouncing uncontrollably "—we, uh…we can expect… Dammit." His arms dropped.

"Hey, it's okay." Maggie placed a hand on his knee. "You've got this. We just need to keep practicing, right?"

He nodded slowly. "You really don't mind?"

She side-eyed him. "All of my antics that you put up with, you really think I'm going to mind when it comes to something that elevates your career?"

He pressed his lips together and exhaled through his nose. His shoulders lowered from kissing his ears as the air escaped his lungs. "Thanks, Mags."

"You've got this! Want to try again?"

He set down the paper. "Maybe later. You hungry?"

"Perpetually."

They headed for the living room. "So tell me for real. How was the date?"

She turned and stared at him, unblinking. If looks could kill, she aimed for the stun setting.

"Damn, that bad?" Garrett winced.

Maggie ran a hand over her hair. "Imagine meeting someone for a mimosa and a chat on a Saturday at noon. I arrive, and his table is being cleared because he ate. We have our mimosas, and he's an okay guy. Works in tech, does something with IT that I don't understand, fine, right?"

"Okay." Garrett nodded, folding his arms across his chest.

"We have some light conversation, order a second round of drinks, and he runs to the bathroom. When he gets back, his phone is in his hand, and he's apologizing—there's been some sort of emergency and he has to go to the hospital. His son's in an ambulance." She gestured wildly with her hands. "He's had some sort of allergic reaction, and it took some time before someone could get to him with an EpiPen."

"Oh, shit."

"Right, so he's sorry, he's rushing, I say no problem, I'll take care of the bill—just let me know once you make it that he's okay."

"Maggie...don't tell me." Garrett squeezed his eyes shut.

"This dude jets out of there and they bring me the bill. Why were there *two* orders for the brunch buffet?" She pursed her lips and stared.

"You've got to be kidding me. He pulled a dine and ditch after having two dates at the same table?" Garrett's head fell back, his mouth wide open. "Wow..."

"First of all, the audacity to lie on your child like that—who *does* that? But second, you scam your way through seatings with two different people, and the restaurant let that slide? Like, why didn't they charge them when the previous person was there?"

Garrett stopped to think. "Actually, that's a good question. Why wouldn't they have brought the check?"

"I don't think he ever left the table. Who knows—he could have pretended that she just got up to go to the bathroom. The restaurant was busy, so they probably weren't paying close attention. Suffice it to say that homeboy is blocked, and the restaurant comped me for everything, because what the fuck?"

"Damn, Mags. I'm sorry."

Her shoulders slumped forward, and she blew out a breath. "Yeah…so I think I'm kinda done with the online thing, at least for the moment."

"Fair. I'm proud of you for hanging in there this long, honestly."

She managed a weak smile. "Thanks. So what did you bring? I heard bags rustling."

He gestured toward the kitchen and pulled a couple of cold bottles from the fridge. "Come on—I'll show you."

A new season of *Yellowjackets* was on the TV screen, and food packages littered the coffee table. "Ooh, what is this? Smells yummy…" Maggie climbed onto the couch, knees first, and folded her legs beneath her.

"Actually…" He grabbed a couple of zafus from a decorative pile. "You might want to sit on the floor closer to the coffee table."

"Oh?"

"Yeah." He smiled secretively as he began opening lids to the packages, displaying injera, a fried fish, colorful lentils, collard greens, cabbage, beet-and-tomato salad and beef sautéed with onions and jalapeños. "I stopped by Little Ethiopia to get some of your favorites from Merkato."

Her mouth dropped open. "I was just saying the other day that I was craving—"

"Asa tibs, a veggie platter, the yawaze tibs and extra mitmita." He pointed to a small container filled with the spice. "I got the Habesha beer and honey wine, too."

"Tej." She nodded. "This is so thoughtful! Thank you. And I can't believe you really held out and didn't watch *Yellow-jackets* without me."

"I've had plenty to keep me busy. I can't believe how many seasons in we are and we still don't fully know what happened. They are writing the hell out of this show."

"Hopefully this season stands up to the rest."

They made it through two episodes with their dinner and beers before they fell asleep on the couch. Maggie woke to Garrett running his hands over her hair, her head in his lap, and she turned to look up at him. His expression was solemn. "Hey, you okay?" She cleared her throat to ease the raspiness.

He sucked his teeth and looked up toward the ceiling. "Do you think that things between us will change if you and Blake get serious?"

"Change how?" Her brows pinched together.

"I mean, he and I still haven't met, but I'd wager he wouldn't want you spending a whole bunch of time with another man. He'd become your person, eventually, right?"

She reached up toward his face and pinched his cheek. "Come on, G. Nobody replaces you."

"You know what I mean." He rolled his eyes.

"Any guy in a relationship with me has to accept you, too. We're a package deal."

"Most of the guys you've dated have had issues with that."

"So? That's a them problem. None of them were the right one anyway." Maggie sat up, moving beside him on the couch. She nudged him with her shoulder. "You're stuck with me, G. No matter what happens. If Blake and I get serious, I'll still make time, but you might have to relinquish a couple of Saturdays."

He nodded. "Just not all of them."

"Never," she agreed. "I'm beat. You want to stay?" She

began picking up food containers and carried them to the kitchen.

"Yeah, I'm too tired to drive. Mind if I spoon with Penny on the couch?"

"You know I never mind, and Penny loves you more than she loves me. Your pillows and blankets are in the hall closet." Maggie stepped behind the couch and wrapped her arms around Garrett's shoulders from behind, plopping a kiss on his cheek. "Thanks again for dinner. Get some rest, okay?"

He nodded. "Will do. Sleep tight, gorgeous."

After running into each other at the gym the next Sunday, Blake had begged Maggie's forgiveness and asked if he could take her for dinner later that night. She agreed, and he sent her a time and address in Manhattan Beach. The street name was familiar, but she couldn't place the building until she parked. "Wow," she breathed.

The building was a house—Blake's house—directly on the Strand, facing the ocean. The roofing of Spanish tiles framed the top of a creamy white house with terra-cotta shutters and an expansive second-level balcony above a hot tub surrounded by lounge chairs and leafy palm trees.

The man lives in my dream house. Maggie's jaw remained slack as she stepped closer, taking in the massive windows on the main and upper levels, the outdoor patio and balcony being perfect places to soak in the sunlight. She pulled the lever to open the front gate and walked down a stone path on the side of the main-level patio. The cover was off the hot tub, steam rising from the water, a yellow rubber ducky floating alone on the glassy surface. As the gate slammed shut behind her, the front door opened, and Blake came out barefoot and smiling.

"You made it!"

"You could have told me." She gestured to the house and out toward the beach.

"I could have," he admitted, "but then I wouldn't have been able to see the stunned look on your face when you pulled up."

"Touché." She smiled. "Hi," she greeted him with a hug.

"You smell so good." His arms tightened around her as his nose tickled her neck. "Wow."

"So what are we doing for dinner? I know there are a couple of walkable restaurants near here," Maggie noted as Blake led her inside. She slipped off her Stuart Weitzman heels and stepped onto his smooth, dark wood floors. "Wow, Blake, this is gorgeous!"

He wasn't quite a minimalist, but everything was neat and clearly had its place. His modern furniture and sleek kitchen suited him. Movement in the kitchen startled Maggie.

"Oh, hello!" She waved politely.

"Hi there, Ms. Jones. Can I get you a glass of champagne?" A curvy woman in a pristine white chef's jacket greeted her with a smile.

"I'd love one, thank you." Maggie smiled, her eyes widening at Blake. "You have a chef?"

He pushed his hands out in front of him, gesturing downward. "Not all the time, just for tonight," he laughed. "It's a special surprise. Cat is a family friend and has cooked up something delicious for us tonight."

Cat nodded, handing Maggie a glass of bubbles in a tulip glass before passing Blake a tumbler of amber liquid.

Maggie's mouth fell open again. "You spoil me far more than I deserve."

He wrapped an arm around her waist. "Maybe *I* think you deserve it."

She looked toward the ceiling coyly. "Well, who am I to argue?"

Blake chuckled. "Dinner needs another fifteen to twenty minutes, so want a tour?"

"Of course!"

He walked her through the house, and every important room had a view—the main living spaces, the master bedroom, even his home gym and office. They stepped onto the balcony and Maggie shook her head as the sun began its descent before them.

"I can't believe that this is your view every night."

"Well, it does get cloudy sometimes, but yes, I'm very fortunate to have this place. With work being as high stress as it can be, I wanted home to feel like a refuge. I fall asleep to the sound of the waves, and I'm rarely more relaxed than when I'm home."

Maggie nodded. "I can't even imagine. You have a whole oasis right here." She leaned her forearms against the balcony's rail. A light breeze fluttered through her crepe blouse, but the sun glowed pink and orange, warming her skin. "If I had a place like this, I think I'd never want to leave. I'd have to find a job where I could work from home."

"I know the feeling. Some days it's really hard to head toward the hospital, but knowing I get to return here makes it a heck of a lot easier." He gazed at her before looking back out to the water. "So, are you hungry?"

"Always." She smiled.

"Always?" he teased, his head tilted slightly.

"Pretty much," she laughed. "I'm not a girl that skips meals." A twinge of anxiety rolled in her stomach as he looked at her.

"Hmm. Okay, well, let's get you fed." Blake held an arm out and led her back inside.

Cat had candles illuminating the dining table, golden flatware bordering white dishes on bamboo chargers. The dining table was a thick wooden slab that had been sanded and stained a dark reddish-brown color, the chairs a muted beige.

"Something smells good." Maggie winked at Cat.

"Thank you!" She smiled as she ladled something into shallow bowls.

Blake held out a seat for her, pushing it in as she sat down. "You look beautiful, by the way."

Ass one, Doctor zero. "Aw, thank you," she replied sweetly.

As he took his seat, Cat carried a small round tray to them. "Okay, folks, so we are starting today with a Greek lemon chicken soup."

"Mmm, thank you." Steam wafted up from the small bowl placed in front of her. "It's so fragrant!" She grinned at Blake, her hands folding on the edge of the table.

He picked up a spoon. "Dig in!" He swirled his spoon around and helped himself, nodding at Cat as he chewed. "Perfect."

Cat smiled wide and excused herself back to the kitchen.

Maggie moved her hands to her lap and bowed her head to pray, whispering over her food. When she had finished and placed her napkin over her lap, she looked up to find Blake watching her expectantly. She grabbed her spoon and tasted the broth, which was luscious and rich, the lemony liquid fragrant with herbs. The chicken and orzo were perfectly cooked; she only wished that the portion filled more of the bowl. "Tasty," she affirmed.

Pleased, he continued eating.

"So how has work been?" She set her spoon down on top of her fork to avoid it touching the surface of the table.

He winced a little. "It's been a rough week."

"Oh, I'm sorry. You don't have to talk about it if you don't want to."

"Thanks." He bristled slightly.

Maybe he lost a patient. Maggie looked out toward the beach. "Have you lived here long?"

"About two years. I have a condo in Culver City where I lived before. I've been renting it out, but I'm toying with the idea of selling it."

Cat cleared their plates and returned quickly with large ceramic bowls in both hands. "Okay, for your main entrée today, you have a Greek salad topped with za'atar-spiced shrimp."

He hired a chef to make salad? Where are the rest of the shrimp? Fresh greens were lightly dressed and topped with thinly sliced red onions, Kalamata olives, banana peppers, bright red tomatoes, cucumber and four measly shrimp. Maggie turned the corners of her closed mouth into a smile as she looked up at Cat. "This is beautiful, thank you."

Blake smiled. "Cat's the best."

Maggie nodded. Cat excused herself and Maggie hoped that dessert would make up for the salad, because though this wasn't all that different from the big Greek salad she ordered anytime Savvy had a craving for her favorite salmon and poached pear pairing over spring greens, the serving size was noticeably reduced.

The door clicked, and Maggie turned to look to see if someone else had arrived.

"Oh, Cat just let herself out to give us some privacy." Blake speared his fork into some greens and a piece of shrimp. "Mmm, my favorite. I don't often have Cat here to cook, but sometimes I'll buy a bulk order of prepped meals for the week. This is probably what I get most, though sometimes I alternate between shrimp and chicken breast."

Damn, no dessert. She took a bite. "Everything is super-fresh. No one can say that, as a heart surgeon, you don't practice what you preach," she quipped.

"Exactly. I'm glad you get me."

Dear God, I was joking. She directed another bite to her mouth and smiled with her eyes as she chewed.

After dinner, they cleared their plates and Blake insisted on running the dishwasher before grabbing them each a raspberry White Claw from a drink fridge below his bar. If it could even be called a bar. He had a bottle of Grey Goose and an unopened bottle of scotch, and that was it. There were a few bottles of wine chilling, but Maggie sensed that he either wasn't much of a drinker or only did so socially.

They carried their beverages to the patio.

"I can't believe you did all of that for me."

"Why shouldn't I? I told you I'd make it up to you." He stepped closer, his hand sweeping against her cheekbone before lightly cupping the back of her head. His lips pressed against hers, their mouths slightly ajar so that they could enjoy the fullness of each other's kiss.

Maggie allowed herself to sink into it, his soft lips applying gentle pressure. She tilted her head to deepen the kiss, but he pulled back.

"Sorry, I'm just acutely aware that we just had those raw onions." He held a hand over his mouth.

She blinked in confusion. "We both had the same thing," she blurted. *Damn, is my breath funky?*

"Oh, I know. I just..." He hesitated.

Maggie held up a hand. "You know what? It's totally okay." She took a quick swig of her drink and looked out onto the water as the last of the sunlight dipped below the horizon. The waves lapped at the shore as seagulls hunted for food near a group of people building a bonfire. "I should probably get going."

Blake's mouth dropped open. "Wait—are you sure?"

"Oh, yeah, listen, it's my busy season at work, so I've got to look over a few documents to prepare for a meeting with a potential new client." *Lie.* She'd read those documents three times, had her notes ready and had rehearsed her pitch more than once. "I am trying to get my bosses to seriously consider me for partner, so I need to do well on this. But seriously, thank you so much for dinner and for the tour. This view is incredible."

"I see. Well, of course." Blake stood, nodding uncertainly. He wrapped his arms around her, dipping his head to kiss her, but she turned her cheek at the last second, plopping one on his cheek as well.

As he pulled back, she lifted a shoulder. "Sorry." She pointed an index finger toward her mouth and wound it in a circle. "Got a little self-conscious," she tittered nervously. "Next time, I'll be sure to bring some mints."

"Right. Well, sugar-free ones if you do. I try to watch my caloric intake," he responded earnestly.

"Of course." Maggie turned toward the gate and glanced back at him quickly. "I'll text you when I get home?"

"Yes, please."

She waved lightly and turned toward her car. As she climbed into her car, her stomach rumbled and she ran her hand over it as she sucked her teeth. *Hmm, there's an In-N-Out on the way home.* "That man would probably think I have a tapeworm or something." Still, the thought of animal-style fries made her mouth water. "Fuck it, I'm going."

13

BY THE TIME LUNCH ROLLED AROUND, MAGGIE HAD NE-
gotiated two settlements and cleared four client files from the
growing pile on her desk. A knock at the door broke her focus
on an email from her contact at the IRS. "Mags? I've got a
food delivery for you." Terry peered inside, a paper bag with
tweed handles in her hand.

"Oh, Terry, I got one for you, too. Feel free to take the package from the top."

"Ooh, what is it?" She opened the bag wide and produced
two identical take-out cartons made of biodegradable material, along with compostable forks, knives and napkins. Terry
set one at the edge of Maggie's desk.

"It's our favorite mixed green salad with sockeye salmon and
extra avocado from that little lunch spot in the building next
door. I've been eating everything but the right thing lately, so
I thought I'd do something healthy but still yummy." Mag-

gie grabbed her salad and fork and began to mix the contents after winking at Terry. *Three of Cat's Greek salads could fit in this container.*

"Thank you—this is just right. Want me to close your door?" She held up her carton in thanks.

"Yes, please," Maggie called, already back in her email.

The door clicked closed, and nothing but the sound of Maggie crunching on lettuce and cucumbers filled the room until Joan burst into the group Zoom. "Hey, girrrl," she called loudly.

The Zoom window had been covered by Maggie's email browser, so she jumped at Joan's screeching, almost dropping salmon in her lap. "Ma'am, what is the matter with you?"

She cackled as Savvy and Beth both logged on.

"Whew, if looks could kill, Mags... What's going on?" Savvy asked.

Maggie pointed at Joan, as if everyone could see who she was referring to. "She plays too much."

"Oh, hush," Joan retorted. "Come on and spill the beans."

Maggie stabbed at her salad, still a little peeved. She shrugged. "What? We had a good time."

"Don't do that, Mags. You scheduled this little squad call so that we could hear all about your li'l date, so drop some details or I'm going back to my wellness research," Savvy threatened.

"Okay, fine." Maggie rolled her eyes, shoving a big bite of salad into her mouth.

Beth's mouth dropped open at the sight, and Joan turned off her video to hide her laughter, though she neglected to mute her microphone. Savvy shook her head as if she'd seen it all before.

"First of all, his house is on the Strand. Remember when we used to walk down there by the beach? One of the houses that we pointed to saying that we wished we had a house like that, with its perfect view of the water for every sunset? Yeah, he owns one of those. And instead of burning dinner or frying me up a bologna sandwich, he hired a chef to cook us authentic Mediterranean cuisine. He's like a Ken doll, but Black."

Savvy snorted but then nodded in agreement. "Right down to the dream house. Good-looking guy, great job, good money. He ticks a lot of boxes so far. How's the chemistry?"

"It's…good. We had a couple of kisses last night, but that's about it." Maggie continued eating while she spoke, bits of dressing coating the corners of her mouth.

"Uh, sis? You missed your mouth a little bit." Joan gestured toward her collarbone while peering into the camera.

Savvy closed her eyes.

"Was he a good kisser?" Beth asked.

"He was," Maggie started. "But I don't know. I can't quite put my finger on it."

"On what?"

"He's kinda boring, and I think he's too much of a health nut for me."

Savvy rolled her hands in front of her. "Say more words."

"I'm not sure we have enough in common. Conversation feels a little stale."

"He has been doing a lot of sweeping gestures, though… the award-winning restaurant with the preset meal, private chef on the beachfront, even the cocoa move," Joanie offered.

"Yeah, but he could be spending all this money to impress you because he is making up for other shortcomings." Savvy held up a pinkie.

"I don't know—maybe." Maggie considered the possibility. "If he'd asked me to stay the night, I probably would have, but I caught a weird vibe toward the end and decided to leave."

"You sure his chef isn't a little side ting?" Beth raised an eyebrow.

"Nah, she's some sort of family friend. All of that effort for a private chef and all we had were teeny portions of soup and salad."

"What are you, eighty? He should have brought you a little cup of Jell-O before your nurse escorted you home for bed!" Savvy exclaimed.

"Okay, right? So it's not just me?" Maggie threw up her hands.

"Why even hire a private chef if you're gonna have a salad?" Joan's perplexed expression was exactly how Maggie felt.

"I ended up getting In-N-Out on the way home."

"I'm surprised you didn't find a street cart for a bacon dog." Savvy popped a grape into her mouth.

"Don't get ahead of yourself. Danger dogs are still my favorite food."

Joan pinched the bridge of her nose. "Your favorite food shouldn't have the word *danger* in its name, Mags. We need to do better. Speaking of, when are you going to grace the tennis courts with your presence? It feels like it's been months since you last came out to train with us."

"No one ups the stakes on the court like you do, Maggie," Beth chimed in.

"Well, that's because they're not as good as me to begin with," Maggie hypothesized, her cheeks full of avocado, bacon and spring greens. "I make them better, because I challenge them. When it's just the two of them playing each other, they're already on the same level—how could they possibly improve?"

Savvy's eyes fluttered before widening, while Joan's narrowed. Beth looked like she was going to burst.

"Talk that talk, Mags. Just bring that same energy when you bring your ass to the court," Joan urged. "Whew, I can't wait to knock you off your little pedestal."

"Mmm-hmm, I guess we'll see."

"Can't we ever just have a successful training session where all of you support each other and cheer each other on?" Beth asked incredulously. "Do you always have to be adversaries on the court?"

"Look here, Beth." Maggie pointed her fork at the screen. "There are guppies and there are sharks. Guppies stick together just like these two do because they're defenseless little creatures. Sharks are apex predators. I don't need to fear being alone, because I'm at the top of the food chain. That's why these two gang up on me all the time—their strength is in numbers."

"If you don't hush your mouth," Joan cautioned, holding up a finger. "You know, God don't like ugly."

"But He does like the truth." Maggie took a bite of food, sliding the fork between her teeth as she pulled it away from her mouth, grinning ruefully.

Savvy rolled her eyes. "Excuse me, Miss Apex Predator, can we get back to the topic at hand? So is it safe to say that you're through with this guy? Blake? You don't sound into him."

"No, don't give up on him yet!" Joanie countered. "Maybe he's just gotta warm up to you."

"I don't know…"

"Just give him a chance," she pleaded. "You're not everyone's cup of tea right when they meet you. Maybe it's the same for him."

Maggie blew out a breath. "I mean, you're not wrong there. I could give him another shot."

Joanie fist-pumped in triumph.

"So when are we gonna meet him?"

"Nuh-uh, we're not anywhere near ready for him to meet y'all or Garrett." She shook her head. "I need to be more sure about him before I bother bringing him to the gauntlet." She gestured toward the screen.

Joan sucked her front teeth and stared at the screen.

"Speaking of G, how's he been with all of this?" Beth raised her hand slightly.

"Y'all are constantly asking about Garrett like he cares. He's doing his own thing, and we are not dating, so there is no reason for him to feel a way. Why would he feel anything but happy for me?" Maggie threw up her hands.

Savvy's head tilted to the side as Joan looked away from the camera. Beth dropped her head and giggled.

"Hello, am I speaking to myself?" Maggie pretended to rap her knuckles against the camera. "Why are y'all so concerned about Garrett?"

"He's a fixture in your life. Remember, it took Rob some adjustment, because he didn't exactly approve of you having a male best friend."

"He got used to it, and Garrett will adjust when I start dating again, just like I have when he dated."

"Uh, he never stopped your Saturday dates when he was dating. You never had to adjust."

"Well, I don't really intend to stop our dates, either."

Savvy pressed her lips together. "Mmmkay, well, let's see how that works out for y'all."

"It's not a big deal," Maggie huffed.

"Not yet," Joan mused.

Beth's and Savvy's cat-ate-the-canary looks in response were too much. "Whatever, y'all. Let me get back to work."

"Love you," they chorused, Joan holding her hands together in the shape of a heart.

Maggie threw them all a neck-twisting eye roll. "Yeah, luh y'all, bye." She logged out and finished her salad in peace, chucking her empty carton to the side so that she could return to her correspondence with the IRS.

"Hey, gorgeous." Garrett gave Maggie a squeeze before walking to his seat. He squirmed a bit. "I never get used to these little plastic chairs. How was your day?"

They had decided to meet up at their favorite spot for a taco Tuesday—a hole-in-the-wall that you could miss if you drove down the street and blinked, but it had some of the best carnitas and lengua in Santa Monica.

"Epic email battle with my government contact." She sat slowly and closed her eyes, taking a couple of deep breaths. "Dealing with them can be smooth or it can go downhill fast. She's relatively new, so she just keeps stepping on land mines with me."

"Again? When is that woman going to learn not to try you?"

"Apparently not today. She was sending all kinds of 'per my last email' passive aggressions and then she tried to add twelve new people to the thread, like that's supposed to make me act any differently."

Garrett leaned forward, his elbows on the table and his head in his hands. "So what did you do in response?"

Maggie smiled sweetly. "Well, I looked at all the people she added, who were all on her same level. Somehow she neglected to include her supervisor or her department head, so I took the liberty of adding them to the email before I hit her with the 'It appears that we have differing expectations as to who is responsible for completing this request, and after reviewing our past correspondence where roles were assigned, I encourage you to reclaim the lead in completing these tasks. Additionally, I noticed that several of our key team members were added to this communication, so I made sure to add the remaining members so that we all have the same understanding moving forward.'"

"Damn, girl. You're merciless."

Maggie shrugged. "She tried it. Who knew diplomacy was my superpower? Anyway, I'm starving."

"No worries. I already ordered some of our faves. I'll let you pick and choose first, and we'll see what else we need."

"*Hola*, Maggie!" Patricia, their favorite server, leaned over to kiss Maggie's cheek. "*Que buena!* Always nice to see you."

"*Y tu, amor.* How have you been?" Maggie fawned over Patricia. "You look good!"

"Gracias, and so do you. I have some of your order still on the way, but here's your two large jamaicas, tacos de carnitas, tacos de lengua, salsa verde, la salsa chile de árbol. I'll bring you some chips y aguacate and los sopes *en un momentito.*"

"*Que rico!* Gracias, *amor.*" Maggie reached for Garrett's hand and they prayed over the food quickly before diving in. The tacos each had a set of thin, fresh corn tortillas, their protein, and ample diced onion and cilantro. Maggie immediately went for a lengua taco, while Garrett reached for the carnitas. She spooned a generous amount of spicy salsa on top. "Mmm, so good. I could eat these every day for the rest of my life."

"You say that about most of the places we frequent." Garrett grinned, a piece of cilantro in his teeth.

"I'm going to ignore that you're poking fun at me and be the bigger person by telling you that half of a cilantro bush is coating your grill right now."

He colored slightly and reached for a napkin to work the herb free. "How big of you," he teased, spooning salsa onto the other half of his taco.

As Patricia dropped off the rest of the food, Maggie's phone rang. "I should take this, G."

He nodded, his eyes rolling toward the back of his head as he sampled a fresh sope.

"Blake. Hi!" She pressed the phone against her ear, turning up the volume to hear him over the bustle of the restaurant.

"Hey, Maggie, how are you?" he called into the phone.

"I'm fine. How are you?" She smiled brightly, hoping her voice carried the right tone.

Someone at the front counter called out a to-go order number over the loudspeaker. "I'm well, thanks. Is this a bad time?"

Maggie bit her lip as Garrett looked away darkly. "No, just having dinner right now."

"Oh, I'm sorry to interrupt. I'll be quick, I promise."

"Yeah, no, it's fine."

"So I remember you mentioning that Saturdays are somewhat sacred to you, and that you and your best friend have your weekend ritual, but I just got these great tickets to see Marsha Ambrosius live this weekend."

Maggie's eyes popped open wide. Garrett stared at her, waiting for an explanation. "You what?"

"I have a contact with L.A. Live, and he normally reserves a couple of tickets for me in case I'm available when some of my favorites come to town. It's over at The Novo, so not a huge venue."

"Wow, that sounds amazing! This Saturday?" She gave a pained look to Garrett. "I've been a huge fan of hers since her Floetry days."

Garrett's head rocked back slowly in recognition. He signaled to Patricia, who brought him a beer.

"I'll call you later with details, but I wanted to run it by you first to see if you'd come."

"Of course, I'd love to! Thank you so much! Okay, I'll talk to you later?" Maggie's voice rose an octave, and she made a face at Garrett, who stared at her with amusement.

"Yes, talk soon. Bye." Blake disconnected the call.

Maggie smiled so hard her face hurt. "Marsha Ambrosius? An intimate concert? How did I get to be so lucky?"

"Magic elves?" Garrett guessed, his tone bored as he set a bottle of Modelo Especial on the table.

Her smile faded. "Wait—you don't mind, right?"

"Doesn't matter now." He dug a tortilla chip into chunky guacamole and shoved it into his mouth. "Besides, I thought you were getting bored with this dude."

"I'm sorry," she started. "I am, but..."

"Mags, it's your favorite artist. You'd drop me for less." He picked up another taco.

"Don't say that," she pleaded, reaching for a sope with carnitas and refried beans topped with shredded lettuce, onion, cilantro and queso fresco. She spooned some of the chile de árbol salsa on top and squeezed a lime wedge over it before taking a big bite. "Mmm, why is this so good?"

"Probably because you know you're about to see Marsha Ambrosius in concert," he deadpanned.

"You know what?" Maggie grinned, balling up a napkin and throwing it across the table. "I'll make it up to you, jerk."

"I look forward to seeing how you're going to accomplish that."

They both reached for the same taco. "I could offer you the last lengua taco?"

"And you think that's sufficient for canceling on me?"

She shrugged. "It's a start."

He waved it off. "You go ahead. I'll take the last sope."

"Deal." She picked up her taco and he his sope, and they tapped the edges of their shells together. "Cheers!"

14

THE INTIMATE STAGE AT L.A. LIVE WAS ILLUMINATED BY candlelight. "Wow, this is gorgeous," Maggie breathed as they followed an attendant to their seats. They'd already had dinner at Fleming's Steakhouse and then walked to The Novo, a small performance venue in comparison to the Staples Center. Maggie's off-the-shoulder black dress with golden appliqués twinkled in the lights. Her hair was plaited into a crown around her head, which, coupled with her smoky eye makeup, made her feel regal.

Blake took her hand to slow her down and pressed his lips against her temple. "You're gorgeous."

She shivered at the contact, her heart fluttering in her chest. *Maybe he's not that bad…* The attendant led them to the VIP area on the balcony, and their seats were front row. "Seriously, Blake?"

"What? You deserve this."

"I can't believe that you were able to get these."

"Oh, it's no big deal. I can't even take credit—this was all thanks to my bro."

"That's a very good friend! I mean, the last time I saw Marsha Ambrosius, she was still *in* Floetry," she gushed.

"Well, now I'm jealous, because I never got to see them while they were together."

"It was amazing. This is gonna be, too." She squeezed his hand. "Thank you again."

People milled in and found their seats. The floor level was standing room only, and the crowd began to pack in. As the lights dimmed, and the announcements were made, Blake kept Maggie's hand in his, holding it in his lap. He traced the top of her hand with his thumb, sending little tingles up her arm.

The stage lit up, and the curtains drew back. Maggie sucked in a breath as even more candles adorned a series of tables and shelves, surrounding Marsha and her background singers. She began scatting to the start of her song "Have You Ever," and Maggie's eyes widened as she leaned forward, immediately beginning to sway when the reggae beat dropped.

Next to her, Blake moved in his seat, and he chuckled as Maggie held a hand in the air, snapping to the music as she sang along with the headliner. Luckily, the woman next to her was the same kind of fan, so they stood and danced to their hearts' content along with most of the people in the audience. She turned and beckoned for Blake to come dance with her, but he waved her off, typing something into his phone. *Maybe it's work.*

After a full set and an encore performance, Maggie and the woman had exchanged numbers and slapped each other five before heading off in opposite directions with their dates. Blake offered his arm and led her back to the car.

On the drive back to Santa Monica, they played the souvenir CD sold by the venue, and Maggie held her own concert in the car. "I'm learning so much about you tonight." Blake smiled as Maggie danced in her seat.

She grinned, her eyes bright. "I am still buzzing from being so close to one of my favorite voices! You sure know how to show a girl a good time."

"I'm really glad that you were able to come out for this. I had no idea what a big fan you were. You danced the entire time."

"I love good vibes, and her music makes me feel good. It's sexy and gritty and soul-stirring." She gestured inward. "I feel the same way about Jill Scott, Jazmine Sullivan... So good." She set her hand on the center console. "Are you not really a dancer?"

He shook his head. "I leave that to the professionals, but I enjoy listening to the music."

Woh wohhh... Maggie looked out the passenger window. "Yeah, such a vibe."

Blake ran his fingers over Maggie's upturned wrist. "Good energy," he agreed.

When they arrived at Maggie's building, Blake found a parking spot right out front and walked her into the building and up to her door.

"I had an amazing time, Blake. Dinner, the concert—everything was spectacular. Thank you." Her heart pounded in her chest as he closed the distance between them. *Is this happening?*

"You are most welcome, Ms. Jones," he whispered, leaning toward her. His lips brushed hers lightly, and she opened her mouth when his tongue trailed slowly across her bottom lip like a brush meeting a canvas. Her arms tightened around his neck as his tongue slipped inside, lightly grazing hers. Blake cradled her face between his thumb and forefinger, his other hand at her lower back, pulling her closer.

"Want to come in for a nightcap?" she whispered against his lips.

He nodded, his forehead bumping hers as he angled his head for another kiss. "Sure."

They stepped inside and Blake stopped short.

"Meow." Penny stared up at them both expectantly, her eyes holding judgment for Maggie bringing someone new into the home without her permission.

"Oh, don't worry. It's just my cat," Maggie said. "I should probably feed her," she laughed nervously as Blake followed her toward the kitchen, his pants featuring an obvious bulge. One that made Maggie close her eyes and thank Jesus as she picked up Penny's food dish. "Come on, Penny," she cooed. "You gonna be a good girl?"

Penny blinked up at her like Maggie was speaking baby talk to an intelligent being.

"Okay, fine. Just leave us alone, will you?" Maggie opened a package of wet food. "It's salmon, your favorite!" She mixed in a couple of Penny's favorite treats, hoping that it would buy her time and that Penny wouldn't lose her shit when she realized that the bedroom door was going to be closed without her inside. As she set the bowl on the counter, Maggie beckoned Blake with a finger toward the bedroom. "Do you want anything? Something to drink?"

"All I need is you right now." His voice was low and hungry. He led her hand to the protrusion in his pants and she gasped at its thickness.

"Big boy," she said coyly. "Follow me."

After closing themselves into her bedroom, Maggie turned to kiss Blake again, wrapping her arms around his neck.

"There's something I should probably tell you," Blake mumbled against her lips.

"Oh, yeah?" Maggie pressed herself against him, running her tongue over his bottom lip until he opened his mouth.

"You know what? It can wait..." His voice trailed off as he pressed his lips against her mouth, her cheek, her jawline. "I can't tell you how many times I thought about you in this way," he whispered.

Maggie ached at her core. She turned. "Can you?" She gestured toward the zipper of her dress.

"Of course." He pulled the zipper down, exposing her lacy garments as he eased the fabric down her body.

Smack.

Maggie's eyes widened at the sensation of Blake slapping her ass. "Wow, that was unexpected," she laughed in surprise. *What in the world? Let me find out he's a closet freak.*

"Sorry, I've just wanted to do that since I saw you at the gym." He laughed lightly, rubbing her where his hand had struck. The rubbing turned to a gentle squeeze. "Better?"

"Mmm-hmm." She turned back to face him. "Here, let me help you." She pulled his blazer over his shoulders and freed his arms, throwing it onto the floor as she began to unbutton his shirt.

"Well, actually, just one sec." He stopped her, reaching over to pick up his blazer and fold it neatly, placing it on the edge of the bed.

Noted. "Sorry." She held his face in her hands and kissed him, willing him to get out of his head. Her hands found his lapels and finished unbuttoning his shirt, opening it to reveal his muscular chest. She smoothed her hands over his skin, lightly grazing until he shuddered.

He closed his eyes. "I like how you touch me," he whispered.

Maggie reached for his belt, but he stopped her.

"Let me."

Huh... "Okay." Maggie stepped out of her heels and lit a

candle on her bedside table. Then she unfastened her bra, allowing it to fall to the floor.

Blake watched, his breathing ragged as he dropped his pants and pulled his shirt off, placing them both on top of his blazer.

The imprint of his dick beneath his boxer briefs made Maggie's breath hitch. "Damn," she whispered. She peeled down her panties and climbed onto her bed, sitting on her knees playfully, beckoning him with a sultry index finger.

Blake reached into a pocket of his pants and grabbed a condom, still wearing his shorts as he climbed onto the bed. "You're so beautiful." The breath from his whisper tickled her skin as his mouth met hers. They fell back against her pillows, Blake running his fingertips from her collarbone to her breasts, kissing them gently as one hand traveled lower and split her apart.

Maggie gasped, relishing the sensation of his mouth and his hands at work.

He settled at her breasts, allowing his fingers to be invited by her slickness into her core.

Maggie whimpered as he touched her, his fingers rubbing against her G-spot, pressure beginning to build. *Of course, the doctor knows exactly where the spot is located.*

Blake pulled back, catching her off guard. He liberated his dick from his boxers and Maggie's jaw dropped.

He's huge. "Wow," she said, gaping.

Blake half smiled, rolling the condom over the head and down the shaft of his penis, guiding himself toward her entrance.

Their eyes met and Maggie nodded.

He rubbed himself against her before gently pushing inside, squeezing his eyes shut as her walls gripped him tightly. "Oh, Maggie."

She inhaled deeply at the pressure, watching his face and

relishing his unhurried entrance. Steady heat built as he dug into her gently.

Lines formed between his brows as he leaned forward, pressing his hands into the mattress on either side of her face. She reached for him, coaxing him to drive more of himself inside. "Are you sure?" he whispered.

"Just go slow to start," she directed, nodding.

As he rocked back and forth, his eyes squeezed shut again. Maggie reached for him, trying to make more of a connection, as her hands grabbed his ass. Her touch encouraged him to move faster, his breathing becoming heavier with each thrust.

Maggie closed her eyes, trying to angle her hips for more stimulation. She wrapped one of her legs around his hip, moving his arm for a moment so that she could put her other leg onto his shoulder. *Just right.*

Blake grunted approval in response, watching her lick her fingers. His mouth fell open as she moved her hand between them, pleasuring herself as he pushed into her, delicious pressure beginning to intensify until she bit her lip to keep from screaming, not wanting the sensation to stop before she reached her pinnacle. Her eyes fell closed as she neared the peak and she moaned as her back began to arch.

"Gah!" Blake exclaimed, startling her eyes back open.

Blake jerked and collapsed on her chest. As he propped himself up on his elbows and kissed her collarbone, Maggie blew out a breath, removing her hand from between her thighs. *What the fuck was that?!*

"That was amazing," Blake whispered as he kissed her.

"Yeah." Maggie smiled weakly.

He pulled out of her and stumbled toward the bathroom. Maggie reached into her nightstand for a feminine wipe, tossing it into the bin after use. She climbed off the bed to get under the covers, scooting over when Blake emerged. He climbed in next to her, wrapping his arms around her to kiss her once more before turning his back against her to be little spoon. He reached back to grab her arm, wrapping it around his middle.

Perplexed, Maggie stared at the back of his head as he fell asleep instantly, snoring lightly. She eventually fell asleep after gently pulling her arm back and turning herself to face the opposite direction.

The next morning, Blake nuzzled the back of her neck as Maggie opened her eyes. "Good morning," she rasped, her voice hoarse. She reached her hand behind her to pat his thigh.

His dick woke up, pressing itself into her lower back. "Good morning, beautiful." He placed a kiss just beneath her earlobe and sniffled.

She turned partway, her torso facing the ceiling. "You okay?"

"Yeah, I'm fine. I just remembered that I was trying to tell you something last night."

"What's that?"

"I'm allergic to cats."

She looked at his face, and his eyes watered and were a little red. "Oh, no, I'm so sorry!" she exclaimed.

"Do you have any antihistamines?" He rubbed at the corner of his eye.

She nodded and got up, padding toward the bathroom, still naked. Her inner thighs throbbed.

"You're a vision." He watched her walk away.

"We put on quite a show." She grinned, throwing her hips farther into a sashay.

"So what about this morning?" he called after her, pulling the covers back for her to join him.

She returned with a bottle of allergy medicine and a cup of water. She perched on the edge of the bed, kissing him lightly as she reached for his shaft. *I wonder if he's into toys...* "I think that can be arranged."

★ ★ ★

Maggie strolled into the restaurant with her sunglasses still on. She pushed them to the top of her head, holding back her curls as she looked for her friends.

"Mags, we're over here," Joanie called.

"How are you doing?" Savvy asked, doing a double take when she spotted her friend. "You're glowing!"

Maggie sat down in a pair of ripped jeans, a tank top and a loose-fitting blazer.

"I like this look—and flats!"

"Yeah, I wore heels last night and we walked from Fleming's to the concert venue and then to parking."

"That's a lot of walking when you're wearing shoes that aren't meant for it, and I know the ones that you like that get you into the stratosphere," Savvy joked.

"Truly," Maggie laughed.

"So…" Joanie nudged her. "Are you gonna tell us how this date was or what?"

Beth smiled as she unwrapped her chopsticks. "The woman just sat down, y'all, damn."

"Thank you, sheesh! By the way, I love how eclectic this place is—sushi and fried chicken, home fries and Mexican food at the same brunch? I never knew that was a thing."

"Okay, it's great, but enough about the menu. Spill it," Joanie snapped. "I need to know!"

"Well, first, the concert was phenomenal. Marsha sang her *ass* off, honey!"

Beth snapped her fingers. "Ooh, we should add Marsha Ambrosius to the reception playlist."

"Yes," Savvy whispered, immediately typing a note into her phone. "Good call."

Maggie rolled her eyes at the interruption. "Anyway, I got up and danced and sang along with her the whole time."

"Oh, Lord," Joan groaned. "Did you allow people around you to actually enjoy the concert or were you bugging them the whole night with your screeching?"

"Shut up, heffa, it was fine. The woman next to me was singing along, too."

"And how did Blake react to your singing?"

"He just laughed and swayed along in his seat, too. He's a little stiff for my taste, but still, it's not like you can do a whole lot sitting down—"

"Dancing in your seat is not easy," Savvy laughed.

"Well, I do just fine, thank you," Maggie replied.

Joan rolled her eyes. "You're a terrible dancer. Anyway…" She rolled her hand to speed forward. "So, you danced, he sat. What happened next? Are you still not feeling him?"

"Eh…well, so after," Maggie continued, "he took me home, he came in for a nightcap, and he ended up staying the night." She accepted a cup of hot tea from a server and sipped while everyone stared at her. "What?"

"He stayed the night, and…" Joan prodded.

"And we had sex?"

"Ooh." Savvy clapped, her smile growing wide. "Give us details. How was it?"

"Respectfully…" Maggie started, clasping her hands together the way her teachers always did when they had to meet with her parents.

"Oh, no," Savvy wailed.

"I mean, the goods were extremely impressive, and he wasn't bad… It was okay." Maggie shrugged, taking another sip.

"Okay like how? Did he take care of business or not?" Beth chimed in, and Joan turned to raise an eyebrow at her fiancée.

"'Take care of business'? What, like it's a chore?"

"It's never a chore with you, babe. I just never understand

why it's so difficult for so many women in heteronormative relationships to receive regular orgasms. I'm always so curious to learn what happens." Beth flashed a flirty smile at her love, propping her elbows on the table and resting her chin in her hands.

"All right."

"Joanie's getting some sex later," Savvy hummed.

"You probably will, too!"

"I'm already well-sexed, girl." Savvy winked.

"I know that's right!" Maggie slapped her five. "Now, what are we eating, because I'm confused by this menu."

"Don't change the subject. So the sex wasn't good?"

Maggie weighed one hand beside the other. "Very vanilla. He finished, I didn't. He's a good kisser. I don't know... It was fine?"

"Jesus. Getting your teeth cleaned at the dentist is fine," Joanie scoffed. "Getting an oil change is fine..."

"So what are you gonna do?" Savvy raised a brow. "You gonna cut him loose?"

"I'm tempted," Maggie admitted, "but at the same time, it's not like he did anything overtly bad. He invited me to Palm Springs for next weekend... It could get better, right?"

The silent lack of enthusiasm was enough to make Maggie pick the menu back up. "So, what's good here?"

"Well, what do you want?" Savvy did the same.

"Chicken and waffles would be amazing."

"They have chicken-and-waffle sliders with a maple sriracha glaze."

"Perfect. Then I'm done." The server returned just then, and they ordered Maggie's sliders, chorizo and eggs for Savvy, a couple of sushi rolls for Joanie and chef's choice sashimi for Beth. "It's insane that this is all at the same restaurant."

"Excuse me, can we also get an order of the honey garlic wings?" Savvy craned her neck. The server nodded in response, jotting it down.

"Ooh, yeah, I had my eye on those, too," Maggie said.

"Nothing matters as long as Mags is fed." Savvy patted her hand.

"And what did Garrett get into since you canceled on him?" Joanie asked.

Maggie shrugged. "I haven't talked to him yet today. Blake left my place right when I started getting ready to meet y'all here, so there hasn't been time. I was thinking about going to the gym later…"

"Why? You didn't get enough of a workout?"

Maggie's face curved into a sinister smile. "Obviously."

Savvy sucked her teeth. "Nasty heffa. You have toys for that." She tossed her hair. "Anyway, have you finished the invitations? Remember, they need to go out by the end of this week."

Shit. Maggie pointed at her. "Right, end of this week."

"Do you need help?" Savvy eyed her friend suspiciously. "I know you're inundated at work, and your calligraphy is gorgeous, but if you need one of us to take over—"

"No! I got it, I promise." Maggie crossed her heart. *I had forgotten all about them.*

"Okay, as long as you're sure. We don't have a huge group that we're inviting, but we still want to make sure that everyone has plenty of time to arrange travel."

"I got you. Seriously, I got you. I'll get them out." Maggie looked down at her phone and quickly sent herself an email reminder to get them done and in the mail. When she put her phone down, three sets of eyes were watching her.

"Did you just send yourself a reminder to do our wedding invitations?" Exasperation blanketed Joan's face.

Maggie's mouth dropped open as her eyes swept the others at the table. "I *promise*. I'll get them done." She crossed her fingers over her heart.

They continued to stare at her.

"I swear!"

15

"HEY, HOW'S IT GOING?" GARRETT'S CHEERFUL VOICE made Maggie smile against her phone.

"Good! I am just trying to get everything ready for the week. It's been just such a crazy day since I got nothing done yesterday." After brunch with the girls, Maggie ran some errands and wrote out a few more wedding invitations before starting some laundry.

"Oh, right, how was your date? How was the concert?" His tone grew more quiet.

"G, it was amazing. It was such an intimate setting—I mean, we were in the VIP balcony area, so it was magical. We were right in the front row, and it was by candlelight. She just stood there and sang her ass off. I—" Maggie gushed, searching for the words. "I had a ball."

"This was your first time seeing her since Floetry, right?"

"Yeah. Remember when we saw them in concert?"

"Uh-huh, I do," he responded quietly. "So…it's worth going, if she comes back?"

"Absolutely, you have to go. Shit, I'll go with you."

"All right, bet. Well, anyway, I was calling to make a plan for Saturday, for the food. I have some ideas in terms of movies as well. We could do another show marathon since the new season of *Wednesday* is out."

"Ooh, that does sound good, but…" She paused. "I have some bad news."

"What? Is everything okay? You talk to your pops?" His voice carried concern.

"No, everything's fine. It's just that…" She took a deep breath, knowing he would be upset. "Blake invited me away for the weekend, and with how hectic work has been and everything, I could really use the getaway. I won't be here for our Saturday date."

"Oh." He was quiet after that. The silence ate at her. It had been a long time since they had a string of Saturdays when they weren't together. "So, where you goin'?"

"He made a reservation at a place in Palm Springs. He knew that work had been stressing me out, and he offered a chance at some respite. He thought a weekend away would be nice, you know, hit up a spa."

"Right… Yeah, I get it. I was trying to do the same thing, making the plan with the movies and everything just to help you unwind—just not on such a grandiose scale," he laughed awkwardly.

"Well, I really appreciate you being so thoughtful and considerate. You've been amazing and, hey, why don't we do dinner later this week? Then we can make a binge-watching plan for the next weekend."

"This is sort of becoming a thing, Mags. Are you sure you're going to be available for the next weekend? You don't want to plan for another weekend that you're going to have to cancel…"

Shit. "Now, don't be like that. I keep my promises, and next Saturday is yours. Period."

"Okay, well, I guess I can save my movie ideas and everything for that weekend, and I will try to keep myself busy this weekend."

"I'm sorry again. I will— I promise I'll make it up to you."

"There's no need for that—you can't be sorry that you're having fun and enjoying yourself while being pampered."

"True, I just… I don't know," she admitted.

"No, seriously, Mags. Don't worry about it."

"Okay, well, I'll see you. We'll make a plan for dinner this week, okay?"

"Yep, you got it." He hung up the line, and Maggie stared at her phone for a moment.

"Luh you, bye."

"Mags, you here?" Garrett called from the front door.

"I'm in the bedroom!"

Penny sat on the bench at the foot of the bed next to Maggie's suitcase while watching Maggie pace back and forth from the closet to what she'd already packed. Penny climbed into the suitcase, sitting on top of a colorful swimsuit, knowing that the suitcase indicated that Maggie would be leaving. *Please don't pee in there like last time.* Penny looked annoyed, but she perked up at the sight of Garrett.

"Hey!" He stepped into the room garbed in his typical casual uniform. "How was your day?" He squeezed Maggie's shoulders as she carried a pair of jeans and a sundress to her bag.

"Penny, move!" She shooed her away with her hand. "It's

been okay, you know. The closer and closer we get to Tax Day, the more people decide to do the most."

"Any more run-ins with the office stalker?" He grinned.

"Not recently," she laughed. "But you never can tell what's going to happen with those ones."

"Fair."

"I am trying to figure out what to pack."

Garrett squinted. "I'm not exactly qualified to give you any kind of fashion advice here."

Maggie scoffed, gesturing toward his comic book graphic tee. "Obviously. What's new with you?"

"Well, I brought some dinner and I have some good news."

"Oh?" She crooked an eyebrow at him as she began folding her clothes, nudging Penny out of the way so that she could pack.

"Yeah. All of that coverage I've been doing for the players' strike, it got the attention of *TIME* magazine, and they want me to write an extended piece to feature in next month's issue."

Her mouth dropped open. "Oh, my God. Congratulations!" Maggie threw her arms around his neck. "That's amazing, G! We are gonna have to celebrate and go get drinks somewhere… just not tonight, of course."

"Yeah, I know. That's fine. I know you need to pack, and you're leaving tomorrow, so I'll collect another day."

"Okay, well, let's see what I've got left." She began ticking things off on her fingers. "My toiletries are done, I've got my shoes in their little bag and my makeup, perfume— Ooh, I need sunglasses… Should I take a hat, do you think?"

"Mags, you never wear hats."

"Well, true, but you know, it's Palm Springs—it's so bright!"

"Yeah, I'm gonna say pass on the hat."

"No, you're right. Hmm…oh, right! Sunglasses." She walked

back into the closet. "I can't tell you how much I'm looking forward to some sunshine and a spa day," she called.

"Yeah, I bet."

She returned with a couple of cases of sunglasses. She dropped one into her oversize tote bag and the other into her suitcase, clapping her hands. "Okay, cool. What did you bring for dinner?"

"Well, tonight I brought some good ole comfort food. I brought you some Cajun wings and fries."

"Potato wedges?" she asked hopefully.

"Your favorite, of course."

"Ooh, extra ranch?" Her eyes widened.

"Come on, Maggie. How long have we known each other?" he quipped.

"Okay, okay, fine." They walked into the living room and Penny followed, brushing herself against Maggie's leg. "Oh, so I guess you're going to come pay attention to me now since you know I'm leaving? Come on—let me feed you." She set out Penny's bowl, and she accepted a few pets before swiping at Maggie to leave her alone while she ate. "I swear, that cat is something."

Garrett laughed, "Yeah, well…she's still the best."

"That's because she favors you," Maggie complained. "Actually, there's one mark against Blake. He might be allergic to her."

Garrett turned. "He was here? In your apartment?"

"Yeah, he, uh…he stayed the night."

"Oh, I didn't realize you guys had gotten to that place in your situation."

"It just kind of happened. We had a really nice date, and he was coming in for a drink and one thing just led to another." She shrugged. She began opening food cartons as Garrett sat staring at her. "What?" she asked once she noticed his gaze.

"Nothing. I'm just processing." His voice had flattened.

"Well, what is there to process?"

"I just, you know... I don't want you to move too fast, and I don't know anything about this guy. I haven't met him yet. I just don't want him to hurt you. Rob really did a number on you, and I'd hate to see you ever have to go through that again." His voice held such conviction that Maggie reached out to hold his hand.

"But what makes you think he's gonna do that? He hasn't given me any indication..."

"True, but I don't want you to run blindly at something because it looks good. I mean, what if it's a mirage?"

"Well, I am grown. I have made it through thirty-eight years of life—it's not like I was just born yesterday. I'm not Boo Boo the Fool." Her tone grew defensive.

"I'm not saying that at all, Mags. You know what? Never mind. I came to bring good news. Let's just celebrate." He threw up his hands.

Maggie took a beat and tried to reset. "Okay, do you want something to drink?"

"What do you have open?"

"I have some bubbles chilling here. I've been wanting to toast to everything that you've got going on with the podcast and your upcoming TV broadcast," she offered. "Now with your *TIME* article, you're absolutely right—we really should celebrate."

She stood to grab paper plates and poured some wine for each of them. "Here." She handed him a glass and a plate with some napkins.

"Thanks," he said tightly. He put a couple of wings on his plate and sat back on the couch.

She added a little more to her glass, eyeing him from the

kitchen. "Let's pray over the food." She walked over to the couch with her own plate.

He held her hand and prayed quickly, releasing her. She dipped a potato wedge into ranch and took a bite, watching Garrett stare at his food. "This really is the best ranch dressing."

"Yeah, it's good." He didn't look at her or touch his wings. He sat as if frozen in place, deeply in thought over ranch dressing.

Maggie crooked a brow as she chewed. "What's wrong? Are you not hungry?"

"I don't know." He looked away, cracking his knuckles on both hands, his leg beginning to bounce. "Maybe I lost my appetite."

Shit, maybe I went too hard. In therapy, one of the things Maggie had been trying to work through was how to convey what she was thinking and feeling without invalidating those things for others. "Listen, I feel like maybe I said something about Blake that described him in a way that bothers you, or maybe you guys need to meet so you can see that he's a good guy, but I don't want you thinking that this guy is bad when he hasn't given any indication that he is."

"I'm not saying that he's a bad guy. I'm just protective of you. You're my best friend, right? So, understand that there's no bad intention here—I'm just protective. That's all." He still refused to meet her eye. "If I considered getting serious with someone, you'd be all over them before I could even introduce them properly."

True. "Okay, but you're also being really negative, and I don't really appreciate that when I'm trying to prepare for a trip with this guy. You know, like you're gonna be all in my head, and I'm trying to figure things out right now. This could be the start of something, and I want you to be happy for me."

"Well, I need more information before I can be happy for

you," he said pointedly. "I'm not trying to upset you, Mags. I'm just being honest."

What the fuck? She exhaled heavily, searching the ceiling for the issue. It took everything in her not to try to shake loose whatever it was that he wasn't saying. "I just don't understand what your problem is, and maybe this isn't a good time to talk about it. Maybe we should just wait until I get back."

"I— Maybe you're right." Garrett set down his plate on the coffee table and stood, only briefly glancing in her direction. "I'm gonna head out."

Maggie's mouth opened to stop him, but he turned and headed for the door. She looked at his plate and then at him leaving. "No, I—"

"I'll see you when you get back," he muttered gruffly. Penny followed him toward the door, mewling after him when it clicked closed softly.

"I didn't mean that you had to leave," she murmured.

Penny turned to glare at her for driving away her favorite human. Maggie began carrying her plate back to the kitchen and stared at the counter until she heard the dead bolt turn. "What the fuck was that?" she whispered.

16

MAGGIE BLASTED TUNES ON THE DRIVE TO PALM SPRINGS
the next day, trying to clear her head, until her phone rang.
She picked up through her car's system. "Hello?"

"Hey, bitch, it's me," Savvy called into the phone on speaker.
"I'm here with Joanie. We just finished up some hot yoga. You
make it out there yet?"

"I'm en route now. I'm just about an hour away."

"You're driving by yourself?"

"Yeah, it's just in case he has another emergency and has
to leave—he wants me to be able to enjoy the weekend trip
either way."

"Well, that's thoughtful. Are you excited? You can be loud
and obnoxious and maybe terrorize your hotel neighbors with
loud sex…"

"Shut up, Joanie."

"What's going on, 'cause you sound funny right now," Savvy
asked suspiciously.

"I just had a really weird conversation with Garrett last night, and he left kind of upset, and I don't understand what his problem is. He seems to think that Blake is going to hurt my feelings or break my heart or something, and I'm not sure where he's getting that 'cause he hasn't even met him yet."

The other end was quiet.

"Uh, hello? I'm sitting here pouring my heart out, and you bitches aren't saying anything." *God, is no one listening?*

"Well, okay, Maggie, just think about this from Garrett's point of view, right? He's your best friend, he's your closest guy friend, he *could* have feelings for you."

"Girl, shut up, we've been over and through this so many times before. You guys are constantly thinking that Garrett feels a way, and he doesn't," Maggie accused.

"We just—" Savvy slowed. "Well, then what reason do you have that he would feel so protective of you when it comes to Blake—or any man, for that matter? He's been coming with you on dates, he's been essentially your number one blocker when it comes to these other men... He didn't approve of Rob when you were with him..."

She hated hearing her ex's name. "Okay, I don't need to be reminded of Rob. I didn't even bring that dude up. Let's not talk about him. I just need to figure out how to deal with Garrett, because at some point I am going to want him to meet Blake and I don't want it to be a disaster."

"Are you *sure* that he doesn't have feelings for you?" Joanie asked. "Because Beth and I, like we've always kind of observed him when he's with us at dinner, and it's in the way he looks at you. It's in the way that you two kind of finish each other's sentences, and you know he's your favorite person to be around. That all *counts* for something, don't you think?"

"Yeah, but why would I want to be with someone like Garrett? You know, like I love him, and I think the world of him as a friend, but look at his dating record—he can't be with anybody longer than two or three months!"

"Yeah, but none of these girls are anything like you, Mags," Savvy offered softly.

"Well, that's because I'm not his type," she huffed.

"No, I don't think that's it," Savvy said. "I just don't think you've let him get a word in edgewise," she chuckled.

"Listen, I promise you that I don't think that he has feelings for me. He's never said anything to indicate that he does. You know we talked about this years and years ago, and we agreed that we wouldn't cross that line..." Maggie frowned.

"Okay...it feels like that sentence wasn't quite over," Joanie guessed. "Besides, does he have to say it explicitly? Maybe he isn't a words-of-affirmation kind of guy. He seems like he's more into gifts or acts of service."

"Hypothetical for you—if you were single right now, and Blake wasn't in the picture, would you be open to dating Garrett?" Savvy asked.

"I don't know. That's weird. The last time I even considered him in that way, we were in college twenty years ago. But that was the last time, and that's not my concern. I'm worried about our friendship. That's what I said back in college, and that still stands today. And our friendship is more important to me than testing out whether we have real chemistry."

"I don't think you need to test that you two have chemistry," Joanie said. "Beth and I can feel the electricity between the two of you, and we're not attracted to either one of y'all."

Ouch. "Okay, thanks for that extremely illuminating pep talk, heffa," Maggie deadpanned.

"Listen," Savvy said slowly. "Just think about it—he might have some feelings and that could bring out some jealousy. It could bring, you know, feelings that he's losing out, and that's something that you two are going to have to talk about when you get back."

"You're right," Maggie agreed. "Okay, well, I'll think about it, but—"

"But don't let it ruin your weekend," Joanie piped in. "Have a good time, get your back blown out if you need to, but just know that we're here for you, and call us when you're on your way home."

"Okay, I will. Love you." Maggie gripped the steering wheel.

"Love you!" Savvy called.

"Luh you, bye," Joanie responded. The call ended, leaving Maggie with her thoughts.

Maggie drove for a long time in silence, passing dusty hills with dry patches of grass and gated communities as she got closer to her destination. Her phone pinged, and she took a quick glance to see that Garrett sent her a text message, so she asked Siri to read it to her.

Garrett: I'm sorry for how I acted. I should have been more supportive, and I hope that I didn't affect your headspace in a way that impedes your ability to enjoy your trip. Have a good time, and let's talk when you get back. Love you.

She double-tapped the screen to send a heart emoji to acknowledge his message, and the tightening in her chest started to loosen, stress beginning to melt from her shoulders. Silence for a long weekend would have been punishment, for both of them.

"Dammit, Garrett. Do you?" she whispered. She shook her head and kept driving, trying to push him out of her head.

"Hey, Maggie, I'm so glad you made it." Blake met her in the lobby of the hotel. "I can't wait to show you our room."

He kissed her lips twice before taking the handle of her roller suitcase in one hand and interlacing his fingers with hers in the other. "You look beautiful! You ready for some respite?"

"I am ready like you wouldn't believe. I'm ready for spa and sleep and room service."

"Well, I can be your room service." He leaned toward her.

Her mouth dropped open playfully. "I wasn't thinking that, but that might be nice."

He regarded her quietly. "Come on. Let's go upstairs for a bit."

Their suite had a view of the pool and some of the surrounding mountains. "This is gorgeous," Maggie observed. They had a sitting area and dining room separate from the bedroom and bathroom. The bathroom had a giant soaking tub in the center of the room and a two-person shower behind it. All modern fixtures and details. "This is perfect."

The bedroom had a king-size bed with rose petals in the shape of a heart on the comforter. "I only massacred one of your flowers to do that. The rest are over here in water." He gestured toward a blue-tinted glass vase.

We're not on a honeymoon, dude. She spotted the roses, long-stemmed red ones, and thought about the white ones her dad sent for her birthday. "That was very thoughtful, thank you." She kissed him lightly, pulling away before things could escalate.

"Let me show you the grounds?"

She nodded. "Sure. Have you stayed here before?"

"Many times. Sometimes I'll meet some golf buddies here— there's a great course nearby." He took her hand and led her to the elevator. On the main level, they walked around and saw multiple pools, a swim-up bar, a lazy river and even a gondolier who took guests on a quick ride while serenading them. "Last time, I visited to celebrate a successful heart transplant."

"Wow." *Celebrate.* Maggie couldn't help but think about her last conversation with Garrett. *Could he really have feelings?*

Blake pointed out some of the restaurants in the hotel and gave her a rundown of others that were nearby. He looked at her for a long minute, and she realized that he must have asked her a question.

"I'm sorry—what were you saying?"

"I was asking you what you wanted to do right now. Rest a little, pool, hang out at one of the bars..."

"If we're going to the spa tomorrow, right now sounds like a great time to spend some time by the pool. We can grab some dinner later, keep things low-key."

"That sounds great. What kind of swimsuit did you bring?" He nudged her with his elbow, making her laugh.

"You'll see soon enough!" She winked.

They went back to the room to change, and suddenly Maggie craved her own space. She gestured toward the bathroom. "I'm gonna go in here and freshen up, maybe rinse off before I get in my suit."

"Okay. Do you want some company?" he offered.

She smiled. "No, I'm okay."

"Okay."

She shut the door to the bathroom and turned on the water for the shower. She looked at her phone but had no new messages. Her fingers itched to text Garrett and see what he was doing. She felt bad that she hadn't stopped to ask more questions about the article that he was preparing to publish. As she stepped into the shower, she tried to wash all of her thoughts of Garrett out of her system so that she could focus.

Once outside, Blake swam while Maggie sat by the pool on a lounge chair, pretending to read a magazine that she'd brought from home. *I wonder if he's on a date right now... Nah, he would have told me. Well...would he?*

A model smiled up at her from the page, holding her hands together in a makeshift heart. *There's no way that he has feelings for me…right?*

Maggie replayed a series of recent conversations in her mind. Garrett's voice rang in her ears. *Hey, gorgeous…* She watched a woman stretched out on a lounge chair on the other side of the pool. Her partner walked over to her and brandished a bottle of wine and a couple of glasses as a surprise, gesturing behind him to the server carrying a charcuterie board. She clapped with excitement, reaching up to pull his face close for a kiss. *Could that be us?*

She shook her head, clawing her way to the present moment. *He doesn't have feelings for me. I'm just tired and burned out.* Maggie closed the magazine and leaned back against the lounge chair, dropping her sunglasses from the crown of her head to the bridge of her nose. *A little catnap might help.*

"Hey, are you getting in?" Blake called from the water.

She shook her head. "Not right now, but maybe later."

At dinner, after they ordered the wine, Maggie noticed Blake watching her quietly.

"What?" She smiled at him.

"Penny for your thoughts."

"Oh, it's nothing." She waved him off. "It's hard to turn my brain off sometimes." *It doesn't help that I want to be somewhere else right now. I need to know.*

"No, your face is telling me that there's something. What is it? Is everything okay?"

"I'm sorry." She squeezed her eyes shut for a minute. "You know, everything at work has been so stressful and that's why we planned this weekend in the first place, but I've also been dealing with this headache and it's probably affected my mood. I apologize. I'll take something to help get rid of it."

"Well, you probably shouldn't have wine if you're gonna take something." He pushed her glass farther away.

"Right, you're right." She took a sip of water and picked at her food, trying to pay attention to the conversation, but unable to engage, her mind racing. *Does he, doesn't he?*

That night she and Blake cuddled in bed, and though he made advances, she turned him down, asking if he would mind if she tried to sleep off her headache. "Of course." He kissed her arm. "That's what this whole trip is about." He held her until she fell asleep.

When she woke, he was no longer in bed. He left a note. "Out for a run."

She paced back and forth in the room, unable to manage her conflicting feelings, but she couldn't get over the fact that she felt like she needed to speak with Garrett. The urgency continued to build inside her until she couldn't take it anymore, so she called the spa to apologize for having to cancel her appointments and offered to pay the full price for the late cancellation. When Blake returned to the room, his eyes immediately went to the suitcase she'd repacked.

"What's going on?"

"I'm so sorry, Blake, but I have to go home. One of my friends is having an emergency, and I need to be there." She didn't feel great lying to him, but she had no choice—she had to see Garrett right away. *I have to know.*

17

"HELLO? MAGS?" GARRETT ANSWERED THE PHONE AS IF he'd just woken up from a nap. "Are you okay?" he asked in a worried tone.

"No, no, I'm fine. I just— I'm headed home, and I want to talk to you, if that's okay."

"Sure, but you're not supposed to be back until Sunday."

"I know. Uh, just meet me at my place in about an hour, okay?"

"Okay, fine." He paused. "Are you hungry? Do you want me to bring food?"

Her stomach growled in response and her voice lowered. "I'm always hungry, Garrett. What kind of question is that?" *Maybe he's not mad at me.* Relief washed over her, and she sped up a little.

"You right. Okay, see you soon," he chuckled and hung up the phone.

She clung to the steering wheel, her stomach doing somersaults at the thought of being in his presence so soon. *Is he getting excited to see me, too?*

An hour later, Garrett unlocked the front door and let himself in. "Mags?" he called.

"I'm right here, on the couch." She watched him veer toward her after he'd kicked off his shoes.

"Hey, are you all right?" He planted a kiss on her cheek.

"Yeah, I'm fine. I just really needed to talk to you." She motioned between them with her hands.

"Okay, what's going on? And why did you cancel your trip?"

"I canceled my trip because I need to talk to you." *I need you to tell me.*

"You canceled your trip for me?" He side-eyed her.

"Yeah."

"But why?"

"Because I want to ask you a question."

He waited.

A knot twisted in Maggie's stomach. *Out with it.* "Garrett, do you have feelings for me?" She looked in his eyes and waited, her heart pounding in her chest and sounding in her ears. She held her breath, afraid of the answer. *What if he says no? What if I was right but I'm the one who actually has feelings? What if I've just ruined everything and he never speaks to me again?* "I just need to know." Her lungs screamed until she inhaled, her heart ready to explode into a thousand pieces.

He put the food on the counter along with his keys before turning back to meet her eyes. "Yes. I do. I have for a long time." He said it quietly but nothing in his eye contact wavered.

It's true. He said it out loud. "Why didn't you tell me?"

"What was I supposed to say? You have made it clear over

and over again that you just want to be friends, and so I've been trying my best to honor that. I haven't made a move, I haven't tried anything—I just *am* your friend."

"You're my best friend," she said. "I'm just so confused."

He sat down on the couch, a full seat between them. "Well, I mean, nothing has to change. This is just how I feel."

"But…how serious are your feelings?" She glanced at him and looked away slowly, only able to watch him in her periphery.

"What do you mean?"

"Is it like? Is it love?" *Do you love me?*

He sighed. "Maggie, we tell each other we love each other every other day."

"We do, but it's a different thing to love someone or to be in love, and you know that." She turned to look at him. "Are you in love with me?"

He licked his lips before pressing them together. "Yeah, I am."

"What are we supposed to do?"

"I'm not sure we have to do anything, Maggie. I mean, you would have to feel a way, too."

"But maybe I do." *I do.*

"Are you saying maybe you're in love with me? Because I don't think that's how that works…"

"No, I don't know. But while I was out there in Palm Springs, all I could do was think about you and what you were doing, and where you were, and that I wanted to talk to you more about your article. About everything. I just felt so bad about the way we left things, and I just was so sure that you didn't think of me that way."

"I've always thought of you that way," he laughed nervously. "Always. Nobody knows me like you do or cares for me the way you do, and I can't imagine anybody else getting as close to me." He moved closer to her on the couch, close enough that the warmth of his body was radiating toward her. If he stretched his fingers, he'd touch her. "Is it at all possible for us to try? To go on one date and just see, and maybe that trial will give you clarity, too, so that you know what you want or don't. If you have any feelings at all for me."

"I mean, I have feelings for you…"

"You know what I'm saying, Mags. I just want to try. I've waited a really long time to tell you this, though I didn't really intend for it to be like *this*… I didn't even bring like the really good food for dinner today. It's not bad food, but it's not special occasion–type food."

I love that he knows there's a difference. "What did you bring?" She sniffed, trying to guess.

"I stopped and got chicken and waffles from Roscoe's."

"I meannn, I'm here for that," she said, her pulse slowing as they returned to familiar territory. "Did you remember to get me smothered potatoes?"

He closed his eyes patiently. "Yes, Maggie, I got you smothered potatoes."

"And an extra thigh, since my order only comes with wings?"

"Maggie, at some point you're going to have to admit that I know your food orders by heart. I *know* you." He looked at her hopefully. "So can we do this? Can we try?"

"Yeah," she said tentatively. "I think so. Let's plan a date."

Garrett's face beamed. "What are you doing tomorrow?"

She grinned back. "Well, I originally planned to be on vacation somewhere, but since I'm not… What did you have in mind?" Her heart thumped in anticipation.

"Don't worry about it. I've got an idea."

A knock at the door made Maggie frown. Her building had a sign-in system and security; one had to have a key fob to get up the elevator, so who could be knocking at her door?

"No solicitors," she called.

The knock came again, and when she opened the door, there stood Garrett. "Hi." He smiled. He held a bunch of peonies in his hand. "I got your favorite. Luckily for me, they're finally in season."

"Oh, my God, thank you." She hugged him and accepted the flowers. "I didn't realize that it was you at the door. Why didn't you just let yourself in?"

"This is supposed to be a date, Maggie."

"Yeah, but I feel like we're kind of already past this."

"I do, too, but we never got to do this, so let's just pretend for a minute that we're on a true first date." His boyish grin made her cheeks warm.

"Okay, you're right. Let's do the date thing. So where are we going?" She turned to put the flowers in water before they left, grabbing some kitchen shears from her knife block and unwrapping the plastic around the flowers. She grabbed a glass vase from a cabinet and filled it with water, dropping in the plant food that came with the bouquet. Garrett watched her as she trimmed the ends of the flowers by an inch, angling the scissors the way her mother had taught her. *I still have no idea why we cut them like this.*

"I got us a table at A.O.C."

"Oh, my God, I love that place!"

The side of his mouth turned upward as his eyes widened. "I know, so let's go." Garrett wore a button-up shirt and a pair of slacks. Neither fit quite right, but it didn't matter.

The image of Blake in his finely tailored suit and loafers flashed through Maggie's mind. Maybe some would think Garrett didn't clean up the same way that Blake did, but he smelled amazing and the smile on his face made Maggie's heart melt a little.

They arrived at the restaurant a few minutes before their

reservation, so they went to the bar to order a drink while they waited. "Hi, folks, can I get you something to drink?" the bartender asked. His handlebar mustache shone in the light.

"Yes. What do you have that's kind of light and refreshing?"

"We have the Bee's Knees with gin, lemon, honey and a little bit of rosemary."

"That sounds perfect, thank you." Maggie wiggled a little with excitement.

"Make that two, please." Garrett reached for his wallet to close the tab.

Their drinks presented to them, Garrett nudged her before wrapping an arm around her shoulders. He'd done it a million times before, but this time it felt different. Maggie sank into his side as he pulled her close.

"Feeling any first-date jitters?" he asked.

She nodded. "I'm hoping the drink will help me relax a bit. I'm overthinking."

"I'm glad it's not just me." He smiled.

They finished their drinks before the table was turned, so they ordered a second round, and once they were seated, a server delivered their drinks and they immediately ordered another round, laughing. "Well, if the second round doesn't loosen us up, the third round will for sure." Maggie raised her glass to tap it against Garrett's.

"Definitely. This was a good idea."

"I think it's a great idea. Thank you." Maggie smiled as Garrett's hand grazed hers as he reached for his water, which sent a tingle up her arm and down her spine. The way he looked at her felt different—the way he took in her face—and she noticed him looking at her lips.

"You look beautiful tonight."

She wore a chambray top tied at the waist with a pale pink

pleated midi skirt. "Thank you. I was trying a little something for springtime."

"It's sexy. I like how pink looks against your skin."

"You do?" She tried not to smile too hard, but the butterflies inside her chest were doing full-on somersaults.

He nodded. "It's soft, like you." She sucked her teeth, but he grabbed her hand. "It's *not* a bad thing, Mags," he stressed. "I'm trying to compliment you. Let me."

He gazed into her eyes so intently that she almost forgot to breathe. "'Kay," she whispered. They stared at each other for a long moment before Maggie lifted the menu to take a look. "Are you hungry?"

Garrett continued to observe her—she could feel his stare radiating from the crown of her head to the surface of the table. "Starving."

They reached for their drinks at the same time. "Me, too," Maggie giggled. She took a big gulp. "So how's work?"

He drained his glass, gesturing to their server for another round. "Work is good. We're getting positive reactions to the podcast so far. Did you tune in?"

"I did." She grinned. "I was really impressed! Your tone was really nice. Very distinct, and you were so knowledgeable on the issues! I felt like anybody who didn't really understand NBA labor relations would be able to follow along really easily—you're making the issues very accessible. It's cool."

Garrett beamed at her. "You think so?"

"You're killing it, love. I'm always gonna tell you the truth—I'm not about to gas you up. Your head's too big already." Maggie sipped her drink, nodding at the server as she delivered the next round.

His glowing smile fell to an annoyed scowl. "Consider me deflated."

Maggie spasmed with laughter, spraying some of her drink

onto Garrett before she could cover her mouth. "Oh, my God, I am so sorry!" She stretched out a hand in apology as she snatched up a napkin and dabbed her face.

Garrett burst into laughter, wiping the front of his shirt with his hand. "I take that back. I guess you're the one who's deflated."

Mortified, Maggie looked around. Several tables tittered and whispered, pointing in their direction. She raised a hand, waving sheepishly. The server rushed over with extra napkins. Mags raised her glass. "You should probably go ahead and put in another round now."

18

MAGGIE LAMENTED ABOUT SOME OF HER MORE ECCEN-
tric clients as they headed back to her apartment hand in hand.

"This feels nice."

"It does!"

"Your eyes are a little low..."

"Yeah, I probably had one too many." He rubbed his face.

Maggie giggled until her laughter was disrupted with the
hiccups, which made Garrett roar with laughter. They reached
Maggie's door and her hiccups hadn't stopped. "You know, I'd
ask you to try to scare me, but I don't think that would work."

"I've got something that might work."

"Something like what?"

"Like this." Garrett leaned forward to kiss Maggie, a quick
press against her lips, but the moment he began to pull back, she
wrapped her arms around his neck and pulled him in for more.

"Oh, my God," she whispered against his mouth, biting his

lower lip before running her tongue over his. "You're a better kisser than you were in college."

Garrett smiled against her lips. "Shut up."

She unlocked the door and they stumbled inside. They approached the couch. "You're gonna have to move somewhere, Penny." Maggie sat down and tried to shoo her away as Garrett sat next to her, leaning toward her for more kisses.

"Yeah, you gotta go," he murmured. He kicked off his shoes as Maggie did the same, and he scooped her legs up onto the couch, kneeling between her thighs as he pressed his body against hers. They kissed each other, savoring each other as he ran his lips down the side of her neck, untying her blouse before unbuttoning it.

Maggie sighed gently as the softness of his lips grazed the space between her breasts. She tried to concentrate on the sensation of his lips, but his hands began to massage her breasts, as his kisses went lower to her stomach. "I love your body, Maggie," he whispered, a hand grazing the outside of her thigh before moving under her skirt to feel her bare skin, the flesh of her inner thigh.

I can't believe this is happening. She opened her legs wider, feeling his hand getting closer to her apex. Then his finger skimmed the heat at her core. "Fuck," she whined, her hips immediately rolling upward for more.

"You're already wet," Garrett observed as he kissed her again, his finger maneuvering past the lip of her panties and nestling between her folds.

Maggie gasped and then moaned, her hips involuntarily reacting to his hand. *Why didn't we think to do this sooner?* The pad of his finger continued to graze her wetness. She whimpered, willing him to apply more pressure until he did. Her hips bucked against him as his fingers entered her. Slowly, they pushed in and out of her as his thumb pressed against her clit.

Her senses overwhelmed, Maggie couldn't help but moan in reaction. "Yes," she whispered.

"Make that sound again, pretty girl," Garrett whispered, running his tongue down her throat to her collarbone before returning to her mouth.

She whimpered and moaned against his lips, accepting more as he pushed inside her, his hands moving faster. Her breath shortened until she cried out against him. He licked her lips and sucked on her neck as she shuddered against his hand. He continued to move inside her with delicious slowness, letting her ride out every spasm until there were none left.

"Good girl. So sexy, Mags," Garrett growled. He began to kiss his way to her breasts, releasing them from her bra before taking her nipples into his mouth one at a time, suckling them, rolling their buds carefully between his teeth.

Maggie's back arched, one leg stretching off the side of the couch, her toes pointed as Garrett lifted her skirt and pressed his face between her legs. "Oh, my," she breathed. She nodded, squeezing her eyes shut as he tasted her, his tongue sliding slowly, parting her before skimming her most sensitive spot, lapping at her. He began applying more and more pressure until she broke again, her hips grinding against his face. Maggie cried out, convulsing, swearing, riding the waves until they slowed. She throbbed with want. "Where did you learn to do that?" she wailed, her pulse racing as she fought to catch her breath.

Garrett grinned and took off his shirt, unbuckling his belt and dropping his pants. As he stood in his boxer briefs, she saw the same outline one might hope for when they see a man wearing gray sweatpants. *The dick print is strong.* She watched him, her head propped in her hands as he looked down at her, admiring how willing and open he was with her—unlocked in every way now.

He took off his boxers and climbed between her legs before tearing a condom wrapper open with his teeth. After rolling it on, Garrett locked eyes with Maggie, his thick shaft grinding against her as he leaned forward for a kiss. "Okay?" he asked.

"Yes." She nodded.

He nestled the tip at her juncture, gliding it against her. He entered her slowly and she sucked in a breath as he pressed into her completely. He hooked one arm under her thigh, cupping her breast in the opposite hand. "You feel so good, Mags." He squeezed the flesh on the inside of her knee, biting it before pushing into her again, her eyes widening at the pressure. As he increased the pace, she lifted her hips to receive him, winding them around slowly, allowing his dick to graze her G-spot, as she ran her fingertips over her breasts, cupping them so that he could lap at them from above. *He just knows what I want.*

"I like it when you touch yourself," Garrett whispered.

I knew you would. Maggie met his gaze, licked her fingers slowly and reached down to rub her clit as he pounded into her. "Damn, Mags. Gimme." She lifted her hand so he could suck on her fingers. "So damn good. Now try again, gorgeous."

She did as he asked, gasping as his hand met hers and he guided her fingers over her bundle of nerves. She bit her lip as he leaned his weight onto her, dipping his head to drag his tongue over her nipple. His positioning applied even more friction to her G-spot. She swore, crying out as their fingers brought her closer to crescendo.

"Good girl, just like that." He nipped at the flesh of her thigh.

The muscles in her arm burned, but she kept going. *I wanna be the best girl...* "Please don't stop, G. Please."

"I'm not stopping." He sank into her.

She moaned, her breath becoming shorter as she got closer to climax, light breaking into a million pieces as she came.

She arched, her hand falling away, but Garrett kept grazing the sensitive bundle of nerves as her body convulsed, giving her everything until she became so sensitive that he pulled his hand away.

"That's right, pretty girl." He pumped harder, coming soon after. He collapsed on top of her. They kissed and cuddled, completely spent.

He lifted himself up onto his elbows and they stared at each other as if they'd just unlocked a treasure hidden within the labyrinth of friendship entanglements. Maggie pulled his face to hers and their lips locked tenderly. When she released him, it was like she was seeing him more clearly than she ever had before.

"Be right back," he whispered. He pushed himself off her, heading through her bedroom into her bathroom. She got up and followed, throwing back the covers and grabbing a wipe, startled when Garrett snuck up behind her. "Here, I brought you a towel."

She smiled, accepting it from him. One end had been moistened with warm water. "Thank you. I thought we might be more comfortable in here." She gestured to the bed, and he climbed in while she cleaned off. She climbed in after him, kissing him softly as he opened his arms to hold her.

"Want me to spoon you?" He nuzzled her neck and she nodded, turning into his arms, her ass pressing against him. "Damn, we might have to try this position next." His breath tickled her ear. His palm grazed her nipples before resting against the flesh of her stomach.

Maggie sighed contentedly, starting to doze off when she hiccuped loudly. They both burst into fits of laughter, her cackles interrupted by several more. When they finally subsided, Garrett tightened his hold on her, burying his nose in her hair, his breath slowly evening out as Maggie's eyes closed.

Maggie woke with a start, feeling the weight of Garrett wrapped around her like a cocoon. His face was buried in her neck; one arm was under her head while the other was over her arm, his hand resting on her belly. The room spun out of focus as she tried to lift her head and her stomach lurched. *Oh, no.* She nudged Garrett awake abruptly. "Wake up, wake up, wake up, wake up!"

"What is it? What's wrong?"

"Get up, get up! *Move!*"

She ran to the bathroom, barely making it to the toilet before she vomited. "Too many drinks," she groaned, wiping the side of her mouth with her arm as she flushed the toilet.

Garrett stood at the doorway of the bathroom, watching her. As she moved away from the toilet and lay on the tile floor, he rushed in.

"What?"

"Watch out!" He fell to his knees and threw up.

The cool tile soothed Maggie's skin, as she lay naked. "I don't know what we were so nervous about… We should have just had sex from the beginning."

Garrett flushed the toilet and moved to shove his face under the faucet so he could rinse his mouth out. He then joined Maggie on the floor. "What was that drink called again?"

"The Bee's Knees."

"Bees are disgusting." They burst out laughing. Garrett wrapped an arm around Maggie before they fell asleep.

Maggie woke on the bathroom tile to the sound of her phone ringing and she groaned. "Where is it, where is it?"

"It's out in the living room," Garrett responded, his eyes still closed.

I'm definitely calling in sick. "Fuck," she lamented, pushing herself up off the floor and out to the living room to answer her phone. "Hello?" she answered slowly.

"Hey, Maggie, it's Blake."

Her eyes snapped open. "Blake? Hi!" She shot a look toward the bathroom, relieved Garrett hadn't followed her.

"How are you?"

"I'm good. What are you up to?"

"I was calling to see if you're going to the gym today. Maybe we could spot each other."

"Oh, not today. I was out a little late last night, and I had one too many, so I'm not in any shape to be in the gym." She ran her hand over her curls, cursing herself for sleeping on the floor and not attempting to put her hair into a bonnet.

"Ah, I understand. I just figured I would call. Are we still on for next week?"

When she'd left Palm Springs early, Maggie had promised Blake that they could go and hang out on Santa Monica Pier. "Yeah, yeah, we're supposed to go to the beach, right?"

"Yes, I think that would be a perfect day."

"Okay, that sounds good to me."

"Well, I will probably give you a call later tonight, if that's okay."

"Sure." She eyed Garrett, who zombie walked from the bathroom in search of his clothes.

"Okay, I'll talk to you later. Bye."

"Bye." She pressed End and looked up at Garrett. "Hey, are you all right?"

"Yeah," Garrett grunted, his eyes half-closed.

"You don't sound okay," she offered.

"I should probably head home." He had dark circles under his eyes, and his hair was flat on one side. He pulled on his clothes and sat on the couch.

"Are you sure? We could hang out for a while, maybe go

back to sleep somewhere more comfortable." She climbed onto the seat next to him, snuggling up under his arm until he pulled her against him. She curled her legs under herself and looked at him.

"I don't know. It's just kind of weird hearing you talk to him on the phone after…" He pointed between the two of them. "Are you still gonna see him?"

She froze. "I don't know. I gotta think about that. I don't think I was thinking that far ahead." She scratched her scalp. *Thinking right now is a fucking chore.* "Can I make you some coffee or something?"

Garrett turned to her slowly, his eyes narrowed. "Do you actually know *how* to use your coffee machine?"

"Okay, fine, I don't know how to use it, but you do, so you can have some coffee if you want to help yourself."

He chuckled. "Come here, girl." He wound his arms around her middle, dropping his hands to her ample ass and squeezing. "I like you naked."

"Keep doing what you're doing and you're gonna turn me on." She looped her arms under his and pulled him closer, pressing her lips against his chest.

"I'm not sure either of us is in the right shape to be able to have sex right now."

"I'd like to think that I am, but I can't promise that I wouldn't throw up on you." She smacked her lips, the faint taste of soured honey still on her tongue.

Garrett made a face. "Well, as sexy as that sounds, I'm gonna pass. I'm going home and am gonna try to sleep this off. Come here, girl." He kissed her sweetly on her lips, her cheek, her neck. "You still taste like you threw up, by the way."

She covered her mouth with her hand and laughed. "Sorry about that."

He waved goodbye and let himself out.

19

MAGGIE ARRIVED AT SAVVY'S HOUSE JUST AS JOAN AND
Beth pulled up. "Hey, y'all," she called to them. Her dark sunglasses shielded just enough sunlight for her not to have to
squint as her baseball cap added an extra layer of shade over
her face. Maggie sipped electrolyte water slowly as she accepted hugs from the couple.

"Wow, must have been some night," Joanie observed.

"Yeah, one for the books," Maggie agreed.

"Did you...?" They stepped onto the porch.

Maggie nodded.

Joan looked impressed. "Okay, well, getting interesting..."

The door swung open. "Hey, Savs." Maggie's voice was
still raspy and thick with sleep.

Savvy leaned against the door. "Dracula, we meet again."

She rolled her eyes. *They really need to come up with something new. You're hungover one too many times around these folks and they never let you live it down.* "Very funny."

Teddy barked a greeting; his tail thumped against the couch as they entered the house and removed their shoes, making their way to the living room. Savvy's bright kitchen was pristine, with one Dutch oven pot simmering on the stove.

"Y'all take a seat. You want anything to drink?" Savvy opened the refrigerator. Maggie held up her bottle of water. "Okay, Mags is covered. Joanie, Beth?"

"Just water for now, but maybe we'll need something heavier a little later." Joan exchanged a look with Savvy, who raised her eyebrows.

"Got it. So got it in, huh?" Savvy sat in an armchair across from her L-shaped sofa after she brought water to the others.

"Yeah."

"Was it good?"

"It was…" She blew out a breath, her head shaking slowly. "I didn't know it could be *that* good. Great," she corrected herself. "He was generous, the package was weighty, he knows exactly what he's doing." Her head continued to shake.

Savvy waved a hand. "Are you in shock?"

"Maybe? This is completely uncharted territory. There's no turning back now."

"Okay…so what's the problem? Any regrets?" Joan prodded.

"Well, the date was a little awkward at first, so we drank to relax. I guess we overdid it."

"Both of you?" Joan raised an eyebrow.

She nodded. "Right after we finished having sex, we both had to run to throw up, one after the other."

Savvy bit back a smile. "Well, that's…romantic."

"No, it's not."

"Okay, it's not. It's actually really disgusting. Still, it's a night you won't forget."

"Ugh, that's what I'm afraid of." Maggie buried her face in her hands.

"Hey, Mags."

"Hmm?"

"You know, we're inside now. So you can take off your sunglasses, let us see that beautiful face of yours."

"Yeah, no. I'm gonna keep these bad boys on for now. The darkness keeps the room from spinning."

Savvy shook her head. "Mmmkay."

"But…what do I *do* is my question."

"What do you mean, what do you *do*?"

"What do I do? How do I do this?" She turned her head to look at each of her friends. "Is we together now? What did I just do?"

Savvy chuckled. "Blame it on the Goose, sis. You're not usually this reckless, but here we are. Pick one. They're both smart guys, they have good jobs, they are both ambitious and they go after what they want." She ticked the items off on her fingers. "One may have an edge when it comes to the bedroom, but it could have been first-time jitters when it comes to Blake. Obviously, there's the friendship aspect…"

Maggie rubbed her temples. "What do I *do*?"

"Are you freaking out right now?" Beth leaned forward.

"A little, yeah."

"I mean, we all want like a good catch, right? You have two, and one of them happens to be your best friend and that's kind of what everybody wants…" Savvy started.

"What do you mean?"

"The perfect partner who's also your best friend? That's goals."

"Well, he's only almost perfect. He doesn't cook like you," Maggie corrected. "And what are you saying? I should choose Garrett?"

Savvy made a face at her and rolled her eyes. "If you're taking it to a vote, he has mine."

"Okay... At the same time, what if something happens and we don't work out, or what if he gets bored with me, or we fight over something stupid and we stop talking to each other? If we lose each other's friendship completely, I would never forgive myself."

"But why do you think that's going to happen? If y'all were gonna fall out, you probably would have by now." Joan leaned forward, her elbows on her knees. "Only love can endure your antics for this long."

"Bitch." *The shade.* "I just know, realistically speaking, that every relationship that I've had thus far has ended."

"Yeah, but if you have the right person, who you're willing to work through your issues with, then you stop the cycle. It's when people go into stuff thinking things are temporary or aren't willing to make the effort to stay together that there are these issues. You tell him 'once you're in it for the long haul, you stuck wit me. I'm a barnacle on that ass, so get comfortable.'"

"Heard that," Spencer called from the kitchen. He was kneeling behind the kitchen island, so they hadn't seen him as they arrived. He popped his head up. "Hey, how y'all doin'?"

"Hey," they responded in unison.

He broke into a smile and dropped back below the counter.

"What's he doin' in there?" Maggie whispered.

"Oh, he's just setting up this new shelving that I wanted for the lower cabinets. And looking good doin' it, too." Savvy eyed her man adoringly.

He looked over at her and winked.

"Mmm-hmm." Savvy smiled at her man.

"Okay, Savs," Maggie scoffed. "Enough making eyes at

your dude. You have a whole fiancé. I'm trying to get on your level, sis. I need you to focus."

She sighed. "Listen, Maggie, what you need to do is decide what you want."

"Why do you say that like it's easy? Surely you each have an opinion here." Maggie finally lifted her sunglasses and used them as a headband to push her hair out of her face.

Savvy sat back in her chair. "You already heard my vote."

"Well, if you *want* for us to weigh in, when you should be making this decision yourself." Joan twiddled her thumbs. "Why don't I play devil's advocate? Your friendship is most important, so maybe you should go with Blake to avoid risking it."

These bitches aren't helping. "Beth?"

"I'm gonna abstain from this one, because I don't think you've known Blake long enough to even put him on the same level as Garrett."

"If they're not even on the same level, isn't that just a vote for Garrett?"

Beth clamped her mouth shut and widened her eyes at Joan.

"Y'all aren't helping me here. I've already risked it with Garrett, haven't I?"

Savvy leaned forward. "Honestly? Maybe. I choose Garrett *because* you can't put Blake on the same level. You could never. There's never gonna be a time when Blake could be on equal footing. You and Garrett are closer than you've ever been— you have built something over the course of nineteen years and some change. You're rock solid. If you *don't* choose him, you run the same risk that you're worried about."

"I just…" Maggie searched for the words. "He's always been such a bachelor, you know? He never lasts with the girls he dates. I don't want to try and completely fall for him, only to be hurt more than I was after Rob."

"Yeah, but like we said before, none of these chicks has been anything like you, and maybe that's the reason. I don't know. I think there's more to it than that, but you should talk to him about it if you're worried about his ability to commit. Have you mentioned it to him?"

Maggie shook her head.

Beth interjected. "Well, okay, so obviously you've been out with both of the guys at this point, but what if you go out again? This time, you and Garrett obviously have figured out that you have limits, so you're not going to drink so much. Just enjoy each other's company and see what happens."

"You're right, okay. Do you think that Blake will feel a way?"

"Well, I mean, number one, what choice does he have if he wants to be with you? Number two, you two have not decided to be exclusive yet. You've only been on a few dates, and yeah, you slept together, but so what?" She shrugged.

Maggie pinched the bridge of her nose. "Yeah, okay. This sounds reasonable enough, I guess, so I'll try this out. Savvy, do you have coffee?"

She nodded and moved to turn on the coffeepot.

"Who are you gonna tell first?" Joan jutted her chin at Mags.

"Well, I guess I need to talk to Garrett, because he knows about Blake, so he's more concerned. Blake has never asked if I'm seeing anyone else, but he probably assumes that I'm not."

"Or maybe he assumes that you are." Spencer spoke up. "When I first asked Savvy out—" he perched on the arm of her chair "—I assumed that everybody was after her."

"Lucky you, that wasn't the case." She smiled up at him.

"Lucky me," he agreed. He placed a kiss on her lips and then her forehead before whistling to Teddy and heading out into the backyard.

Savvy grinned at the others. "He's building an arch for our pre-wedding trip photos."

"That's cute, Savs." Maggie's face softened. She pulled her sunglasses off. "All right, well, I feel better. What do you have to eat?"

Savvy cackled. "Come on. I packed you a bunch of food."

Maggie squealed, jumping up from her seat, wiggling her fingers. "I love coming to your house, Savvy. It's like Christmas!"

Joan rolled her eyes.

"Hey, G." Maggie sat on pins and needles, anxiety churning through her veins like adrenaline.

"Hey, you. What's up? How are you?" His voice softened. "I've been thinking about you."

"Me, too." Maggie's cheeks warmed as she pressed her phone to her ear. "So I just wanted to touch base with you since you had to leave so abruptly earlier. Make sure you were feeling okay."

"Yeah, we were both looking pretty green. I'm good, though. How are you?"

"Yeah." Maggie smirked. "I'm okay. That was some night, huh?" *My good girl.* She bit her lip as she thought about him referring to her in that way. His praise was burned into her psyche and she squirmed in her seat.

"It was. I'm glad we didn't have more to drink, because I would hate to have forgotten any of it. Though I definitely want to make it up to you," he assured her.

"Me, too…" Her mind went to their moments on the couch, and she had to shake the images out of her head to focus on the conversation. *Come over.* "I, um, I did enjoy myself. You know, before we got sick. That part was *not* a normal occurrence."

"Yeah, I did, too. I'm sorry that happened. I wish that we'd just acted normal." He laughed. "I can't believe we were so nervous. It's not like we were out with strangers."

"I know. We were acting brand-new, and for what?" she agreed. "Yeah, but lesson learned. Even if there are some jitters next time, I know you, and you know me."

"Right. Wait—so we really can do this again?" He sounded hopeful, and something about that made Maggie's stomach flutter.

"Of course!" *He thought I'd just act like nothing happened?* "I think we should go out again, but basically, I want to do another date with each of you so that I can just be sure that I know what I want, because I feel like our last date wasn't... In a lot of ways it was wonderful, but I'd like to have another date without the awkwardness, where we don't throw up, so that I can make a more educated decision."

"I see. I guess I just thought you'd feel more certain after... you know." He sounded disappointed. "I mean, you've been out with him before..."

She bit her lip. "Does this make you uncomfortable?"

He sighed into the phone. "I'm in a place, Maggie, where I don't want to share you, so yeah, I'm uncomfortable, but I respect that you need to do this for yourself. I want you to be sure when you choose me."

She smiled. "Okay, G, talk your shit. I like the confidence."

He chuckled. "You've gassed me up over the years, so you only have yourself to blame."

"Hmm," she replied.

They sat in silence for a few minutes, something that happened frequently on their longer calls. Maggie was always comforted by the silence with Garrett. She could hear his breath, and it calmed her down when she was feeling anxious or overwhelmed. It soothed her.

"So, um, who you gonna go out with first?"

"You, if that's okay?" *Say yes.*

"Really?" His voice perked up.

"Yeah. Maybe we can do something during the week? Maybe Wednesday or Thursday?"

"Okay, that works. I can do either of those," he offered. "Or both…"

She laughed. "Okay, greedy."

"So what if I am? I know what I want."

Maggie shut her eyes, all of the ways he could be greedy popping into her mind. *Girl, get your head out of the gutter!* "I appreciate that. I want to be sure what I want, too, so I don't think we should have our Saturday date this week. I'm going to need some time to think after I see the both of you."

"Yeah, all right," he agreed sullenly. "Well, I'll make sure to plan something fun, and what, should I pick you up from work or your place?"

"From my place so I have some time to change out of my work clothes, if that's all right?"

"I can't wait. I'll plan something good," he promised.

"I'm sure we'll cut up regardless." She smiled into the phone, wondering if he could hear it.

"Bet."

20

AFTER SEVERAL DAYS OF GRUELING WORK, MAGGIE WAS
a bundle of nerves as she primped for her date with Garrett.
He'd recommended that she keep her clothing casual for their
date, so she'd trusted the recommendation—didn't mean she
couldn't look cute. She fluffed her pineappled curls, which
had a cute, checkered scarf tied as a headband to help create
some makeshift bangs. She smoothed a bit of edge control to
capture her baby hairs before using an edge styler to lay them
down in loops at her temples and kiss curls at her sideburns.
She donned some chunky gold earrings and gave herself an
extra spritz of her favorite Kayali combo. At the sound of the
front door unlocking, she headed out toward the living room,
waving to Penny, who lay sprawled on the bed.

"Mags?" Garrett let himself into her apartment.

"Hey!" She sashayed over to him and gave him a big hug.
"Wow, you look nice."

He wore a pair of dark jeans and a V-neck sweater. "Thanks. I just thought I'd try something different. You smell really good, by the way."

"Thank you," she laughed. She motioned toward his 'fit. "I like this. It's great to see you outside of your usual uniform."

His hands stretched out by his sides. "This isn't all *that* different, Maggie. You look beautiful."

"Thank you." She twirled, wearing a snug pair of jeans and ankle boots. Her starched white button-down blouse was partially tucked in to show off her curves. Her wide gold hoops and other jewelry accented the simple look and matched her highlighter. She pulled on a floral kimono-style duster just in case it was breezy and they had to stand outside. "So, what are we doing?"

"Well, first, we're gonna shoot some pool, and then we're gonna go crack some crabs." Garrett ticked two of his fingers. *Brilliant.* "Ooh, that sounds perfect!" Her eyes lit up. "But let me go change my shirt real quick," she laughed. She returned a moment later with a snug black tank tucked into her jeans instead, the same duster finishing the look. "It's always so hard to get that Cajun butter sauce out of a white shirt." She grinned.

"Yeah, I should have warned you, sorry. I think I actually like this a little more anyway." He closed the distance between them and grazed his finger from her collarbone to her sternum. "You're not so covered up."

Maggie shivered. "Okay, damn, swag."

Garrett tossed his head back and laughed, offering her his elbow. "Let's go."

They hit up a pool hall while they waited for a table at The Boiling Crab. The popular restaurant didn't take reservations, and the wait could easily be over an hour. Savvy had put them onto the hall as a great way to pass the time, and anything that appealed to Maggie's competitive side was great for date night. So long as he wasn't going to be a sore loser.

"You know, it's been a long time since I've seen you run a table." Garrett's mouth curved to one side.

"Well, I haven't had the need to hustle anybody in a long time," she laughed. "Remember, I used to collect lunch money and meal cards from everybody in the dorm?"

"Yeah, you had like three different meal plans."

"Well. I found that if I had one for each of the cafeterias on campus, I was able to have a variety that not everybody had access to."

Garrett shook his head. "You know, it's kind of uncanny how you're like a foodie but you don't cook and you're not as adventurous as someone like Savvy."

"Listen, I have an appreciation for good food, whether that is considered a foodie or not. It is what it is. I just know that I enjoy it, and I'm not one of those people who's like 'oh, I don't live to eat, I eat to live.' No, I do live to eat. I *want* to. Give it to me," she demanded playfully. She grabbed a cue stick from a rack and prepared to break. "You wanna put some money on this?"

He exhaled deeply, marveling at her. "You don't even need to warm up before you say something like that?"

"You think I need a warm-up to beat you?"

His mouth dropped open, but his eyes twinkled.

"I mean, I'm just asking." She strolled toward the other end of the table. "You don't have to say yes."

He chalked his cue. "How much?"

"Ten bucks?"

"Deal."

She positioned herself and slid the cue stick forward in a sharp, fluid motion, the cue ball breaking the triangle apart, sending solids and stripes rolling every which way. Two dropped into the corner pocket.

"Both of those were solid," Garrett observed. He sipped on a pint, watching her move.

In less than five minutes, all that was between Maggie and Garrett's wallet was the eight ball. "Eight ball in the corner," she said quietly, grazing the top of her cue with the chalk.

Garrett nodded slowly, watching her.

She lowered her torso toward the cue ball, fixated on the spot where she wanted to hit it, and then adjusted her gaze to see where she wanted it to connect with the eight ball for it to slide into the pocket without making the cue ball drop, too. Her eyes took in the angles as she ran the cue stick through a loop created by her thumb and forefinger gently before tripoding her other fingers against the felt of the table.

"You sure you're not gonna scratch?" Garrett teased.

"I know what I'm doing," she replied without turning. She slid the cue stick forward smoothly and it tapped the cue ball, which barely kissed the eight ball, sending it into the corner pocket as the cue ball slowed and stopped against the end rail. She turned and extended her upward-facing palm. "Pay up, Mr. Bailey."

He shook his head, smiling at her. "Yeah, okay. I'm good for it."

"Double or nothing?"

"I'm not doing this with you, Mags. We are just playing here, because if you hustle me out of my money, how do you expect me to pay for dinner?" he teased.

"Fair enough," she laughed. "Come on. Go ahead and rack 'em."

Once the restaurant hostess texted Garrett that their table was ready, they closed out and headed downstairs to the restaurant, the smells of garlic, toasted paprika and butter filling their nostrils.

They ordered crab legs and green mussels, shrimp and andouille sausage, and potatoes and corn with their specialty sauce on it, along with a pitcher of beer.

Maggie properly tied the plastic bib around her neck and laid a row of paper towels across her lap.

"You look like you've done this many, many times. Almost like you're getting ready to do an eating contest."

"Well, it's no contest, but I'm definitely a winner." She grinned.

"Smooth," he laughed. His dark eyes met hers and stayed there. Like no one else was even in the room.

"Do you remember the first time we went to shoot pool?" Maggie asked.

"Yeah, of course. There was some girl who was totally trying to hustle me, and you came and whooped her ass so badly that, by the end, she and her mom *both* owed you money."

"Yeah, that was great. That ended up paying for my flights for spring break."

"I remember just being in awe of you. I was always in awe of you." He smiled at the memory and Maggie watched him reminisce.

"I just can't believe that you kept your feelings to yourself all this time." She shook her head, resting her arms on the table in front of her. "Has it been hard for you watching me date for so many years?"

"Yeah, it's hard, but I've always been honest with you in terms of the guys you dated. There were some that I liked and others that I didn't think deserved you, like Rob," he admitted. "But I always hoped I'd get to shoot my shot."

"Ugh, don't remind me. You really did tell me about that one, and I should have listened." She sipped her beer.

"I didn't bring him up to say 'I told you so.'" He leaned forward.

"No, but you did tell me and I should have listened. I thought you were being silly, and I was so into him, and since I had met him through Beth, I thought he was okay, but even Beth didn't know that he was dogging out her other friends while dating me."

"He was a tool. But enough about him. Remember the day that we met?"

"Yeah." Maggie smiled wide as Garrett drank his beer. "We lived in the coed dorms that first year. I got there the day before you. I walked into your dorm and greeted you. Welcomed you to the building and told you I was your next-door neighbor and introduced myself. And you just looked at me like I had three heads."

"I thought you were hot and I didn't know how to handle it. Do you remember what you were wearing?" he asked, while Maggie shook her head. "You had on a bikini and jean shorts. You were getting ready to go to the pool."

"Oh, right! I had met your roommate a day or two earlier, and I came to invite him to the pool, but only you were there, so I invited you instead."

"Yeah." The server carried their food over and poured it out over butcher paper, the steaming boil fragrant with garlic and spices. "This looks great, thank you." Garrett nodded at the server before returning his attention to his date.

"That was a good day." Maggie smiled, remembering playfully splashing him once they got into the water until her mind redirected. "Wait—you thought I was hot that first day?"

Garrett's brows knit together and he closed his eyes, nodding emphatically. "Of course I did."

"Wow, I had no idea."

"Did you think I was cute back then?"

"I was already kind of blinded by my infatuation for your

roommate, but wow, if I hadn't been…" She shook her head. "I mean, obviously you were attractive—you always have been—but I was so focused on school that I really wasn't thinking about getting into anything else after the breakup. Come on—let's pray."

They joined hands, the warmth of his spreading up her arm as they bowed their heads and Garrett took the lead. Maggie exhaled deeply, listening to his prayer and squeezing his hand as it concluded. "Amen." She smiled at him, not yet letting go.

Garrett's thumb drew circles on the back of her hand. "Remember the first time we went to the movies?"

"Yeah. We saw *Think Like a Man* or something like that." She gazed at the ceiling, trying to recall.

"Yeah. I tried to make a move but then I got nervous."

"You did?" Maggie's eyes widened.

He laughed. "I tried to put my arm around you but then you stretched and needed more space, so I took it back."

"Aw, I'm sorry," she said. "I must have missed the cue."

"Well, either way, I landed right where I'm supposed to be." He gently rocked her hand.

"Yeah, almost twenty years later." She shook her head in disbelief.

"Chess, not checkers," he quipped. "Now, let's eat."

After their meal, they kissed passionately in the hallway outside her condo unit. Garrett squeezed Maggie's ass, moving his lips to her throat. "You wanna go inside?"

She nodded. As they stepped into the apartment, their lips continued to explore each other's, and they hungrily began to peel off clothing the moment the front door closed. In seconds, Garrett tugged at Maggie's tank top and she'd pulled Garrett's sweater over his head. Her hand grazed his belt before they heard movement, startling them. Penny stared at them lazily from the couch, an annoyed look on her face as if they'd disturbed her.

Garrett grabbed Maggie's hand and led her to the bedroom. "I've been wanting to do this all night." He kept his hands on her arms as he trailed kisses from her jawline down her neck to her collarbone, eventually peeling off her tank top. He turned her around, pressing himself against her ass and wrapping his arms around her as he slowly unbuttoned her pants and dragged her zipper downward, exposing lacy fabric beneath. "This is sexy," he observed as he slowly peeled her jeans off.

Maggie's strapless bra and panty set were delicate black lace and they showed off her shapely posterior, and she leaned back into his hands as he cupped her ass. They roamed forward over her belly to her full breasts before returning to her back to unclasp her bra.

"I wanna devour every inch of you," he whispered into her ear, pressing his lips to the nape of her neck. "Will you let me?"

She nodded slowly, anticipating his touch as his fingers came forward to graze her nipples. She melted against him, the juncture between her thighs throbbing. Ready for whatever he had in store for her.

"Come over here." He led her toward the bed.

With her arms free, she relieved him of his sweater and unbuckled his belt.

"You want me in your mouth?" he asked. The gravel in his voice reverberated between her legs.

"Yes," she replied. *Call me your good girl.*

He sat down on the bench and she unzipped his pants and released him from his boxer briefs, her fingers barely able to meet as she held him in her hand. At her touch he made a guttural sound, almost a growl, which lit a fire in her. The head of his dick barely fit in her mouth, so she spit and used her hands to moisten and massage his shaft as she sucked on him, running her tongue around the tip. "That's a good girl." His voice remained low, throaty.

Every time he spoke, giving her words of encouragement, she went harder, sucked harder, held him tighter, undulating until his breath hitched and he said, "Okay, that's enough, my good girl. My turn. Come here."

She stood with her body facing him as he gripped the edges of her panties and pulled them downward. He kissed her stomach, and once the lace hit the floor, his hands pulled her closer, guiding her breasts to his mouth. He kissed and teased and suckled, rolling one nipple between his fingers as he sampled the other.

"I want you," he said slowly. His fingers trailed down from her breasts, over her belly, to her thighs. One hand slowly crept up the flesh from the inside of her knee, grazing her most sensitive spot. "Maggie," he breathed heavily.

She held her breath, waiting for what was to come.

The pad of one finger began to tease her clit as Garrett continued to speak to her. "I want you to sit on my face. Will you do that for me, my good girl?"

The sensation of tiny circles building pressure short-circuited Maggie's ability to think or speak, so she nodded, crying out as his finger dipped into her.

Just as quickly, he pulled his hand away, tasting his finger. "Yeah, I like that. Now come over here." He stood and moved to the foot of the bed. Keeping his feet on the floor, he lay back against her duvet cover. "Come on up here." He held her hand as she climbed on top of him, initially straddling him, grinding against the hardness of his erection until he squeezed her ass and guided her forward.

Her knees on either side of his head, she lowered herself gently until his mouth grazed her sensitive skin. His hands held her in place as he lapped at her, suckling her clit, savoring her like a delicacy. Maggie moaned, biting her lip as she wound her waist, riding the waves of his tongue, savoring every movement. He squeezed her ass, pressing her farther against him. She whined that it was too good, rocking her hips back and forth over his mouth. The heat became almost unbearable.

When Garrett clutched her ass and flipped her over onto her back, his hands gripped the flesh on the backs of her thighs and pushed her knees toward her chest as he pressed his face into her juncture once more. Maggie's toes rested on his back as he continued to press her thighs into her belly, folding her to expose her tender flesh. She held the backs of her knees as his tongue began to lap at her faster. She cried out as his tongue dipped inside her. When he replaced his tongue with his fingers, she lifted to meet him. He pushed inside her with deliberate slowness as he continued to wind his tongue around her clit. Maggie cried out, convulsing as she came hard. Lights twinkled behind her closed eyelids, but he didn't stop—he merely slowed, sensations became gentle, waiting for her body to allow him to bring her over the brink again.

"Oh, my God," she breathed.

"Nope, just me." Garrett stood, dropping his pants and boxers, allowing all of him to be on display. His smooth skin, the sheen of her essence on his beard, his thick arms and soft belly. He pulled a condom from his pants. "Okay?"

"Yes, please." She still couldn't get over what she'd just experienced, but she knew she was ready for more.

"Scoot back on the bed, bae," he instructed huskily.

She did as she was told and he followed her. After he put on the condom, he ran his fingers down her smooth brown skin, picking up her leg by the ankle and setting it on his shoulder.

"That's my good girl," he growled, wrapping her other leg around his waist. "Are you ready for me, bae?"

"I'm ready," she said, nodding. He pushed into her slowly, in and out, a little bit more each time until she could feel the pressure building. "Oh, my God," she whispered. *We must have been really drunk the other night, because I don't remember it being like this.*

Holding her in place with her pelvis slightly tilted, Garrett rubbed directly against her spot with slow deliberateness.

"You're gonna make me come again," she whispered, staring up at him.

"Would that be so bad?" He pressed his hands into the mattress on either side of her head.

She shook her head as the pressure continued to build. She wound her hips in a circle and he grunted.

"Yeah, I like that. Do it again."

Each rotation caused the pressure against her G-spot to build and him to groan. "I'm about to come," she whispered.

"Come for me, then. Come for me like a good girl should," his voice rumbled as he slid against her core.

That was all she needed to hear before she broke into pieces, crying out, her back arched. He began to pick up speed. "That's my good girl." He kissed her leg as it rested on his shoulder and continued to drive into her. "You're so perfect," he whispered. "Wet. Warm. Mmm. You wanna turn over for me?"

Maggie nodded, ready to display her posterior. She turned over, pressing her face into the mattress as she arched her back and lifted her ass to meet him, wiggling as she felt his erection against her.

His hand held her waist as he used his other one to guide himself inside her. "All this ass…"

She giggled. "Mmm-hmm."

He pushed inside her and she gasped. His hand slid from her waist to the front of her thigh, moving below her belly to play with her clit. "Your body is so beautiful, Maggie, so soft." He kissed her spine.

She rocked herself back against him, the dampness of their skin clapping at the impact. "Fuck…"

"Tell me what you want."

"I want to make you come."

"Well, that feeling is mutual." He continued to draw circles around her clit with his finger. "Will you do that for me, my good girl?"

"Mmm-hmm," she moaned. She continued to throw it back at him, the rhythmic clapping getting faster as he applied more pressure to the circles. Her breath became ragged as he growled.

"Yes, I'm 'bout to—" Garrett moaned loudly. Maggie pressed her hands into the mattress and rocked against him, the sounds of their rhythm at an all-time high. His body shook behind her as he emitted a low noise from his throat, but his hand never stopped moving, not until she shattered completely.

Maggie cried out, her body spasming beneath him as he continued to pound into her. With her last spasm, he withdrew from her, also removing his finger from her clit. As she looked back at him, he tasted the digit that had pressed against her.

"Perfect meal," he said and turned toward the bathroom.

Maggie pulled herself up long enough to peel back the covers and climb into bed. She heard Garrett flush the toilet and run water to wash his hands while she turned down the covers on his side of the bed so that he could climb in. "Wow." She smiled at him as he crawled up the mattress, her head resting against his chest as he pulled her close. His heart pounded in her ear.

"That was…"

"Yeah," she giggled.

He laughed. "I can't wait to do that again."

"Well, you let me know when you're ready, because I can't,

either." She yawned and nestled herself closer against him, feeling him smile against her throat.

"Neil, thanks again for the heads-up. Next round of drinks are on me." Maggie grinned against the telephone receiver. "Seriously, you made my day."

"I'm gonna hold you to that, Mags. Congrats again!"

Maggie hung up the phone and did a little dance behind her desk. "Yes, yes, yes!"

Terry peeked her head in the door. "Was that the call I think it was?"

"Yep, the presentation went so well that Neil's client wants to work with me across all of their start-ups." Neil was an estate attorney whom Maggie referred business to often when individuals were looking to build living trusts or otherwise get their affairs in order when it came to passing down a family business. In return, he often passed her business that could use guidance on tax matters. "This one is big for us."

Terry punched the air. "That's what I'm talkin' 'bout!" She leaned over Maggie's desk to slap her five, clasping her hand and shaking it exuberantly. "Proud of you, girl. You gonna go give Stewart the good news?"

"You know it!" Maggie looked into a compact and fluffed her hair, pressing her lips together to make sure her gloss coverage was still intact. Her mother taught her to always approach her superiors as put together as possible—she believed it was far easier to reward hard work when someone was put together. A sloppy appearance, in her opinion, was a precursor to poor performance.

"Good luck!" Terry whispered.

"Thank you!" Maggie twiddled her fingers and strode down the hall, her posture becoming more upright and strong as she reached the last office. She rapped her knuckles on the open door twice. "Hey, Stewart, do you have a second?"

"Sure, Maggie. What's up?" Stewart looked up from a document he was redlining, no doubt for the third time. He was a man of short stature, with very little hair remaining on the top of his crown, and his piercing gaze still had the paralegals running for cover. He sat back in his chair to give her his full attention.

She stepped just across the threshold of his doorway. "Two things. First, that client with the eight start-ups? He's signing on with us this afternoon."

His mouth dropped open. "I wasn't sure we were gonna land it since you mentioned he was considering our competition over in Century City."

"I know. It was a little touch and go, but I gave him a piece of advice about the living trust that my friend Neil set up for him, and that sealed the deal."

"Resourceful." He nodded approval. "What was the second thing?"

"The Meyer case?"

Stewart pinched the bridge of his nose. The Meyers were a pain-in-the-ass couple who, at the advice of their former tax accountant, had paid only business taxes, neglecting their individual obligations, and were audited within an inch of their lives. "What now? You know, every other day my life is filled with regret for introducing those two to our firm."

Stewart had met Mr. Meyer on a golf course in Long Beach, and after hearing about some of what the man was experiencing, he encouraged a meeting to talk it all out. When Stewart realized how involved the case would be, his eyes had glazed over and he'd assigned it to Maggie as a test of her experience and patience.

Maggie worked with the Meyers for two years, scouring

all of their receipts and documents, speaking to her contact at the IRS almost weekly. Worst-case scenario, the couple faced the possibility of jail time for tax evasion, and Maggie fought hard to demonstrate that they were acting under the guidance of a professional and did not act maliciously or with the intent of avoiding their individual taxes. "They were found negligent. No intent to defraud or evade."

Stewart put his palms on his desk and pressed himself up out of his leather chair. "Maggie, that is fantastic work. Wow, well done." He didn't smile often, but he was cheesing so hard it looked like his cheeks hurt.

She clasped her hands in front of her. "Thank you. I wasn't sure which way that was going to go. Honestly, I was worried they were potentially going to face some jail time."

"I was worried, too. Wow." He sat back down. "Why don't you come in for a sec. I've been wanting to chat with you anyway, and this is as good a time as any." He waved her inside. "You can shut the door behind you."

Oh, shit. Her stomach did a little flip. She did as she was told and planted herself in a seat across the desk from him, crossing her legs at the ankles. She folded her hands in her lap to keep from fidgeting.

"Maggie, you've really outdone yourself here. We are extremely impressed with your initiative to bring in these clients, and on a personal note, I'm very proud of you." Stewart smiled at her, this time a little more relaxed. "I think that I'm ready to give my recommendation to the others."

"You mean, you're recommending me for partner? Seriously?"

"Seriously." He nodded. "You've really outdone yourself here, and I think that we probably should have done this a while ago."

"How long do you think it will take for all of the partners

to determine whether they want to move forward or not?" She bit her lip nervously.

"I don't think it will take much time at all considering we've been talking about this for the last six months, and just wanted to see how you would approach bringing on new clients if you knew that you were up for partner, and you have not disappointed. Honestly, they were convinced a while ago, but I wanted to see how you handled yourself with the Meyers.

"You've really proven yourself, Maggie. You are professional, you are obviously hungry and you're looking to build. We would be lucky to have you here as partner," he assured her.

Maggie felt a flutter in her chest, her smile growing wide. "Wow, Stewart, I can't believe it!"

"Believe it, kiddo, and let me be the first to welcome you, partner." Stewart extended his hand to her, which she gripped tightly, looking him directly in the eyes.

"Thank you, Stewart. I won't let you down."

"I know you won't."

Maggie practically skipped back to her office, shutting her door behind her so that she could leap and dance around the room. She grabbed her phone and sent a text message to Garrett.

Maggie: Hey are you busy?

Garrett: Hey just doing some research right now for an article, what's up want me to call you?

Maggie: Yes if you have a sec.

Garrett: OK give me two minutes.

Maggie: Bet.

Maggie danced around her office for another minute before she sat down to catch her breath. She sipped on some water and looked to the ceiling as if to make eye contact with her mom. "We did it," she whispered, holding a hand toward heaven. "Thank You, Lord, for this blessing, and thank you, Mama, for encouraging me to go after it."

Her phone rang, and Garrett's photo illuminated her screen.

"Hey, gorgeous, what's up? Are you okay?" he asked quizzically.

"Yeah, I'm fine. I just wanted to talk to you really quickly."

"Okay, shoot."

"I just wanted to let you be the first to speak to the new partner at the firm." She waited a beat before proceeding to emit a high-pitched squeal as she swung her fist into the air.

Garrett whooped loudly into the phone. "Oh, my God! Are you serious? I knew it was gonna happen, but wow, I'm so proud of you! You did that, Mags. That's amazing! How does it feel?"

"Honestly, I have no idea," she laughed. "I spent the last couple minutes dancing around my office, though, so joy is definitely in the room."

"Did anyone see you? You're a terrible dancer," he deadpanned.

"Don't throw shade at me in this moment," she retorted. "If I remember correctly, you're the one that doesn't have any rhythm." Garrett couldn't even two-step without looking like he'd trip over his own two feet.

He chuckled. "This is why we work so well together. Good dancing is clearly not a requirement for either of us."

She cackled. "True. We're lucky that Savvy and Joan aren't requiring us to take dance lessons before the weddings, because they'd be sorely disappointed."

"Can you imagine?"

"Actually, I can. We would get kicked out of class within the first five minutes," she giggled.

"Sure would. Listen, Mags, we have to celebrate."

"We can definitely do that. I probably have a long day ahead of me, but let's plan something. By the way, do you have a new article out today?" She typed in her password to unlock her computer.

"Yeah, it's a precursor to my next podcast for ESPN. We're talking to a couple of the players who are being really vocal about the upcoming strike. It gives a pretty good account of what's happened so far and what each side's demands are."

"Oh, I definitely want to read that," she murmured. She typed his name into the search bar to pull up his most recent update on the NBA players' stance on the renewal of their collective bargaining agreement with the association.

She heard him snap his fingers. "By the way, can I borrow that USB microphone that you don't use?"

She leaned an elbow against her desk as she held the phone receiver, trying to picture where she'd last seen it. "Sure, you can have it if you want. I think it's in my office."

"Okay, thanks. Do you mind if I stop by to pick it up sometime this week?"

Maggie heard the faint sound of a pen scribbling something down and pictured Garrett writing himself a reminder on a Post-it. "Not at all. Grab it whenever. I probably will have a couple of late nights this week, so you don't have to schedule that around me. I'm playing hooky tomorrow to go surprise my dad."

"He'll love that—he's gonna shout, Mags! And will do. I'll get it tomorrow or the next day. Hey, listen, I need to get going to go and prep for this interview. Call you later?"

"Sure, that sounds great."

"I'm really proud of you, Mags." The tone of his voice

was serious. "You worked really hard to get to this level. You should be really, really proud of yourself for all of the work that you've put in. You earned that, and you deserve that recognition."

Butterflies swooped around in her chest. "Thanks, G. I really appreciate you saying that and for you encouraging me when I felt really unsure."

"Always."

"Okay, I'll let you go. Talk to you later."

"Count on it."

21

"HEY, DADDY!" MAGGIE STOOD ON THE STONE PORCH in a sundress, a jean jacket hanging over her shoulders.

"Hey, pumpkin, what are you doing here?" he asked incredulously, unlocking the screen door to swing it open and invite her in. They embraced in the doorway.

"It's been too long since I put eyes on you, and I needed a squeeze. What you been up to since you got back? How was Mexico?"

"Oh, you know, just kind of putzing around the house today. Got a couple of little tinkering projects. Mexico was nice. We ain't bought property just yet, but we saw some promising little condos."

"Nice! I hope y'all took some pictures."

"Oh, even better. Courtney got some video for you. It's too bad we didn't know you were coming, because she went out to run a bunch of errands. She would have loved to see you."

"I should have called, but I wanted to surprise you. I've got some good news."

"Uh-huh." He eyed her. "Well, come on back here. Let's grab a seat. You thirsty?" He refilled his coffee mug as they passed through the kitchen into their sunroom.

"Nah, I'm okay." She followed him and plopped down onto the daybed while her father sat in his favorite rocking chair.

"So, spill."

"Well, first. I wanted to tell you in person that I've officially made partner!"

His eyes lit up. "Oh!" He laughed heartily and jumped to his feet. "You were so somber coming in here, I thought something had happened." He wrapped his arms around her again. "Congratulations! See, and you were worried that it wouldn't happen."

"That's true. And you were right."

"Well, more than anything, I'm just happy that you're happy." He released her. "You *are* happy, right?"

"Mmm-hmm." She looked up at him, her eyes wide as saucers.

"Okay, Magnolia." He grew serious. "I knew there was something. Why don't you sit down and tell me what's going on, because you never show up out of the blue. If I recall, I pulled that once on you when you were in college and you freaked out on me for not giving you proper notice."

Maggie's face grew hot as she laughed. She sat back down on the daybed, the sunlight streaming through panoramic screened windows. "Okay, you're right. You've got me. I just wanted to talk to you for a bit. I can't really stay. Did you have plans?"

He shrugged. "Maybe a bit of fishing off the coast, but that can wait."

The beauty of him living in San Diego was his ability to

keep a boat and go out on the water whenever he pleased. "That sounds like a good day," she offered.

His stern gaze spoke for him. *Get to it, baby girl.*

Maggie blew out a breath. "Dad, did you ever get the sense, you know, from the time that you've known Garrett as one of my friends… Did you know that he liked me?"

His eyes widened. "Of course. He followed you around like a puppy dog."

"Dad, be serious," she chided.

"Listen, do you want the truth or do you want me to lie? He's always been in love with you. From the very first time I came to campus to see that he was okay for you to hang around with, I knew then that he liked you. He wasn't trying to pounce on you like that roommate of his." He sipped his coffee, staring at her pointedly.

Lord. "But…how? How did you know?"

"Well, he told me."

Maggie tilted her head as her eyes squeezed shut. "Wait— he told you back then that he liked me?"

"Yeah. I asked him point-blank what his intentions were with you, and he said, you know, that you two were very close friends, and that you were really intent on the two of you maintaining that friendship, but that he had his sights set on more. I told him that was fine but that he should wait until he had more to offer you before he tried to pursue anything, and he agreed, especially since y'all were still in college and trying to figure things out for yourselves in terms of what your careers were going to be and how much money you were going to make and where you were gonna live—you know, all the things. I mean, as luck would have it, you both landed in LA, but for the longest time, we all thought that he was gonna be in Chicago." He cupped his mug in his hands.

"Yeah, or New York," she said quietly. A gentle breeze

flowed in from the open windows, ruffling the bottom of her dress.

He snapped his fingers. "Exactly, New York, so I've always known."

She processed slowly. "What are your thoughts on that?"

"Well, what are *your* thoughts on it? I mean, that's why you're here. You didn't drive all the way down here to ask me for my blessing."

"Would he have your blessing, Daddy?" Maggie's voice was barely above a whisper.

Mr. Jones's baritone voice only got deeper when he laughed— it reverberated from deep in his belly. "He's always had my blessing, baby girl! I like the way he treats you. I like the way that he makes sure that he understands you. The two of you communicate well. You know, after the sex is gone and everything else, you got to be able to spend time with that person. He's your person, in that way. Why do you ask this now?"

"Well, 'cause he and I went on a date the other day, but there's also someone else."

"Who?" he asked incredulously.

Maggie took a deep breath. "His name is Blake. I met him at the gym. He's a heart surgeon that's done really well for himself and has a home in Manhattan Beach that overlooks the water. I don't know a lot about his family but he seems like a good guy. Obviously, he's not Garrett."

"So which way are you leaning and what's holding you back?"

"Honestly, I think I'm leaning toward Garrett, but that's scary. What if we ruin our friendship?"

"Do you really think that's possible?"

Her phone pinged, and she frowned as she saw Blake's name flash on her screen. "I'm sorry—what was that?"

He eyed her. "Who is that? Is everything okay?"

"Yeah, it's one of them now. Just wanting to talk, and I don't know what to say. Blake is a great guy, and if Garrett wasn't in the picture, I might try to pursue things. I mean, I'm still getting to know him, so I don't feel as sure. He's nice, though. And Garrett is amazing—he's Garrett—but what if he loses interest in me?"

"Maggie, it's been twenty years. Just be honest, especially with yourself—that's all you ever have to be. It doesn't matter what they want to hear. Go after what you want."

"You're right. I guess I'm just stuck in my head, thinking about all of the what-ifs."

"Don't let those automatic thoughts cancel out your opportunity for happiness," he cautioned. *He's always good for a note from his therapist.* "I can't tell you the right answer here, babe. You have to decide that for yourself. You are an intelligent woman, and you have everything that you need to make this decision."

"But what do I base it off of?"

"I think this one can't just be about logic, baby. You can't reason this one out or do a pros-and-cons list and think that's going to tell you an answer. Have either of them given you any red flags?" He leaned forward, his elbows on his knees.

"Maybe. Nothing crazy blaring, but I'll have to think on it." She shrugged.

"Well, your intuition has always guided you in the right direction, and you have always made sound decisions because you don't make them on a whim. You think them through by giving yourself the time and the space to do so. So don't let anybody rush you. Take your time, talk it out if you have to, but you'll know what to do when the time is right."

Maggie nodded, rising from her seat to hug him. "Thanks, Daddy."

"That's my girl. Can you stay for lunch?"

She eyed him playfully. "What do you have and can I take it to go?"

He burst out laughing. "I can always count on you to have an appetite."

Thursday, Blake and Maggie enjoyed a leisurely day at the beach. They walked up and down Santa Monica Pier, Maggie ate junk food and they soaked in the bright California sunlight. He tried to convince Maggie to get on the Ferris wheel, but she threatened to throw up her hastily eaten cheesy popcorn on him if they did. He laughed it off, but Maggie sensed that he really wanted to get on there. He relented when she shared her propensity for motion sickness.

As they strolled, Blake held her hand, leading her toward sites that interested him. They stopped at a trivia booth, and they flipped through old vinyl at a cart playing Marvin Gaye on an old Crosley record player. When Maggie pointed to a tarot card reader, Blake pulled her away, instead checking out a mobile free library. They stopped to observe different street performers, but Maggie's mind wandered. The legendary tin man stood statuesquely next to her, and she didn't notice until he sneakily tapped her on her shoulder.

As they rounded the Promenade, Maggie couldn't help but think about Garrett.

"Hey, do you wanna stop here for dinner?" Blake hitched his thumb toward a sushi spot.

"Sure, that sounds great." She smiled thinly.

Inside, he ordered sashimi while she ordered assorted tempura and a dragon roll. They ate quietly, Maggie mostly poking at the shrimp tempura with her chopsticks. *I'm always hungry. What's wrong with me?* She ordered a small bottle of sake to help her relax and had a second when the first didn't ease her anxiety. The crisp liquid had notes of melon and citrus.

"Hey, are you okay?" Blake asked at the end of dinner.

"Hmm?" she responded, meeting his gaze. "Oh, I'm sorry. I've just been busy with work and everything," she stammered. *Liar.* "I'm just so inundated right now. I think my mind is just, you know…" She laughed nervously, waving her hand up over her head as if everything were scattered. "I'm a bit fried. I'm sorry if I haven't been great company today."

She'd gone back and forth on whether to mention that she was also dating Garrett, but they hadn't discussed anything in terms of exclusivity, so she didn't feel like she owed him that information. That didn't mean she'd stop thinking about it, though.

"No, I understand," he said. "But are you sure that's it?" He leaned forward on his elbows. "You can talk to me, you know. I like you, Maggie," Blake started slowly, "and I know I'm not the only one you're seeing, but I know what I want and I think that we could be really great together."

Maggie looked down at the table before meeting his eyes. "You're right. I am seeing someone else, too, and I'm—" She breathed. "I'm just trying to find my footing. I'm not really sure which way to go. You're both great guys and I just—" She stopped. "I just don't want to hurt anybody." *I don't want to hurt Garrett.*

Blake reached out a hand and took Maggie's in his. "I think at the end of the day, you just have to be true to who you are and what you want. Otherwise, you're doing multiple people a disservice, right?"

She nodded. "Yeah, I suppose that's true."

"Do you want anything for dessert?" He searched her face.

She smiled weakly. "No, thanks. I think I'm good. I should probably get home."

Blake took care of the check and reached out a hand as he stood. "Come on. I'll take you home."

They strolled back to her building and Blake saw her to her door. He kissed her gently, immediately going in for seconds, deeply savoring her lips before pressing his mouth against her neck. "Let's go inside," he whispered.

Maggie pulled away gently. "Not tonight, love. I think I should just…" She gestured toward her door.

"No, come on," he pleaded.

"Next time, okay?" She smiled at him, attempting to unlock the door.

Blake wrapped his hand around her wrist and she bristled, snatching her arm away. "Maggie, just for a little while."

Before she could say anything, the door to her apartment swung open and Garrett charged toward them. "No means no, asshole. You should go."

"Garrett!" Maggie held her hands up, stepping between them to defuse the situation before it could escalate.

"And who's this guy? Is this— He's the other one?" Blake blinked rapidly, assessing Garrett from head to toe. "What is this? You planned to see both of us in the same night? I take you out and then you have this guy waiting for you at home?" He gestured to Garrett, in his jeans and graphic tee. "You're a little more 'equal opportunity' than I thought you'd be."

Maggie stared at him, shocked. "Excuse me? What is that supposed to mean?"

"Hey, you don't talk to her that way," Garrett interjected.

"Why? What's it to you?" Blake goaded him. "What's *she* to you?"

Maggie stared at him, completely flabbergasted. *Is this the same dude?*

"I'm her best friend, and she's mine. I love Maggie, and I have for a long time."

"Well, obviously, you should move on, bro. She clearly doesn't feel the same, because if you were always an option, she slept on you for a reason. *You're* the one who doesn't have a place here, so why don't you leave?"

Garrett stepped back, Blake's words landing like a body blow.

Blake turned to Maggie. "I'm right, aren't I? Are you gonna tell him what I did to you? I guarantee you he can't do you like I can. He can't touch you—"

"Shut up, Blake. You have no right, and besides, you don't have any clue what I thought about that experience," she interjected.

"You and I both know you weren't acting, Maggie." His eyes narrowed.

Garrett paled, blinking at the sting of Blake's words. He stepped toward him, glowering. "It doesn't matter. You're barely getting to know her. Just walk away, man."

"It's Maggie's choice," Blake retorted.

"G, just relax." She put her hands toward Garrett. "Don't listen to him. It wasn't like that," she pleaded.

"Oh, so you're more worried about this guy than you are about me," Blake accused.

"Listen, dude, just go," Garrett repeated, his expression stony.

"I know what I want, and I'm not going anywhere until she tells me I need to go."

"Blake...please," she started.

Garrett and Blake stared at each other, Blake's eyes wide. He puffed out his chest. He was wider, but Garrett was taller. Maggie looked back and forth between the two, unable to find the words to deactivate the bomb being primed to go off.

"I'm gonna ask you one more time," Garrett said calmly, holding out a hand to reduce the tension.

Blake bristled, pushing Garrett back into Maggie and then punching him in the face before he could react. Garrett landed against Maggie, bumping her back into the door. He held his eye as Maggie yelled from behind him. "*Hey!* Both of you leave!"

The pair turned to her, sputtering out their excuses.

"I—"

"Mags—"

"Let me talk—"

"We should go inside…"

"No. I'm not going to be with either one of you anytime soon if you're going to act like this. Now, get out." She stepped inside her condo and slammed the door behind her.

She heard the sound of something brushing against the door for a moment, as if someone pressed their hand against it but thought better of it before they knocked. Whoever it was left.

Maggie stepped out of her shoes and stalked to the couch, plopping down next to Penny. "I could use some love," she said, her voice glum.

Penny stepped into her lap and pressed a paw on Maggie's arm.

"Thank you, my sweet girl." She scratched behind Penny's ears and let Penny nuzzle her head against Maggie's neck. Maggie dragged her nails along Penny's back as it curled before picking her up and carrying her to the kitchen. "Come on, sweet girl. Let's get you some food."

Maggie's phone began to ring, and she turned it off, not wanting to deal with either of the guys or their inevitable excuses for what just took place. After setting Penny's bowl on the counter, she changed into her pajamas and returned to the living room to feel like she wasn't alone.

Unable to think or even process what just happened, she climbed back on the couch and promptly fell asleep.

22

WHEN MAGGIE WOKE, SHE CALLED SAVVY, WHO PRO-
ceeded to phone tree Joanie and Beth for an emergency
brunch. Savvy picked up Maggie on the way to the restaurant. Maggie came out of her building wearing a denim jump-
suit, sandals and oversize sunglasses, her curls piled on top of
her head in a pineapple. Savvy wore a printed midi dress with
spaghetti straps and a jean jacket—her signature style. As they
drove to the restaurant, Savvy reached across the console and
squeezed Maggie's hand.

"I can't believe this is my life, girl," Maggie said, her tone
resigned. "You were right. I should have made a decision
sooner."

Savvy kept her eyes on the road. "One never wants to be
right in a situation like this."

"No, I know, but you were. There's no getting around that."

"Well, let's see if we can find a silver lining, huh? Two

great guys are fighting over you, vying for your attention."
Savvy tapped the back of Maggie's hand with her index finger. "You're *that* bitch."

"Gas me up, sis." Mags smiled a little, cutting her eyes to
her friend.

"Just remind me to stop before it goes to your head."

Maggie rolled her eyes, feeling almost normal for a moment.

When they reached the restaurant, Savvy dropped her keys
with the valet. Joanie and Beth were already inside, and each
embraced Maggie tightly before greeting Savvy.

"The table's ready for us," Joanie said, and they were led by
a hostess to the restaurant's patio, which was lightly shaded by
a massive pergola. The sun had already burned through the
marine layer of fog, and Southern California was prepared
for a warm spring day. Beth wore jean shorts and a tank top
that showed off her muscular physique, while Joanie sported
tailored cigarette pants and a sleeveless blouse. They ordered
pitchers of mimosas and bellinis, chocolate chip pancakes, a
chorizo-and-egg scramble topped with sliced avocado, home
fries, extra bacon and coffee.

"Okay, so we're all here, we've all gotten pieces of this,"
Savvy started slowly. "Tell us everything."

Maggie recounted the day from the pier to dinner to the
house. "I was definitely distracted," she admitted. "And, yes,
I was thinking about Garrett, but I never expected that these
two on their first meeting would be coming to blows. I just
didn't want company for the night so that I could figure out
where my head was at, and then Garrett popped up and Blake
lost it."

The table fell silent, and the group tried to wrap their heads
around what had happened the night before.

"Well, only one person swung," Savvy said gently. "I don't
think Garrett was actually there to start a fight."

"Listen, I know you have a soft spot for Garrett," Maggie acknowledged. "But neither one of them should have acted the way that they did last night. It was not cute, and what was Garrett even doing there?"

A familiar voice chimed in from behind her. "I can answer that."

Maggie's spine stiffened at the sound of him, and she turned to look into his eyes. "What are *you* doing here?"

Garrett stood with his hands in the pockets of his jeans—the same clothes he had been wearing the night before. There were bags under his eyes. "Spencer let me know where y'all would be."

Maggie shot a look at Savvy, who narrowed her eyes at Garrett. "He did what?" she asked. "Oh, he gon' hear about that from me."

"No, please don't let me get him in trouble. It's not his fault. It's mine," Garrett admitted.

"You shouldn't be here. I think you should leave," Maggie said slowly. *But please stay.*

"I promise you I will do whatever you want me to do. I'm just hoping you'll allow me to apologize to you and then I'll go, okay?" He eyed her anxiously. "Please, Maggie."

She looked down at the table and nodded, and he grabbed a chair to sit so as not to bring more attention to the table. A few people glanced in their direction, trying to assess what was happening from the expressions on their party's faces.

"Listen, and I'm saying this in front of the people you care about most, so you know I'm telling you the truth. All of those times when you would kind of tease me for not lasting with any of those girls I dated? Of course I could never have a serious relationship with any of them. Maggie, I have been in love with you since we kissed in college. I have compared every girl I have ever dated to you, because *you* are the standard and nobody beats you.

"I don't care if you are shoving down pastrami fries with extra onions, I don't care if you're slurping on Orange Bang, I don't care. I don't care if we're throwing up in the same toilet because we're hungover. I just know that I need to be near you."

A hint of a smile tickled the corners of Maggie's mouth at the mention of Orange Bang, but as fast as it appeared, it was gone. She stared at Garrett devoid of emotion.

"You make my day better. You make *me* better. I know everything there is to know about you—even the things you like to hide from me." Garrett smiled. "Like when you hit my car and pretended not to know anything had happened."

Others around the table hid their smiles.

"I know you already, so I don't need to date you. I don't *want* to date you—I want a relationship with you. I want to be your partner. But at the very least, I want our friendship back."

"Why did you show up last night?" she asked quietly, not looking him in the eye.

"Remember I needed to get that USB microphone from your place?"

She snapped her fingers. "Dammit, I had completely forgotten about that."

"Please tell me you're gonna stop seeing that guy," he pleaded.

"Why?"

Garrett lifted his hands in surrender. "I don't have a reason. It's not like he ever did anything to you, and I know that, because you would have told me, but I just— I know he's not the right one for you."

"How can you know that when I don't know that?" *Maybe I do.* She stared at him, hurt in her eyes. "You said you would let me come to a decision, and at every point you have tried to sway it in your favor."

"No, I—"

"All the people that you swiped on—some of those were good guys. And every time you talked about Blake, it was just you being jealous, feeling inferior. And you're not at all inferior, but I know that's how you felt."

Garrett hung his head. "You're right. Please just don't give up on me, Mags. Not after all this time."

"I need time to think—" she gestured around the table "—and whatever this little intervention is, it's doing exactly what I didn't want it to do. I gotta go." Deflated, she stood and grabbed her purse.

Savvy jumped up. "Wait, Maggie, no. This isn't what we had in mind."

Maggie squeezed her hand. "No, I'll call you later. I just— I just need to be by myself." She walked away and just kept walking until she found her way home.

One thing that Maggie prided herself on as an attorney was her ability to make the case for both sides before arriving at a conclusion—it was always necessary to consider what opposing counsel would argue, even if her client had the stronger argument. Monday she sent texts to both guys, asking them for time to think so that she could make a decision. Both Garrett and Blake had been calling and texting, trying to apologize, trying to get their explanations in, but she didn't want to hear any of it. She wanted to decide based on her own feelings.

With work and her social life being so busy lately, and Tax Day quickly approaching, Maggie hadn't done much in the way of shopping, but she still made it a point to schedule a Zoom lunch with the girls right before the meeting. She poured hot water from an electric kettle in the break room into a cup of spicy ramen noodles. Anytime Savvy came to visit her office, she'd drop off pantry items that she could eat when she got too busy to order anything. There was no way she was going to attempt to cook anything, and Savvy thought having food delivered all the time was a waste of money. When Maggie considered washing down her ramen with her fourth cup of coffee, Savvy was the first one to log on.

"Hey, sis, you okay?"

Maggie nodded. "Better today. This is weird, right?" she laughed slowly.

"It's unique, that's for sure," Savvy giggled. "I don't know. As far as situations go, could be a lot worse." She smiled brightly. "You'll get through it like you always do."

Maggie nodded again. "I just still can't believe they almost fought."

Beth and Joan popped on then. "Hey, Mags." They each waved. "Everyone is lookin' fly. What did we miss?" Joan sipped on a bubble tea.

Savvy took her cue. "Well, so we never got to finish our convo at brunch, but I think they're both good guys. I think they both made some bad choices recently, but I think they're still good guys…"

"Come on, girl. We all know that you're team Garrett," Joan teased.

"I mean, I am." She closed her eyes for a minute. "I just… He wasn't wrong when he said that he knows you better than any other guy ever could, 'cause he does. It's true. He knows you better than your father knows you, he cares for you, he listens, he's thoughtful. He is invested in your success, and to me, that's what you need from a partner.

"And it's not to say that Blake's not capable of that. I just don't know him like that."

Maggie nodded slowly, considering her words. "You still playing devil's advocate, Joan?"

Joanie's head swayed side to side as she grimaced, as if she was ping-ponging between the two. "You know y'all have been friends for so long, it just makes me nervous. I don't want you to lose your friend."

"True," Maggie agreed, "and that's why we made that pact all those years ago."

"Yeah, but you were like nineteen then," Savvy argued. "You're thirty-eight now. You know him, he knows you and knows what your deal breakers are, so you know what he would have to do to cross that line with you. Is he even capable of doing that to you?"

"I mean, I don't think so," Maggie replied slowly, "but aren't we all capable?"

"Listen, if you're going to go all philosophical, I can't help you," Savvy snapped.

Joanie jerked her thumb in Savvy's direction on the Zoom grid and burst out laughing. "Not all philosophical! Damn, Mags, don't break Savvy."

Maggie cracked a smile and began to giggle until it built to full-on laughter.

"Shut up." Savvy regrouped. "Listen, love, you've got two sets of friends here who have found the people that they want to spend the rest of their lives with. If you had to choose to spend your life with one of these guys today, and I get that that's an unfair question to ask since you're still in such early days with Blake—we know that—but if you had to choose today, how would it not be Garrett?" Savvy implored.

"And, now that he has made how he feels plain, are you also risking it all by not acting?" Beth asked.

"Now who's getting philosophical?" Joanie teased. "Look, like Savvy said, they're both good guys. Obviously, you know

Blake has his stuff together, he likes to pamper you—and you deserve that—you seem like you have good conversations, he seems like he is interested in who you are as a person, and nothing has indicated that he's trying to change you in any way."

"It's so weird with him," Maggie shared. "It's like he's the Black Ken doll. He's got a dream house with a perfect view, he's got this incredible job, he doesn't want or need for anything, he takes good care of himself, he's disciplined, kind, generous…"

"So what are the cons?" Joanie nudged.

"He's a little boring, but irrespective of that, he's not Garrett." She shrugged.

"Go on." Savvy leaned toward her screen, giving a nod of encouragement.

"I mean, there are things I know I would tell Garrett today that I wouldn't necessarily share with Blake, and it's just because we've had almost two decades to get to know each other and be comfortable enough to know that he's not going to judge me. With Blake, I still don't know that. I feel like he's capable of saying some real reckless shit, but we had been drinking…"

"Yeah, but alcohol makes you tell the truth. It doesn't make you lie and say ugly shit on purpose. Like, you say that shit 'cause you're already thinking that shit and you no longer have the filter to stop you," Savvy pointed out. "Did Garrett say anything crazy when y'all were drunk?"

"No, he just told me he loved me a lot."

"So are you really upset with Garrett, then? I mean, yes, he hid his feelings for a long time, but we've been trying to tell you for years that he felt a way. It's not been *that* well hidden."

"It's really been that obvious?"

Three heads bobbled on her screen.

"Honestly, when I first met him, I thought y'all were old flames and stayed friends when it didn't work out. The chemistry is off the charts," Beth shared. "Feels like you've got an answer, sis."

"Yes, so speaking of answers, let's talk wedding stuff for a minute, Ms. Maid of Honor," Savvy interjected. "Do you have your dresses?"

"Yes."

"Okay, have you booked your flights, hotels and done all the things?"

Such a Capricorn. "You already know I have."

"Okay, shoes?"

Shit. Maggie scrunched up her face. "Mmm. Aren't we going to be on the beach?"

"Ma'am."

"Fine, I'll get them," she relented.

"Okay, you've got hair and makeup taken care of... Jewelry?" Savvy continued to tick things off of her list.

"I've got that," Joanie said.

"Okay, am I forgetting anything?"

"Well, are you sure you don't want to do a bridal shower? Just the bachelor/bachelorette? The latter is already planned, by the way. It's day two after everyone arrives in Phuket," Maggie advised.

"Ooh, noted. And I don't think I need a bridal shower," Savvy said slowly. "We'll all be together on the honeymoon, which will feel like a fun retreat, but I might need something else soon." Her eyes shone.

"What?" Maggie leaned forward. Beth and Joanie did the same.

Savvy rolled her office chair backward so she could point at her belly. "We just confirmed it this morning. I'm pregnant." Savvy grinned.

Maggie's eyes began to water. "Oh, my God, you are? Why didn't you tell me?"

"I'm telling you now, heffa."

"Congratulations, Savs!" Joan squealed.

"I know, but oh, my God, you've been letting me just live in my own little world…" Maggie wailed.

"Well, but there's some things that you need to figure out, and that's okay, and we don't have to deal with the baby shower until we're back from the wedding."

"Oh, wait. You'll be okay to make the trip, won't you? Have you told your mom?"

"Yeah, we'll be right at the very tail end of it being okay to travel, but my doctor confirmed we are good. I'll probably be showing in my dress, but thank God it's so flowy, it won't make a big difference. Mom knows and she's super-excited. She wants us to go and get a special blessing while we're in Thailand."

"That's amazing, Savvy. We're so happy for you!" Joanie gushed, and Beth nodded, clasping her hands together.

"And now I get to be TiTi Mags!" She beamed.

"TiTi Mags, TiTi Kotter, TiTi Beth, yep, y'all better get ready!"

"Well, that's the best damn news I've heard in a long time." Maggie's face balled up as she started to cry.

Savvy threw up her hands. "Oh, God, here we go again. You know, for as bad and bossy as you are, you really are a cream puff on the inside."

Maggie emitted a series of high-pitched sounds since she couldn't form words. She covered her mouth as she sobbed. Maggie whined into her hand unintelligibly.

Savvy rolled her eyes. "Okay, well, I can't understand you once you go all supersonic, so I'm going to log off. Kotter, Beth, I'll see you on the tennis court later."

"You got it! Congrats again, Mama Savs!" Beth exclaimed.
Savvy waved and blew air-kisses. "All right, love y'all!" Her image disappeared from the screen.

"Love you!" Maggie sobbed. "Ugh." She reached for tissues. "I've gotta pull myself together."

23

"HEY, MAMA JUNE, IS THIS A GOOD TIME?"

"Maggie! It's great to hear from you. I'm so glad that you called, because I have been wanting to talk to you about some of the wedding arrangements." Savvy's mother, a true alpha personality, had been like a second mother to Maggie since her mom died. Having known Maggie for most of her life, she was often willing to tell her the hard truths that others tried to hide from her.

Even outside of the wedding, Maggie had regular conversations with June about work and her love life—things she would have confided in her own mother about had she still been alive. Tough as June could be, she was quick to acknowledge hard work or effort and she was always generous with her time.

"Oh, great. Savvy mentioned that you had some thoughts about the ceremony?" Maggie had a pen and paper to take notes. June was detail oriented with her ideas.

"Yes, I did. I really wanted to see if we were already committed to having the ceremony at the hotel, because if we have some wiggle room, one of our family members has access to this beautiful botanical garden nearby, and I thought that that could be a prettier venue."

"You don't like the beach?" Savvy and Joan had agreed to a joint wedding on a stretch of private beach owned by the hotel in Phuket. Though they were staying at a luxury property, the wedding ceremony itself was relatively informal. The families and friends were intended to form a circle of love around them as they shared their vows with each other. June's husband, Max, had agreed to officiate the weddings, having done so for several couples over the years.

"The beach is beautiful, you know, but it's so messy. The sand gets everywhere, and then we'll track it into the reception area. I just thought that maybe the garden could be a little more refined." Miss June didn't often get her way when it came to imposing her will on her daughter, but it never stopped her from trying.

"Now, Mama June." Maggie smiled into the phone. "You and I both know your daughter. She is such a water baby, I can't imagine that she would consider moving the ceremony away from the beach. Plus, remember that this is also Joan's wedding, and her whole plan was to get married on a beach."

"Hmm. I hear what you're saying. Would you be a dear and ask them anyway?"

There is no way they'll say yes. Maggie burst out laughing. "Sure, I can do that for you."

"Thank you, dear. So what else is new?"

"Aside from you getting ready to be a grandmother? Congratulations, by the way!" Maggie squealed.

"Ah! I'm so glad she's shared the news. Thank you. I am

beyond excited," Mama June laughed. "I've been waiting a long time for this."

"Savvy is going to be an amazing mom. Just like you."

"You're sweet. Now, tell me."

"Well, I just made partner at the firm." Maggie's smile widened.

"Oh, my goodness!" she exclaimed. "How extraordinary! I am so proud of you, Maggie. Your mom would be, too."

Maggie's eyes teared up at the mention of her mother. "I think she would be, too."

Mama June's voice softened. "I know she would be, sweetheart. She always shared how proud she was, even when you went away to school. Well done. You worked hard for that."

"Thank you. I needed to hear that," Maggie sighed.

"By the way, have you decided on your date for the wedding yet?"

Right back to business. Her mind moves a mile a minute. Maggie sighed again. "No, but I've been thinking about that a lot, actually, and I think I'm leaning in one direction, but I haven't confirmed anything yet."

June was quiet on the other end for a moment. "What is your hesitation? You've always struck me as very sure of yourself, so what is it that is holding you back?"

Maggie stretched her neck, leaning her head to one side. "The decision that I make could impact a very important friendship of mine, and I'm afraid to risk what we've built over the course of twenty years."

"Ah, so you're considering Garrett as your choice, of course," Mama June acknowledged.

She sure does cut to the chase. Maggie laughed awkwardly. "Well, yes, to put it bluntly."

"Let me tell you something, Maggie. Twenty-year friendships last as long as they do because the foundation remains solid. As long as you two communicate honestly with each other and respect each other's boundaries, I don't believe that your friendship is at risk. It will only get stronger."

"You think?"

"I do. You two have a great respect for each other, and you know each other like the backs of your hands. I understand your trepidation, but I think that because you have such great care for each other, that will be reflected in the way that you both approach this relationship. Unless either of you gets into this and starts acting brand-new, it'll only get better."

"That makes a lot of sense, actually. Thank you for that." Relief washed over her.

"Well, just think about it this way," she chuckled. "Knowing everything that you do right now, how would you feel if you never got the chance to pursue anything?"

The weight of her words hit Maggie square in the face. "Wow, I guess I never thought about it like that." The thought of it made her sick; her stomach churned and her cheeks grew hot. "Thank you, Mama June."

"You are welcome. Now just one more thing."

"What's that?"

"I want you to help me surprise Savvy with something for the wedding."

"Oh? I'm always here for a good surprise. How can I help?"

They talked through the details of Mama June's surprise, and Maggie promised to set everything in motion. "Excellent. I can't wait for November!" she exclaimed. "It's such a perfect time to visit, and this will be your first time, yes?"

"Yep, it sure will be. I'm really excited to see Thailand and of course to eat all the yummy food."

"It's so good and so cheap, Maggie. You're going to love it. Anyway, I should get going. Max and I are going to drive down to Monterey. Good luck, dear!"

"That sounds fun! And thank you. You two be safe and I will talk to you soon."

"Sounds good, sweetheart. And congratulations again!"

"Mags, are you here?" Garrett called into the apartment.

"Yeah, I'm in the office. I'll be right out," she hollered. She had brought work home with her at the end of the day and had spent the past hour reviewing tax documents for a client. *Nothing like the week taxes are due to light a fire under their ass.* She closed the folder on her desk and pushed back from its surface to stand up and stretch her legs. She stepped into the living room to find Garrett in a full suit and stopped in her tracks. "Wow, look at you! You are lookin' sharp!"

"Shut up, Maggie. I'm already self-conscious enough," Garrett growled. "You're not helping, you know." Sweat beaded on his forehead, and his wide-eyed expression registered somewhere between terrified and ready to run.

"It was just a compliment," she laughed. "Anyway, you ready?"

He blew out a breath. "I am." He handed Maggie a packet of papers containing the CliffsNotes version of his report. He eyed her warily. "You know, I was also hoping that maybe we could talk…"

She held up a hand and shook her head. "If it's anything having to do with us, I'm sorry, but I'm just not ready to talk about it. We will, though, I promise."

"I understand." He looked away from her, his voice solemn. "Okay, then, we should probably get to it, and I'll leave you be."

A sharp stab pierced Maggie's gut as she regarded the hurt in his eyes. "I know I've taken a while. I just don't want to make any rash decisions, especially ones that could end up hurting you. You mean too much to me."

His shoulders drooped a little. "No, I get it. I would never do anything to hurt you, either."

I don't believe you would. Maggie perched on the arm of the couch, waiting for Penny to move before sliding over onto the seat and pulling her legs underneath her. "Okay, well, why don't you have a seat, and I'm gonna lead you in." He nodded in response, choosing an accent chair across from the sofa, and she brought her finger to her ear as if to hold an earwig in place. "Okay, and we are coming to you live from the studio. I am Maggie Jones and I'm joined today by Garrett Bailey, who is here to provide an update on the NBA players' strike, which has now been scheduled to begin next month. Garrett, what's the latest?"

"Well, thank you for that introduction, Maggie." He spoke haltingly, awkwardly enunciating unusual syllables. "Today, representatives from the National Basketball Association have announced plans for another lockout, as they did in 2011, at the close of the playoffs."

Maggie nodded. He made attempts to look up at her every few words, but anytime he looked away from the page, his hands clenched onto it, causing it to rustle.

"As some of you may recall, uh, there, uh, there was a players' lockout back then, access was limited to training facilities and teams could not trade, incentivize or contact players in any way."

His voice began to shake slightly and Maggie bit her lip. With the broadcast being just a couple of days away, she didn't want to fan the flames of his anxiety. In the moments that he glanced up in her direction, she gave a thumbs-up and nodded encouragingly. *If only he could talk this out the way he did on the podcast.*

"The lockout dragged on for months, with team owners and the players unable to reconcile their demands, causing the season to be cut short." He coughed, bringing his fist to his mouth and clearing his throat. "Could I have some water?" he asked.

"Yeah, of course." She jumped up and jogged to the kitchen, her filtered water pitcher sitting on the counter. She grabbed a clean glass from the cupboard. "Do you want ice?" she called.

"No, thanks."

She handed the glass to him carefully before sitting back down. Garrett took a couple of swigs before setting it down on a coaster on the coffee table. "Thanks." Penny jumped onto the arm of his chair, resting her paw on his arm as if to show her support. He rubbed her back and looked to Maggie. "Should I continue?"

"Yeah, go for it."

"According to one player, who wished to remain anonymous, the goal of beginning the strike much earlier this time around is to hopefully avoid having to eat into training camp or preseason games. The players do not want to eat into the season." He looked up from the page. "From there, I go into the details of some of the meetings that were shared with us by an anonymous source. It's like no one wants to be identified as having spoken to the press right now since it's still early days and the strike hasn't officially started yet."

"Yeah, that makes sense. How long is the segment?"

"About ten to fifteen minutes, I think, but I was just told today that we're likely to have to do some follow-up segments that are more Q and A style, potentially over the full weekend."

Maggie beamed at him. "Wow! How do you feel about that? Are you excited to already be asked back to do more?"

He laughed anxiously. "I want to be excited, and I know that this is something I have wanted for a long time. It's just hard to reconcile the fact that my nerves get the better of me anytime I speak in public." He glanced down at the paper again.

"Do you want to go over a little bit more?" She jutted her chin toward his notes.

"Sure." He cleared his throat and rolled his shoulders back from being up by his ears. "According to several sports agents, this time around, no one is discussing the possibility of disbanding the union. If you recall, that was something suggested by several agents back in 2011, but players like Derek Fisher spoke out against disbanding the union, which would remove certain protections for the players." Garrett's voice was a little shaky.

"Wow, this is really interesting," Maggie observed.

Garrett's knee began to bounce, causing the papers in his hands to rustle. His eyes scanned the words on the page. "Sometimes I just wish that I could step out of myself so I could just do this. I don't want to miss out on opportunities because of this." He pointed at his shaking knee with a will all its own.

"Hey," Maggie said gently. "You're going to do fine. Just pretend that all you have is a microphone in front of you and you're just recording for the podcast. Just talk like there are no cameras and you can be your normal self."

"Yeah." His expression was unreadable, so she decided not to push it.

"Do you want to go through your report again? Or maybe we could practice some Q and A in case any of the anchors wanna ask you anything?"

Garrett shook his head. "No, I think I've had my fill already." He ran his hand over his hair, visibly stressed. "Honestly, I wanna wake up and have this already behind me."

"Maybe your feelings about it will change over time," Maggie offered. "Maybe you'll get used to it a little faster than you think you will and it'll become comfortable."

Garrett shrugged. "That feels a long way off."

"How is the podcast going?" Maggie asked gingerly.

Garrett shrugged again. "Pretty well. Especially with things starting to amp up in terms of the strike. We've already gained a ton of listeners and we're receiving all kinds of questions that they want us to answer. So far, so good."

"That's great! I'm so proud of you."

Garrett looked at Maggie intensely. "I…"

"Still not ready," she replied gently.

He nodded. "Okay, well, I should probably go, then."

She couldn't remember the last time they'd hung out and hadn't shared a meal. Watching him leave drilled a hollow space in her stomach.

Garrett rubbed Penny's back one more time. "Listen, Maggie, I don't know what you're going to choose or what you're thinking, but I know how I feel about you. And I know I've wanted to be with you pretty much the whole time I've known you. But if you decide that you don't want to take the chance, or that you want to try with Blake——" he looked down into the floor "——I would respect that and honor your wishes. At the end of the day, you are my best friend and I just want you to be happy. Even if it's not with me." His face clouded over, and he looked away.

Maggie's heart dropped in her chest and she didn't know how to respond, so she just bobbed her head in response. "Thanks," she croaked.

He stood to leave. "Will you text me when you get home?" she asked.

"Sure. I'll talk to you later." He turned and left, shutting the door behind him quietly. She heard the key insert into the dead bolt, and once it clicked, he was gone.

"Mrs. Bailey?" Maggie held her cell phone to her ear, squeezing her eyes shut.

"Maggie, is that you? Hi, honey, how are you? And please

stop calling me Mrs. Bailey. After all these years, you can call me Janet."

"Now, you know that I was raised better than that, and I can't just call you Janet," Maggie reasoned with a laugh. She'd been trying for the better part of two decades to get Maggie to call her something other than Mrs. Bailey. When Maggie's mom died, Garrett's mom, like Savvy's, made it a point to check on her regularly, give her advice and just be there as a motherly figure. Maggie sent cards more often than she called, but hearing Mrs. Bailey's voice was like a balm to her frazzled nerves.

The woman sighed. "Very well. How are you doing, dear?"

"I'm okay. I—I'm not really sure how to jump into this," Maggie laughed nervously.

"Well, I can tell you that I've spoken to Garrett recently, if that helps," Mrs. Bailey chuckled into the receiver. "I've been expecting you."

"Well, yeah, so Garrett and I... I'm just not sure what to do."

"I'm not sure I'm the best person to advise you on this one. I already see you as my daughter, you know."

"Yes, but you know Garrett."

"True, but you know him better than I do—he calls me daily, yes, but he doesn't tell me everything."

"I'm just so thrown for a loop. I didn't know he had these feelings and..."

"Well, Maggie, he's...he's always had these feelings," she replied gently. "He's had feelings for you really since he met you. I started hearing about you well before the infamous kiss happened, and by the time that happened, he just wouldn't even shut up about you."

"Really?"

"Yeah. He's been waiting a really long time to tell you that, and I think he was scared to tell you, but he's also relieved that at least you now know." She paused. "I hear that there's another young man as well."

"Yeah," Maggie confirmed. "And he's nice…"

"Right," Mrs. Bailey caught on. "He's just not Garrett."

"Exactly. I'm just— It's not that I don't have feelings for Garrett, because I do. I'm just afraid, and it's like…quicksand."

"I understand that fear completely, dear. You two have been best friends a long time and it feels like a major risk to try to do something new with your friendship."

"Precisely!"

"You know, Garrett can't take back what he said. He means it."

"Yeah…"

"You risk the friendship no matter what. And if you move on with this other guy, I can't imagine that he will feel all that excited for you to spend a bunch of time with Garrett."

"So with that route, then, our friendship has to end."

"Not necessarily, but it'll be different, and I think you have to consider how that changes things for you—if your friendship has to be different, in what ways would you want it to be different? Yes, think ideal world, but also think realistic world, and think about your happiness. You don't have to make a decision that makes Garrett happy. You have to make the best decision for you. But I do want you to know that when he makes his decisions he always has you in mind."

"He does?" Maggie's eyes began to water.

"Did you know that he was offered a job in New York after he finished his master's?"

What? "No…he never told me that."

"He decided to take the Los Angeles job because that's where you were gonna be after law school. I think he was afraid to be too far away from you."

I'm afraid of that, too. "Wow. Thank you, Mrs. Bailey. I really appreciate you sharing that with me."

"Anytime, dear. And make sure you come out and visit sometime soon. It's been a long time."

"Yes, ma'am, I will."

At home, she took a long, hot shower, and though her dad had advised against it, she mulled over pros-and-cons lists for each of the guys. She wasn't quite sure where the value lay in all of her notations when she'd finished. "I guess Dad was right," she mumbled. Penny had been dozing by her side, but she looked up at Maggie for a moment before setting her head back down and falling asleep.

"Yeah, you're right. It's time for bed. I'll figure this out tomorrow."

24

MAGGIE CHANGED INTO SOME WORKOUT CLOTHES AND
sneakers and drove over to the Strand. She desperately wanted
stress relief, but she figured she would be safer walking the
beach than potentially having to face Blake in the gym. Instead of walking on the paved sidewalk, she decided to go
down the stairs and walk on the beach, so that if Blake were
home, he was less likely to spot her.

She stared out at the ocean as she walked, her shoes digging into the sand making her exert extra effort. She liked
the burn in her quads, nodding at the lifeguards on duty as
she passed the tower. Eventually, she decided to sit down in
the sand, which was warmed from the sun. She picked up a
handful of granules and squeezed them from one hand to the
other, thinking of a clock as the sand fell from between her
fingers. *Time is running out.* "What am I going to do?" she
whispered to herself, going back through the conversations

with her friends and family. The incident that happened between Garrett and Blake, and how both of the men carried themselves in that moment.

She thought about how Blake had grabbed her and how Garrett stepped between them to protect her. She thought about Blake's words in the moment, and how apologetic all of his texts had been. She pulled out her phone and began scrolling through the strings of messages she'd received after that night.

Blake: Maggie, I owe you an apology. I acted out of character, and that will never happen again.

Garrett: Mags, are you okay? I know that I should have come by last night, and I'm sorry that everything went down the way that it did. I know that I bumped into you when I got hit. Are you hurt? Please talk to me.

Blake: Did you go to sleep? Please call me when you get this.

Garrett: I'm up if you want to talk. If not, I'll check on you tomorrow. I hope you get some rest.

Blake: Hey, good morning. Think you'll have time to chat?

Garrett: Hi gorgeous. Checking on you. Are you okay? Anything I can do? I really am sorry for getting in the middle of things yesterday.

Garrett: I just want to apologize again. I know that I shouldn't have shown up at your brunch with the girls, but I just had to see you. I'll be here when you're ready to talk. Thanks again for your help with the practice sessions.

Blake: Hey, you busy?

Blake: We really should talk, Maggie.

Heaving a heavy sigh, she picked herself up off the sand and continued walking. Toward the end, she stopped and faced the ocean. The sun sparkled, kissing the waves, as a couple of dolphins poked their heads up for air before diving back under the surface of the dark water. Maggie smiled to herself.

Heading back in the direction of her car, she decided to detour to Blake's house, banking on the chance that he was home when he sent her that last text just a few hours ago. As she neared, she spotted him on the patio and waved a hand in his direction. He stood abruptly, moving toward the gate to let her in. "I didn't expect you to show up," he laughed awkwardly.

"Hey, Blake," Maggie said meekly, giving him a quick hug. "I'm glad that you're here."

"Well, you know I wanted to make sure that we had a chance to talk and I know it took me a bit to think things over and I haven't been responsive, but I just needed some space from the situation to really be able to think about it."

He gestured to a couple of patio chairs facing the water. "No, I understand, and I apologize. I really acted out of character and I want you to know that that's something that I'm working on."

"It is?"

"Yeah, I'm always considering ways I can improve. I try my hardest and I work out as hard as I do to be disciplined. But there are moments where I maybe say the wrong thing and this time I just let my temper get the better of me, and I should have greater control over that."

"Wow, I'm really glad to hear that you're that self-aware. Thank you for acknowledging that."

He nodded. "So is your friend okay? I really am sorry about that and if you could communicate to him that I apologize."

Maggie tilted her head. "Normally, I would probably just make you apologize yourself," she laughed.

He hung his head. "So I guess that means this is it?"

She nodded slowly. "Listen, you're an amazing guy. In a lot of ways you are the guy that so many of my friends would dream for—you have a beautiful home, a beautiful life, you're smart, you're successful, you're sexy. Whomever it is that you choose to be with will really be lucky to have you."

"But you don't want to be the one that I choose," he deduced quietly, his eyes fixed on her.

She looked at the water wistfully. "If someone didn't already have my heart, I absolutely would want to be in consideration. You're such a good guy and you treated me so well. I was very spoiled, and you were damn near perfect," she laughed. "Keep working on you, and I think the right one will find you."

He nodded. "So it's not *that* moment that made the choice for you?" He looked relieved.

Maggie bit her lip and shook her head. "No, I think this choice was made years ago and I just didn't realize that I'd made it. I've just been running scared for a long time."

"So you two go way back?"

"He's been my best friend for almost twenty years."

Blake exhaled, whistling through his teeth. "There's no competing with that."

She shook her head slowly. "No hard feelings?"

"None whatsoever. Well then, I guess I'll see you at the gym." He stood to hug her.

"Yeah, definitely. You take care." She squeezed him tightly before turning to leave.

"Yeah, you, too, and hey, if the status quo changes…"

"Oh, I will be at your front door," she laughed.

He grinned, nodding as he used two fingers to salute and turned toward his house.

Maggie crossed the street and sat down on the bench where they'd had hot chocolate on her first day and watched the sun set.

"You know." A voice behind her startled her. It was Savvy and she had Teddy, her chocolate Lab, on a leash. "People say that when the last little bit of the sun dips below the horizon that there's a green flash of light. Have you seen that before?" Savvy asked as she sat next to Maggie.

"I should have known you'd show up."

Savvy held out her open palm and Maggie put her hand in her friend's. "I'm always going to show up, and I think that that's why you made the choice that you made, because you know he will, too."

"Always." Maggie nodded. "Doesn't make this feel any better, though."

"I know it."

Teddy rested his chin on Maggie's knee and she stroked his ears as she leaned her head onto Savvy's shoulder. "You're the best."

The next day, Savvy's name and face appeared on Maggie's phone. "Hey, girl, what's up? I'm just about to head to the office."

"Girl, I need you to turn on the television," she urged.

"Why? What's going on? What channel?"

"ESPN. Hurry!" Savvy nagged.

"Okay! Gimme a sec. Oh, my God, is that…is that Garrett?"

"Yeah."

There he was in his full suit, but he had dark circles under his eyes, his hair was a little longer than it usually was and his beard wasn't as well-groomed as it normally was. Maggie's mouth dropped open.

"He looks kind of tired and mad nervous," Savvy said.

The back of his chair was moving. *His leg must be bouncing like crazy.*

"Yeah, he does." If Maggie were being her usual, blunt self, she'd say he looked haggard.

"He looks miserable," Savvy said.

As he was speaking to the other correspondents, he sounded tired and distracted, and almost a little shaky. All Maggie could do was think about how long he had dreamed of this moment, and how she did not want to be related to the reason why he fucked up his chance. *I've gotta fix this.*

"Savvy, I'm gonna have to call you back." Maggie hung up the phone and dialed a number that she didn't often call. "Kenny, hi, it's Maggie."

"Well, hey, Mags. I haven't talked to you in a while. How you been?" Kenny's easy smile carried in his voice.

"I know, I know," she laughed awkwardly. *I hate small talk.* "I'm good! Listen, I just wanted to reach out—"

"You see our boy on TV?"

"Yeah, I see him," she laughed nervously.

"He looks like hell, don't he?"

Fuck, everyone is noticing. "That's kind of my fault…"

"Well, I can't imagine what you did to make him look like that, but maybe I don't want to know," he chuckled. "And he's got two more segments to do today. They asked him to go live for Q and A twice, so he's there all day. They even added some extra slots for him over the weekend. He gon' have to do better than this if he's gonna get to keep 'em."

"Oh, no," she groaned. "So, listen, I need your help. I want to… I need to talk to you."

"Okay, okay. It sounds like maybe we should meet up. Do you want to grab some coffee?"

"Yeah, that would be great. Do you have time today?"

"Sure. You still work in the same building?"

"Yeah, I'm headed there now."

"Okay, how about we meet at the café next door at eight thirty?"

"That's perfect. I'm on my way."

"Okay, bet I'll see you there."

25

THE ESPN STUDIO WAS NOTHING LIKE WHAT MAGGIE expected—everything was out in the open. There were glass windows that allowed people to look in. Someone was standing in front of a green screen, giving a report. She didn't see Garrett, but Kenny confirmed he was inside.

Kenny had arranged for her to visit the studio with a special access pass.

She stood by the wall trying to make herself as invisible as possible, not knowing where he was going to come from. Her heartbeat thumped rapidly in her chest, threatening to burst through. She tried to stabilize her breath.

"Excuse me, can I help you?" a woman called out to her from behind a reception desk.

"Oh, hi, thank you. I'm here for one of your correspondents. Garrett Bailey." Maggie stepped forward slightly. She hadn't intended to come to the studio that day, but Kenny couldn't get the pass for the weekend segments, so after they met, she'd rushed from a court hearing to the studio in her dress suit. And she had changed out of her heels into flip-flops because her feet were hurting. To make matters worse, her curls had chosen not to cooperate and were out of control. She pulled her hair back into a ponytail puff and tried to smooth her edges, but she knew she looked a mess.

"He should be right out," the woman called to her.

"Okay, no worries and no rush. Thank you," Maggie responded.

"Is he expecting you?"

Maggie shook her head slowly.

The woman winked at her, understanding. "He's just recording a voice segment for this weekend in one of our studio rooms. He's almost finished."

"Ah, thank you."

She stood in front of the green screen with her hands folded in front of her. *What to say…what to say.* She hadn't rehearsed anything on the ride over—she had been singularly focused on driving at the speed of light.

"Hey, Sylvia, um, I might need to do that last bit over again. I'm not sure that I pronounced those names clearly enough. Can you let me know if—"

"Garrett." Maggie waved nervously.

"No problem, Garrett. I'll check the tape and let you know."

"Thanks." He stepped toward Maggie, his eyes searching her face. "What are you doing here? Are you okay?"

"Kenny got me access so that I could come and see you."

"But why here? I could have come to you. It's literally the busiest week of your year."

True. The week of Tax Day felt like the Olympics. "I know, I know, but I just didn't want to wait, and you know you've been so patient with me the last few days." She looked down at her hands. "And then I saw you on TV, and I just had to see you."

His frown lines melted. "Okay, so...so you want to talk now?"

She nodded. "Is that okay?"

"Yeah, sure." He stepped closer to her, blinking as if he were processing.

"I just need to say this, okay?"

"Say what you need to say." He looked like he was bracing himself for the worst.

"Listen, I know that I have had a lot of worries about what we should or shouldn't do because of our friendship, but over the last few days I learned things about the both of us that I didn't know previously."

"Oh? Like what?" He scrutinized her face.

"Why didn't you tell me that you had a job offer in New York when we got out of school?"

It was his turn to look down at the floor. "I didn't feel the need to stress you right before the bar, and I already knew what I was going to do."

"But you wanted that job."

"Yeah, but I wanted to be near you more and so it was an easy choice. There wasn't anything for me to think about, really, and I've been happy here."

Maggie exhaled deeply. "Is it true that you had feelings for me before our kiss in college?"

"You must have talked to Mom." Garrett's lips turned upward in a half smile.

The corners of Maggie's mouth twitched but she held back a smile.

"Okay, Mags, now I officially have no secrets from you," he said. "What do you want to do? You lead, I'll follow."

"You don't really mean that." Maggie shook her head.

He frowned. "What do you mean?"

"You can't possibly always want to follow my lead. What do you want, G?"

"Well, sure, if I can have it my way, I don't just want to be with you. I want you to feel the same way I do."

She stepped closer to him, his eyes widening. "Well," she replied softly, "I do."

"You do?"

She nodded. "And have for some time. I just… Somehow I missed the signs." She shrugged. "I think we've been in a relationship this whole time and I just didn't see it. You are the highlight of my week, of my day. You're the voice that I hear when I know I should be doing something and I'm not—you'd tell me to go out and reach my full potential. But you're also the voice that I hear cheering me on when I do something great. Like every time I win a case…" She looked down and reached into her purse.

"I had gotten these, and you and I had talked about the possibility of someone else being in that seat, but this ticket is yours. Our seats are together, and I don't want to travel with anyone else by my side but you." She held up their plane tickets to Thailand.

Garrett looked down, reaching for Maggie's hands so that he could hold them in his own. "So what are you saying, Mags?" His lips pressed together into a boyish smile.

"I'm saying that I want to be with you. I'm saying that I want you to be my date to the weddings. I'm also saying that I love you and have loved you, and if you're down, then I'm sayin' we go together heavy."

Garrett's mouth twitched and then widened into a broad smile. "You're for real right now?"

"For real, for real."

"Well, come here, girl. You know I already told you all of that weeks ago." He pulled her close, wrapping his arms around her shoulders, kissing her cheek, her forehead and finding her lips. "Nineteen-plus years, Maggie. I have waited over nineteen years for you to tell me that you *love me* love me," he whispered in her ear.

"They say patience is a virtue," she responded, her face buried in his chest.

He chuckled. "Well, I'm no saint, but when it comes to you, I would have been willing to wait even longer. I'm glad I don't have to, though."

She lifted her face to kiss him. "No, you sure don't."

26

MAGGIE SAT AT THE BAR FOR HAPPY HOUR TEXTING THE girls on the group thread, each of them out for date night. As she sipped her martini she observed others greeting each other and finding their dates among all of the singles. Tax Day was finally behind them, and she'd made it to the end of the week. The first part of the day, she'd run errands and cleaned house, and now Maggie felt like celebrating doing her favorite pastime: people watching.

Maggie: Y'all, you're not going to believe what I just saw!

Joanie: Ooh what??

Maggie: So I am at the bar now, and across the room, I saw this woman on a date with a guy. They walked out to the valet stand, and his car came first. After he drove off, she came back inside and some other dude goes and buys her a drink. She left with the second dude!

Savvy: SCANDALOUS

Out of the corner of Maggie's eye, someone drew near. "Excuse me, miss. I couldn't help but notice you here, glowing. Would it be okay if I offered to buy you a drink?"

Maggie turned and smiled. "Thank you, but—"

"But her date just arrived. Sorry, man." Garrett slid in behind her and kissed her shoulder, one of his arms wrapping around her, his fingers intertwining with hers.

"That's you, man?"

"Yessir."

He looks so proud. Maggie smiled brightly.

He gave Garrett a pound and walked away. "Respect."

"Would you like another martini?"

Maggie shook her head. "We should get the check."

"Yeah? What are you thinkin'?"

"Well, you just look so good today. I think—" she looked up toward the ceiling before playfully batting her lashes at him "—that we should order some takeout and have a Saturday date at home."

"So the usual, then?" He smiled wryly.

"I think we're creatures of habit."

He tilted his head. "You think that's why this has worked as long as it has?" He dipped to kiss her lips. Once, twice. "I think you're right. Do you know what you wanna eat?"

"No, but you always do."

They ordered rice plates from a local Hawaiian restaurant along with fruit tea and a couple of pieces of Spam musubi, because Maggie was obsessed. Back at Maggie's condo, they set up on the coffee table per usual. Penny tried to snuggle against

Garrett, peddling for attention as he attempted to make plates. "Come on, Penny. Relax." He playfully swatted at her to get her to stop sticking her nose into the bags of food.

"She's been so attached to you now that you're around so much more," Maggie observed, relaxing on the couch, folding her legs underneath her and propping an elbow on the back of the sofa to gaze at him. "She really likes having you around."

"Yeah, I like it, too." He scratched Penny's neck and then moved to wash his hands so he could finish putting plates together.

"Well, have you thought at all about consolidating?" Maggie eyed him.

He froze. "Like move in?"

"Yeah, or we can find another place if you want."

"But you love this building!" He rested his hands on the counter.

"Yeah, but would this be big enough for both of us?"

"I don't see why not. You have that home office that you barely use. Would you be okay with me using it?"

"Of course." She shrugged.

"And some space in the closet for my clothes?"

"Okay, see…this is where we might have some issues." She held up a finger and he rounded the kitchen island.

"You know what?" He wrapped his arms around her waist and pulled her to him. She stepped into his embrace, resting the side of her face against his heartbeat. "You betta give me some closet space, girl," he teased, nuzzling her neck until she cackled.

She kissed him, wrapping her arms around his neck. "Okay, I'll give you space. This will be *our* space."

"You're really sure about this?" He pulled back enough to look her in the eye.

"Yeah. Why go home when you'd rather stay here anyway?"

She grinned ruefully. "I know it's tough whenever you have to be away from me."

He rolled his eyes, smiling. "I mean, I guess that's true. It's torturous to be away."

"Besides, you're paying rent. We could save money and use it to travel or eventually get a bigger place..."

"Wow, we're really adulting now... We 'bout to be shackin' up." He nodded. "Yeah, let's do this."

They kissed again and the food was growing cold on the counter. Garrett steered Maggie backward into their bedroom. "Well, Ms. Jones, I know that I definitely have an appetite, but right now I'm craving you," he whispered against her lips and kissed her shoulder. "Why don't you let me help you out of this?"

She turned around so that he could unzip her dress. He kissed down her spine as he dragged the zipper downward vertebra by vertebra, making her shiver. Once she had stepped out of the garment and turned to him, he held her face in his hands and kissed her again, running his tongue on the inside of her lips before tilting her head for more access. "Hey, gorgeous." He massaged the back of her neck, kissing the tip of her nose and her forehead.

"What do you think about a shower?" she whispered.

"That sounds nice..."

"Mmm-hmm." She nodded, biting her lip as she pulled his hand toward the bathroom. She turned on the water and the jets blasted in the showerhead. "Now, you come here," she demanded, removing his tie and unbuttoning his shirt. "I really like when you dress up like this."

"Really?"

"Mmm-hmm. It's very sexy."

"Well, maybe I should dress like this more often."

"Maybe you should." She looked up at him.

"You look at me like that, and I'd do just about anything."

"I'll keep that in mind," she chuckled. They finished undressing each other, and she nudged him into the shower. "Get in there!"

"Ah!" The spray barely skimmed his skin and he jumped back toward her. "What the— Do you shower in boiling water?!" he exclaimed as Maggie burst out laughing and turned more of the cool water on.

"I like to feel clean!"

"Yeah, by burning off a layer of skin?" He rubbed his arm and then tested the water with his hand before stepping in.

"I'm sorry. I didn't realize you were so sensitive," she teased.

"Ha ha, very funny. Come here, you." As the water ran down their skin, Garrett's hands roamed Maggie's body.

"So beautiful." He dipped his head to kiss her mouth before trailing butterfly kisses along her jawline to her throat, and as he reached her shoulder, he turned her around, pressing himself against her back, his hands cupping her breasts, capturing her peaks between his fingers.

"You're so tall," Maggie murmured, his erection nudging her lower back.

"Yeah, but you have this bench here." He sat down, widening his legs so that she could sit on his lap.

He guided her backward, edging her legs apart and splitting her folds with his fingers as she gasped. Holding his thick erection in one hand, he grabbed her hip, lowering her slowly until his tip met the warmth of her entrance, gliding into her until her ass landed on his lap.

Maggie rested her hands on Garrett's thighs as she sank onto him, gasping at the pressure. "Oh, my God."

"Just right, my good girl," he whispered in her ear.

She whimpered, nodding as she rocked back and forth, her nails digging into his flesh. She kept moving as he massaged her breasts, squeezing them gently before rubbing her nipples between his fingers. Maggie threw her head back against his shoulder as she began to pick up speed, her back arching.

Garrett kept one hand on her breast and brought the other between her legs.

"Yes, play with it," she purred. "You always know what to do."

Garrett kissed the space between her shoulder blades and she curled her back toward his mouth. As his fingers grazed her clit, he began to apply more pressure in a swift, circular motion.

"Just like that." She nodded, moaning and picking up speed as his fingers began moving faster over the sensitive flesh. "So fucking good." Her ass clapped against him, and he moaned as she rotated her hips.

"Yes, good girl. Come for me," he murmured in her ear. His hand continued to apply pulsating pressure to her delicate mound.

Maggie's eyes closed and lights flashed behind her darkened eyelids, and she cried out. Her head rolled back as she rode out the waves.

After her last spasm, Garrett moved his hands to Maggie's hips, guiding himself into her with more force, their bodies pounding together as droplets of water splashed from the impact. "Oh, I'm close." CLAP. CLAP. CLAP. He lifted his pelvis to meet her as he pulled her down, pounding into her. He moaned as she threw it back on him, pumping into her as hard as he could.

Maggie adjusted her hands on his thighs and held him tight. "Yes, yes," she gasped.

Garrett's breath became erratic, his body clenching before his release. "Oh, Maggie," he breathed. He took control of the momentum, allowing her pussy to slowly devour his shaft. He wrapped his arms around her tightly, one hand moving upward to her throat. As he gripped her lightly, he pulled her back to him, kissing her shoulder blades and the nape of her neck.

"That," Maggie said, standing, "was an excellent appetizer." She smiled, leaning forward to rest her hands on Garrett's thighs to kiss him gently as the water dampened her hair. She pulled him to his feet and began lathering his skin with bodywash and a loofah, the scents of botanicals wafting up in the steam.

"Mmm, I like this." He smiled.

"Yeah?"

"Makes me feel like royalty. We gotta try the bathtub next."

Maggie giggled. "I can't give you the *Coming to America* experience, if that's what you're picturing. Not in *that* tub."

"You know that's what I was thinking." His grin widened.

"Well, I can take care of your royal penis for you, though," she said with a glint in her eye.

"Give me a few minutes, and I'll take you up on that." He took the loofah from her, rubbing it against her back as he kissed her.

"I can't believe it took us this long to get to this place." She nuzzled her face into his neck.

"I blame you."

"Ah!" she exclaimed, smacking his damp skin playfully. "Honestly, I blame me, too."

"Nah, there's no blame here." His finger traced her jaw as he lifted her gaze to meet his. "Nobody can tell you that you're ready. You just have to be ready. And besides, you were worth the wait." His mouth closed on hers as the steam enveloped them.

27

Months later…

THE SPRINTER VAN LURCHED, MOVING QUICKLY OVER
the roads to their destination, the traffic congestion chaotic with
the morning bustle. Maggie was hunched forward, her head near
her knees. "Oh, my God, what was I thinking?" she groaned.

Garrett chuckled, rubbing his hand across her back.

Savvy, being pregnant, had won the right to call shotgun
over anyone else. She turned back carefully to look at her
friend, one hand resting on her stomach as the other gripped
a handrail. "You okay back there, Maggie?"

"No," she croaked.

"You look like you're gonna turn green. Well, figuratively
speaking, anyway."

Maggie flipped her off as the sounds of snickering surrounded them. "The things I do for my friends," she muttered.

"Would you at least tell us where we're going?" Joanie reached forward from the back row to rest a hand on Maggie's arm.

"How does that help me?" Maggie squeezed her eyes shut, gripping one hand on Garrett's leg.

"Do you need a bag to throw up in?"

"Respectfully, sis. Shut. Up." She pivoted slightly to the side, resting her cheek on Garrett's leg.

Beth, on the other side of the narrow aisle from Mags, patted her thigh. "Sometimes, for me, when I get a bout of motion sickness, my best defense is trying to get myself to sleep through it. On flights and trains, I can be out before we start moving. Why don't you stretch out? You can recline the seat and try to get more comfortable."

Maggie nodded, leaning back into the chair, her head against the headrest. "Phuket isn't a huge place. We should be there soon."

"Is that true?" Savvy turned to their driver, who smiled brightly.

"Yes, ma'am. We should arrive in another thirty minutes."

Savvy turned to peer back at her friend. Maggie squinted her eyes open slightly before squeezing them back shut. "Guess it's a good thing we left before breakfast."

"Please don't even think about discussing food. I will throw myself into oncoming traffic," Maggie groaned.

"It's gonna be okay, bae. We're almost there." Garrett's hushed tone was soothing as he kneaded his thumb into her shoulder. He reclined his seat next to her and ran his hands over her hair, which she had braided for the trip. Her long box braids were dark at the roots and a honey blond toward the tips, which reached the small of her back. "Just try to rest," he murmured, pressing his lips against her temple.

She nodded, focusing on his hands moving through her

hair. She drifted off to sleep, and the next thing she knew, the van had stopped. "Please tell me we're there," she squeaked.

Savvy threw up her hands. "But *where* is 'there'?"

The driver ambled out of the van and came around to the other side, opening Savvy's door and helping her out before sliding open the large door for all of the back passengers. "We are just outside of Rassada Pier Terminal. I will grab a cart for your belongings, and we can make our way to your guide."

Spencer wrapped an arm around Savvy, his hand palming her belly. "Are we going on a tour?"

Maggie smiled cryptically, lifting her hands. "Sort of?"

"Mags, come on," Joan whined. "We're already here. What are we doing? For this bachelor/bachelorette?"

The driver came around with a cart loaded with totes and backpacks. Maggie had instructed everyone to bring a bathing suit, an all-white outfit, sunblock and any toiletries they might need for a full-day excursion. "Right this way."

The group trailed behind the cart through the terminal, exiting to a breezeway along a massive pier with speedboats, catamarans, yachts and sailboats lined up for people to board. "Whoa." Joanie's mouth dropped open. "You chartered an entire boat and didn't tell us?"

Maggie's eyes sparkled, her fingers intertwining with Garrett's. "A yacht, actually. One with a very strong stabilizer, thank God. We're headed to Phi Phi Island, and on board, we have a chef and a couple of massage therapists so that each couple gets their own couples massage experience in one of the lower cabins. Once we get to the island, there's kayaking and paddleboarding, a sunset meal and a full bar."

"Maggie! I've never even been on a yacht before," Savvy gushed. "How did you pull this off?"

She shrugged. "I have my methods."

"This way!" their driver called. At the end of the pier, an

eighty-foot yacht was docked, with several crew members waiting to greet them.

"That's the *Phoenix*." Maggie pointed, turning to look at her friends as their collective jaws hit the pavement.

Once they reached the crew, the captain introduced himself and the others, and they helped everyone on board after they all removed their shoes. The main deck gleamed, and the captain gave them a quick tour to familiarize them with the different cabins, the galley and the toilet facilities. One cabin had been set up for the couples massages, while another was a changing quarters. There was one with several bunks in case anyone wanted to rest their eyes. The galley was brightly lit, and glasses of champagne were poured as everyone nibbled on trays of fresh fruit. The chef took omelet orders and everyone made their way back up to the main deck, which was sectioned into a large dining area, comfy couches and lounge chairs facing the bow.

"We'll be underway momentarily, so if you all would like to get comfortable, I believe the chef will bring your breakfast to you here." Captain Chai Son gestured to the table.

"Thank you." Maggie nodded, grabbing a seat.

"Are you gonna be okay on the water?" Beth eyed her carefully.

"I'm actually better in open-air situations. Plus, I think it's more the jolting and jerking that bothers me more than the waves. Should be okay." Just then, the yacht pulled away from the dock, and everyone turned to look at her. "I'm fine, I promise!"

The chef began to bring out dishes, assisted by a couple of other crew members. Soon the table was packed with omelets over rice, skewers of grilled pork, and bowls of jok—thick rice porridge topped with minced pork and other proteins, a soft egg, scallions, ginger and cilantro. Another tray of fresh mango, papaya, lychee, dragon fruit and pineapple was set in the center of the table along with lettuce leaves and dipping sauces to accompany the other dishes.

The table was quiet aside from the occasional crunch, everyone digging into the food. Maggie dived into the jok, seasoning hers heavily with white pepper, fried garlic and onions and some dark soy sauce. The silky texture made her dance in her seat, her mouth watering as the bright orange egg yolk broke and spread over the other contents of the bowl. "I think this might be my favorite dish so far in Thailand." She shoveled another scoop into her mouth, the unctuous yolk adding another layer of richness to the porridge. Lost in the moment, she let a soft moan escape her lips as her head fell back.

"Uh, Mags, should we leave you alone with the jok?" Savvy pulled the seasoned pork off a skewer with a piece of lettuce and dipped it into a spicy sweet fish sauce before popping it into her mouth. She gave a thumbs-up to the chef, who peeked out to check on them. "The moo ping is exceptional!"

The chef beamed and pressed his hands together before retreating to the galley. After finishing their meal, Savvy and Spencer followed crew members to have their couples massage below deck, and the others changed into swimwear and lounged in the sunshine.

Maggie had donned a pair of aviator sunglasses and a hot-pink bikini, a sheer sarong wrapped around her waist.

Garrett kissed her shoulder. "I don't think I saw this suit before." He tugged playfully on one of the strings, which she'd knotted to keep the girls in place.

Maggie grinned at him over her shoulder. "You like?"

His arms wound around her as he pulled her close. "I love."

They soaked in the sunlight, laughing and joking while Joan and Beth napped in their chairs, the balmy air sweeping over them as they neared the island. Once they dropped an-

chor, Savvy and Spencer emerged from their massages looking serene—Savvy's hair was tousled and fragrant.

Beth and Joan went for their massages while the rest of them
jumped into the water and swam to a small beach. The crew
paddled over in a kayak with snacks and towels to sit on. Garrett
attempted to paddleboard, losing his balance each time he tried
to stand, Maggie taking joy in watching his legs wobble until he
landed back in the water again. "You know, I'd like to see you
try this," he called.

"Nah, I'm good." She waved.

Next to her, Savvy nudged her with her shoulder as she
sipped a cocktail from a hollowed-out coconut shell. "You did
good, Mags. You happy?"

She nodded. "Very. I'm not sure what I did to deserve it."
She shrugged. "What do you think of your bachelorette party?"

They turned to see Spencer in one of the kayaks playing
turkey with Garrett, who had resigned to sit straddling the
board. "It's perfect. I couldn't have asked for anything better."

"Good. Make sure to keep that same energy when it's my
turn."

Savvy sucked her teeth and glared at her friend. "You know
what? Let me remind you that Karma is waiting for your ass
in that Sprinter van. We still have to get back to the hotel,
you know."

Maggie's face clouded over, having completely forgotten the
return ride. "Fuck," she complained, drawing out the word
as she kicked her foot in the warm sand.

Savvy shook her head and stared out at the bright blue
water. "Do better," she tsked.

"You right."

"Maggie, will you put yourself together?"

"I'm sorry," she sobbed. "I'm just happy for my friend. Are
you really mad at me right now?"

"I'm not mad at you but you need to turn off the waterworks—you just had your makeup done," Savvy chided her.

"Okay, Mama Savs, I need you to chill."

"Mama Savs." Joan cracked a smile. She and Beth had chosen to have a joint preparation room where everyone in the bridal party got ready together, though a slight divider wall kept them from seeing each other until the ceremony.

Joan decided to wear a white linen suit, her fresh twist-out curls were coiffed into an updo, and an orchid was pinned on her lapel.

"You look great, Joanie." Maggie kissed her friend's cheek, rubbing any residual lipstick off with her thumb.

Savvy sat in a comfy armchair, her hand rubbing on her growing belly.

"Savs, you are glowing. You look so beautiful, mama!" Beth exclaimed from her side of the partition. She glowed, looking happier than ever.

"Come on now, sis." Savvy waved. Beth's wedding dress was a simple but breathtaking backless white gown with thin straps and a low-cut bodice in the front. The hem kissed the floor and a cathedral train pooled behind her. Atop her pixie cut, she wore a white fascinator headband with a magnolia to one side and just enough netting to cover half of her face like a veil. Her dark brown skin shone with the perfect amount of highlighter and a crimson lip. "You are a vision," Savvy said from her seat. "I'm sorry I can't be of more assistance right now, but the tiny human is dancing all over my bladder and I'm gonna have to pee again. Baby Morgan can't seem to stop jumping around."

"Go calm the baby." Joanie jutted her chin toward Savvy.

Maggie had become the baby whisperer. "Hi, baby. This is TiTi Mags, and I'm gonna need you to relax for a little while, 'cause I'm gonna need your mama to stand in this wedding without needing to pee. Yes, I do," she cooed.

Savvy scrunched up her face for a moment and then re-laxed. "I don't know how you do it, but it's like she knows to reposition herself and take a seat."

Maggie brought her face closer to Savvy's belly, speaking in full-on baby talk. "Because she knows that TiTi Mags don't play. That's right! That's my good girl!"

"Ugh." Savvy rolled her eyes. "Please don't talk like that to my child."

"That's right," Maggie continued, ignoring her friend. "You're gonna come out smart like your TiTi Mags. That's right."

Savvy and Joan exchanged a wide-eyed glance, which Maggie ignored.

"Hey, y'all," Garrett called from the door, in a tan linen suit. "They just sent me to let you know that everything is all set up and we're ready for you out here, Joan."

"Okay." Joan blew kisses to Savvy and Mags and stepped closer to the partition. "I'll see you soon, babe. Close your eyes until I get outside."

"Okay! I love you."

"Love you."

Maggie stepped to the other side of the wall. "Jesus Christ, who could pull off that dress but you, B? Joan is a lucky, lucky lady."

"Okay, we should line up." Beth and Maggie stepped to either side of Savvy to help her up. Her bump had grown enough to show, but she was still safely within the travel win-dow. "I am so happy that we are on a beautiful island enjoying each other's company, but I have to admit that I will be really excited to go home." Savvy grinned, picking up her bouquet.

Music started and an acoustic version of Tamia and Eric Benét's "Spend My Life with You" began to play.

"That's my cue." Savvy grinned. Maggie pushed open the

door slowly, and Savvy began the processional toward the altar with her uncle Joe as Beth's dad stepped into the room.

"My baby, you are stunning." He kissed Beth's cheek.

Maggie grinned as she stepped out, clutching her bouquet. Ahead of her, she could see Spencer's reaction to Savvy's procession. Maggie followed slowly, smiling at Garrett in the second row as she walked solo. As she reached the altar, she plopped a kiss on Joan's cheek and stepped aside for the second bride, the rings in the pocket of her dress.

The music changed and John Legend's "All of Me" began to play. Beth and her father stepped out of the building, her clutching her dad's arm, and Joan's mouth immediately went slack. Her eyes welled up as her soon-to-be wife and father-in-law proceeded toward her. Maggie reached into her pocket and handed Joan a tissue.

When Beth reached her space across from Joan, Joan and Beth's dad embraced. "Proud of you, kiddo."

"Thank you, sir." Joan held out her hands to Beth, who placed hers on top, as they stood before their friends, making vows to be together forever. Maggie stood to the side of the two couples, distributing rings to both when the time came.

After the ceremony, the couples jumped a broom as they made the processional back toward the dance floor. Before the music was in full swing, Maggie stood by the DJ, who handed her a microphone. "Excuse me, everyone, may I have your attention?"

The family turned toward her, and Maggie waved. "It's me again."

The crowd laughed.

"As you know, I am the very lucky best friend to two of our brides, and first I just want to thank you all for being here and for showing these couples so much love. I have had the pleasure of knowing both of these ladies for most of my life, and my world wouldn't be the same without either of them.

"Spencer, I am so thrilled that I forced your wife onto a dating app and that you two matched on there. Soon after that, you had your first date, and the rest is history. I'd like to take credit for bringing the two of you together."

Savvy began to open her mouth.

"And, yes, I recognize that the two of you met before I forced you onto the app, but you didn't agree to a date until after you matched." She brought the mic closer to her mouth. "Check. Mate."

The crowd erupted with laughter.

"Similarly, Joanie, while I wasn't there when you initially met Beth, I was absolutely present the day that Beth asked you on a date, and——" she gestured "——because Savvy's so modest, I take full credit for encouraging you to go out with her."

"Of course you do." Joanie grinned.

"As a result, Savvy, Joanie, Beth——any firstborn children should be named after me. Obviously, daughters should be named Magnolia, Maggie for short. There's only one Mags, of course." She pointed to herself. "For sons, it's a little old-school, but Magnus will do."

Savvy's look of horror made the crowd laugh even harder. She shook her index finger in response.

"It's okay, I know you'll need a moment to warm up to it, but at the end of the day, you'll remember how thankful you are that I helped you both find your soulmates, and then you'll name your babies after me. A win is a win. Am I right?" She nodded into the crowd. The tittering began to fade. "On a serious note, Savs, Joan, you are my rocks. Your love and belief in me has carried me to heights I wasn't sure that I could reach, and blood couldn't strengthen our sisterhood. I am honored that I was allowed to stand with you both on your special days, and I hope that, one day, you'll do the same for me.

"Before we raise our glasses to toast our happy couples, I have a special request from the mother of one of the brides."

Savvy and Joan looked at each other and then back at Maggie.

"A few months back I received a call from Mama June, asking if I could help her with something special." Hotel staff members began to pass out paper lanterns to each person along with a pen. "These are *khom loi*, or *sky lanterns*. They're made out of rice paper, so yes, eco-friendly, and I'd like to ask that each person write a wish, a message or a prayer for our lovely couples before we light them and release them toward the heavens."

Savvy clutched a hand to her chest, as she reached her other hand out to squeeze her mom. Ms. June patted Savvy's belly before accepting her own lantern.

A few moments later, after everyone wrote out their messages and well wishes, bridal party included, staff members walked around with small torches to light the lanterns.

"Now remember, everyone, you should watch your lanterns ascend until it disappears." She nodded to the staff to begin lighting them. The lightweight lanterns were large but extremely light. Maggie held hers up and a woman lit the bottom. Maggie raised hers higher, watching it float into the air as she released it. She watched the lanterns rise, mesmerized by the number of them lighting the night sky. As hers disappeared from view, Maggie closed her eyes and wished.

The lanterns moved through the sky, circling almost like a school of fish until they funneled out of sight. The hotel staff returned with trays of champagne flutes.

"To Savvy and Spencer, to Joan and Beth, may your unions be built on the strongest foundations, may they endure, may they grow and may you continue to learn and love one another from each day forward. May you be slow to anger and quick to forgive. May you find your way to each other in this life and the next. I love you all. To the happy couples!" Maggie raised her glass high.

"To the happy couples!"

The DJ started the music, and everyone made their way to the dance floor.

As Maggie followed, she grabbed Garrett's hand so that he could walk with her. On the dance floor, the DJ played every group dance song and traditional Black wedding song they could think of, including the Electric Slide, the Wobble and the Cupid Shuffle. Garrett couldn't find the beat, and Maggie had forgotten half of the steps, but it didn't matter.

Maggie, Joan and Savvy came together at the center of the dance floor and grasped each other's hands, forming a circle. They laughed and body rolled to the photographer's delight, as Maggie gushed, "I am so happy right now. This moment is absolutely everything, and I love y'all so damn much! Everything I've wanted is here right now."

"Maybe not everything." Savvy smiled mysteriously.

"No, everything's here!" Maggie assured her.

"Everything's here, but maybe it's not quite as it should be," Joan replied. She tilted her head, gesturing for Maggie to turn around, and as she did, she found Garrett on one knee. The music faded as she stepped toward him, her mouth agape at the sight.

"Maggie, you are my dream," he said simply. He looked around them at the family and friends circling the dance floor. "When you were in law school and I was in grad school, we walked past this old jewelry store and you pointed to a ring that you thought was beautiful. You said something like 'when I get married, my husband will pick out a ring just like that,' and what you didn't know was—" he pulled a box out of his pocket "—I bought that ring the very next day. Magnolia Felize Jones, I have loved you every day since I met you and I will love you until my final breath. Would you do me the honor of being my wife?"

Maggie burst into tears. She nodded her head because she couldn't get words to come out. Garrett slid the ring onto her finger as she proceeded to ugly cry. "No one better take a picture of me like this," she threatened.

A photographic flash burst in her face in that moment, and she whirled around to see Savvy holding the camera. "It's not like you're gonna hurt a pregnant lady." She smiled. "Besides, I can still take you."

Maggie threw her head back and laughed, wiping the tears from her cheeks as she turned and kissed Garrett. "Yes," she finally said. Then she turned to her friends and threw her arms around them. "Did y'all know?"

"When are you gonna realize that we always know?"

A slow dance began to play, and couples held hands, two-stepping on the dance floor. Maggie wrapped her arms around Garrett's neck. "You know, I just remembered something."

Garrett ran his fingers over her bare shoulders, sending a delicious shiver down her spine. "Yeah? What's that?"

"You know, it's been months now and I still haven't deleted my dating profile. I should do that when we get home." She looked up into his dark brown eyes.

He shrugged. "I'm not that worried."

"No?"

He pressed her hand against his heart and pulled her close. "Not at all. Besides, all the good ones are taken anyway." He smiled at her, planting a kiss on her lips as they danced the night away.

★ ★ ★ ★ ★

ACKNOWLEDGMENTS

First, last and always, Father God, I thank You for another day and another opportunity to connect with others through love and joy.

To Jemiscoe Chambers-Black, my agent extraordinaire, I couldn't be more grateful for you. I appreciate and value your insights, your encouragement, your friendship. Jem, thank you for your friendship and for being my greatest champion. To film agents Debbie and Alec and foreign rights agent Taryn, thank you for your enthusiasm and for believing in my projects. To everyone at Andrea Brown Literary, I am so grateful for a powerhouse squad!

To my editor, April Osborn, thank you so much for loving Savvy enough to allow space for Maggie. To the team at MIRA, thank you for supporting my dream!

To Noa Denmon, your artistry inspires me, and no one else could do Maggie justice.

To my family: Mom and Pop, thank you for cheering me

on, for reading scenes that I'm sure made you uncomfortable and for being okay with me not killing off a character on page (yet). To Uncle Stuart, thank you for always being there. To Uncle Kirk, Kira, Jess, Mykel, Grett, Yvette, Ariana, the Mc-Coys, the Welches, the Adamses, the Harts, the Grimeses, the Batistes—I am blessed. To my nieces, MacKenzie and Leila, and my godsons, Lucas and Ka-ton, I love you and am always proud of you. And, no, y'all should not be reading this.

To Lane Clarke, I'm a better writer because of you, and I am grateful to call you my sister. Shout-out to Brother G, Pax and Pickles. To Kiki, Morgan, Madi, Kai, Regina, Nikki, Jayce, Tanisia—thanks for writing sessions and letting me pick your brains.

To Charish Reid, Catherine Adel West, Jasmine Guillory, Courtney Kae, Darby Baham, Lane Clarke, Myah Ariel, Riss Neilson, Tracey Livesay, Suzanne Park, Jayci Lee, Tif Marcelo, Elle Cruz and Danielle Jackson: thank you for reading advance copies of my work! I am in such awe of your talents and am honored to get to know (and stan) each of you.

To Becca, Kelly, Analieze and Rees Literary Agency—thank you for another year of growth.

To my writing community, thank you for the writing sessions, the Slack talks, the advice, the love. Thank you for being incredible, brilliant, encouraging friends and good human beings.

To my DC fam: Ka-ton, Meesh, Neil, Sammy, Charles, Shelby, Ka-el, Elisha, Jazmine, Lawrence, Zoma, Katie, Corrie—I love and appreciate each of you. To the Buzzsaw: Everett, Amir, Matt, Octavius, John—thank y'all for supporting me and always having my back. Thanks to Trev and Bert—I'm so grateful for how you show up for me.

To my law school admissions tramily and my higher ed community—words can't describe my love and gratitude. The chosen family trope is one of my favorites for a reason. Love you.

To community!

<3 TJM